4/08

THE SPEE

BY THE SAME AUTHOR

The Tenant & The Motive
Soldiers of Salamis

THE SPEED OF LIGHT

Javier Cercas

Translated from the Spanish by Anne McLean

BLOOMSBURY

Published by Bloomsbury USA, New York
Distributed to the trade by Holtzbrinck Publishers

All papers used by Bloomsbury USA are natural, recyclable products made from
wood grown in well-managed forests. The manufacturing processes conform to the
environmental regulations of the country of origin.

LIBRARY OF CONGRESS CATALOGING-IN-PUBLICATION DATA HAS BEEN APPLIED FOR.

ISBN 1-59691-214-6
ISBN-13 978-1-59691-214-4

Originally published in Spanish as *La Velocidad de la luz*
by Tusquets Editores, Barcelona, 2005
This English translation first published in the UK
by Bloomsbury in 2006
First U.S. edition 2007

1 3 5 7 9 10 8 6 4 2

Typeset by Hewer Text UK Ltd, Edinburgh
Printed in the United States of America by Quebecor World Fairfield

For Raül Cercas and Mercè Mas

Evil lasts, mistakes do not,
the forgivable is long forgiven, the knife cuts
have also healed, only the wound that evil inflicts,
does not heal; but reopens at night, every night.

Ingeborg Bachmann, 'Gloriastrasse'
Unveröffentlichte Gedichte

'But what if we're overwhelmed?'
'We shan't be overwhelmed.'
'But what if we're smothered?'
'We shan't be smothered.'

Jules Verne
Journey to the Centre of the Earth

CONTENTS

ALL ROADS

NOW I LEAD A false life, an apocryphal, clandestine, invisible life, though truer than if it were real, but I was still me when I met Rodney Falk. It was a long time ago and it was in Urbana, a city in the Midwest of the United States where I spent two years at the end of the eighties. The truth is that every time I ask myself why I ended up precisely there I tell myself I ended up there just as I might have ended up anywhere else. Let me explain why instead of ending up anywhere else I ended up precisely there.

It was by chance. Back then — seventeen years ago now — I was very young, I'd just graduated and a friend and I shared a dark, dank apartment on calle Pujol, in Barcelona, very close to plaza Bonanova. My friend was called Marcos Luna, he was from Gerona like me and in reality he was both more and less than a friend: we'd grown up together, played together, gone to school together, we had the same friends. Marcos had always wanted to be a painter; not me: I wanted to be a writer. But we'd done two useless degrees and we didn't have proper jobs and we were as poor as could be, so Marcos didn't paint and I didn't write, or we only did in those rare spare moments we were left by the more than full-time job of surviving. We barely got by. He gave classes at a school as dank as the apartment we lived in and I did piecework for a publisher run by slave drivers (copy-editing, correcting translations, proof-reading), but since our miserable salaries combined weren't even enough to keep ourselves housed and fed, we took on anything we could scrape up here and there, no matter how peculiar, from proposing a list of possible names for a new airline to an advertising company to putting the archives of the Hospital del Vall d'Hebron in order, as well as writing unpaid song lyrics for a floundering musician friend. Otherwise, when we weren't working or writing or paint-ing, we wandered around the city, smoked marijuana, drank beer and talked about the masterpieces with which we'd one day take our revenge on a world that, despite our never having exhibited a single painting or published a single story, we felt was blatantly ignoring us. We didn't know any painters or writers, we didn't go to art openings or book launches but we probably liked to imagine ourselves as two bohemians in an era when bohemians no longer existed or as two terrible kamikazes ready to explode cheerfully against reality; in fact we were nothing more than two arrogant provincials lost in the capital, lonely and furious, and the only sacrifice we felt unable to make for anything in the world was to return to Gerona, because that would amount to giving up the dreams of triumph we'd always cherished. We were brutally ambitious. We aspired to fail.

But not simply to fail any old way: we aspired to total, radical, absolute failure. It was our way of aspiring to success.

One night in the spring of 1987 something happened that would change everything. Marcos and I had just left the house when, right at the intersection of Muntaner and Arimon, we ran into Marcelo Cuartero. Cuartero was a professor of literature at the Autonomous University of Barcelona whose dazzling lectures I'd attended with enthusiasm, despite being a mediocre student. He was a heavy-set, short, red-headed man in his fifties, a sloppy dresser, with a big, sad turtle face dominated by bad-guy eyebrows and sarcastic, slightly intimidating eyes; he was also one of the foremost experts on the nineteenth-century novel, had led the university protests against the Franco regime in the sixties and seventies and, it was said (though this was difficult to deduce from his classes or his books, scrupulously free of any political content), was still a heartfelt, resigned and unrepentant communist. Cuartero and I had spoken once or maybe twice in the corridor when I was a student, but that night he stopped to talk to me and to Marcos, told us he was coming home from a literary gathering that met every Friday in the Oxford, a nearby bar, and, as if the meeting hadn't satisfied his conversational craving, asked me what I was reading and we started talking about literature; then he invited us for a drink in El Yate, a bar with huge windows and burnished wood where Marcos and I didn't often go, because it seemed too posh for our skimpy budget. Leaning on the bar, we spent a while talking about books, at the end of which Cuartero suddenly asked me where I was working; since Marcos was there, I wasn't brave enough to lie to him, but I did all I could to embellish the truth. He, however, must have guessed, because that was when he told me about Urbana. Cuartero said he had a good friend there, at the University of Illinois, and that his friend had told him that next term the Spanish department was offering several teaching-assistant scholarships to Spanish graduates.

'I have no idea what the city's like,' Marcelo admitted. 'The only thing I know about it is from *Some Like it Hot*.'

'*Some Like it Hot?*' Marcos and I asked in unison.

'The movie,' he answered. 'At the beginning Jack Lemmon and Tony Curtis have to play a concert in a freezing Midwestern city, near Chicago, but due to some trouble with gangsters they end up running away to Florida disguised as girl musicians and living it up like crazy. Well anyway, Urbana is the freezing city they never get to, so I guess Urbana must not be too wonderful or at least it must be the total opposite of Florida, supposing that Florida is so wonderful. Anyway, that's all I know. But the university is good, and I think the job is too. They pay you a salary to give language classes, just enough to live on, and you have to enrol in the doctoral programme. Nothing too demanding. Besides, you want to be a writer, don't you?'

I felt my cheeks flare up. Without daring to look at Marcos I stammered out something, but Cuartero interrupted me:

'Well, a writer has to travel. You'll see different things,

meet new people, read other books. That's healthy. Anyway,' he concluded, 'if you're interested, give me a call.'

Cuartero left not long after that, but Marcos and I stayed in El Yate, ordered another beer and spent a while drinking and smoking in silence; we both knew what the other was thinking, and we both knew that the other knew. We thought that Cuartero had just said in a few words what we'd been thinking for a long time without saying it: we were thinking that, besides reading everything, a writer should travel and see the world and accumulate experiences, and that the United States – any place in the United States – was the ideal place to do all those things and become a writer; we were thinking that a steady, paid job that left time to write was much more than I could dream of finding at that moment in Barcelona; too young or too naïve to know what it means for a life to be going to hell, we thought our lives were going to hell.

'Well,' said Marcos eventually and, knowing the decision was already made, drained his glass in one gulp. 'Another beer?'

So it was that, six months after this chance encounter with Marcelo Cuartero, after an interminable flight with stopovers in London and New York, I ended up in Urbana just as I might have ended up anywhere else. I remember the first thing I thought when I arrived, as the Greyhound bus that brought me from Chicago entered a succession of deserted avenues flanked by little houses with porches, red-brick buildings with meticulous flowerbeds that shimmered beneath the burning August sky, was how tremendously lucky Tony Curtis and Jack Lemmon had been in *Some Like It Hot*, and how I'd write to Marcos to tell him I'd travelled ten thousand kilometres in vain, because Urbana – a little island of barely a hundred and fifty thousand souls floating in the middle of a sea of cornfields that stretched unbroken to the suburbs of Chicago – was not much bigger and didn't seem much less provincial than Gerona. Of course, I didn't tell him anything of the sort: in order not to disappoint him with my disappointment, or to try to modify reality a little, what I told him was that Marcelo Cuartero was mistaken and that Urbana was like Florida, or rather like a mix of Florida and New York in miniature, a vivacious, sunny and cosmopolitan city where my novels would practically write themselves. But, since no matter how hard we try, lies don't alter reality, it didn't take me long to discover that my first impression of the city was accurate, and so I let myself be overcome by sadness during the first days I spent in Urbana, unable as I was to shake off my nostalgia for what I'd left behind and the certainty that, rather than a city, that unrelenting furnace lost in the middle of nowhere was a cemetery where I'd soon end up turning into a ghost or a zombie.

It was Marcelo Cuartero's friend who helped me to get over that initial depression. His name was John Borgheson and he turned out to be an Americanized Englishman or an American who hadn't been able to give up being English (or just the opposite); what I mean is, although his culture and education were American and most of his life and all of his academic career had been spent in the United States, his Birmingham accent was still almost pure and he hadn't been infected by North Americans' direct manners, so he remained an Englishman of the old school, or he liked to imagine himself as one: a shy, courteous, reticent man who vainly struggled to hide his true vocation, which was for comedy. Borgheson, who was about forty and spoke that slightly archaic, stony Spanish often spoken by those who've read a lot of it and spoken it rarely, was the only person I knew in the city, and upon my arrival had been kind enough to take me in; later he helped me find an apartment to rent near the university campus and get settled in there, showed me the university and guided me through the labyrinth of its bureaucracy. During those initial days I couldn't avoid the suspicion that Borgheson's exaggerated friendliness was due to the fact that, by some misunderstanding, he thought I was one of Marcelo Cuartero's favourite students, which I couldn't help but find ironic, especially since by then I was beginning to entertain well-founded suspicions that if Cuartero hadn't sent me to a more remote and inhospitable place than Urbana it was because he didn't know of a place any more remote and inhospitable than Urbana. Borgheson also took pains to introduce me to some of my future colleagues, students of his and assistant professors like me in the Spanish department, and, one Saturday night, a few days after my arrival, he arranged a dinner with three of them at the Courier Café, a small restaurant on Race Street, very close to Lincoln Square.

I remember the dinner very well, among other reasons because I'm very much afraid that what went on there reveals the precise tone of what my first weeks in Urbana must have been like. The three colleagues, two men and one woman, were more or less the same age as me. The two men edited a biannual journal called *Línea Plural*: one was a Venezuelan called Felipe Vieri, a very well-read, ironic, slightly haughty guy, who dressed with a meticulousness not entirely free of affectation; the other was called Frank Solaún and he was a Cuban-American, well-built, enthusiastic, with a gleaming smile and slicked-back hair. As for the woman, her name was Laura Burns and, as I found out later from Borgheson himself, she belonged to an opulent and aristocratic family from San Juan de Puerto Rico (her father owned the country's foremost newspaper), but what most caught my attention about her that night, apart from her unmistakable *gringa* physique – tall, solid, blonde, very pale skin – was her intimidating propensity to sarcasm, reined in with difficulty by the respect Borgheson's presence inspired. Otherwise, he gently imposed his authority for the duration of the dinner, channelling the conversation into themes that might be of interest to me or that, he imagined or wished, at least wouldn't make me feel excluded. And so we talked about my trip, about Urbana, the university, the department; we also talked about Spanish writers and film makers, and I soon realized Borgheson and his students were more up to date on what was happening in Spain than I was, because I hadn't read the books or seen the movies of many of the film makers and writers they mentioned. I doubt the fact embarrassed me, because back then my resentment at being an unpublished, ignored and practically illiterate writer authorized me to consider everything being done in Spain to be garbage – and everything done anywhere else pure art – but I don't rule out that it may explain in part what happened when we were having coffee. By then Vieri and Solaún had been talking for a while with unrestrained devotion about the films of Pedro Almodóvar; the ever attentive Borgheson took advantage of a pause in the enthusiastic duo's exchange to ask my opinion of the films of the director from La Mancha. Like everyone, I think I liked Almodóvar's films back then, but at that moment I must have felt an irresistible urge to try to sound interesting or make my cosmopolitan vocation very clear by setting myself apart from those stories of drug-addled nuns, traditional transvestites and matador murderers, so I answered, 'Frankly, I think they're a pile of queer crap.'

A savage roar of laughter from Laura Burns greeted the judgement, and my satisfaction at this reception of the scandalous comment kept me from noticing the others' glacial silence, which Borgheson hurried to break by changing the subject. The dinner soon concluded without further incident and, on the way out of the Courier Café, Vieri and Solaún suggested going for a drink. Borgheson and Laura Burns declined the invitation; I accepted.

My new friends took me to a club called Chester Street, located appropriately enough on Chester Street, beside the train station. It was an enormous, oblong place, with bare walls, a bar on the right and in front of it a dance floor bombarded with strobes and packed with people at this hour. As soon as we got in, Solaún wasted no time in losing himself among the heaving throng on the dance floor; for our part, Vieri and I made our way to the bar to order Cuba libres and, while we waited for them, I began a half-mocking, half-perplexed comment to Vieri about the fact that there were only men to be seen in the club, but before I could finish a guy came up to me and said something I didn't understand or didn't entirely understand. Leaning towards him, I asked him to repeat it; he repeated it: he asked me if I wanted to dance with him. I was just about to ask him to repeat it again, but instead of doing that I looked at him: he was very young, very blond, he seemed very cheerful, he was smiling; I said thanks and that I didn't want to dance. The boy shrugged and, without further explanation, he left. I was going to tell Vieri what had just happened to me when a tall, muscular guy, with a moustache and cowboy boots, came and asked me the same or a similar question; incredulous, I gave him the same or a similar reply, and without even looking at me again, the guy laughed silently and also left. At that very moment Vieri passed me my Cuba libre, but I didn't say anything and I didn't even have to read the smug and slightly vengeful sarcasm in his eyes to feel like Jack

Lemmon and Tony Curtis arriving in Florida dressed as girl musicians or to understand the stupefied silence that had followed my verdict on Almodóvar's films. A long time later Vieri told me that when, the morning after that triumphal night, Frank Solaún told Laura Burns they'd taken me to a gay fiesta on Chester Street Laura's shriek resounded through the halls of the department like a fulmination: 'But that guy's such a Spaniard his brain must be shaped like a *botijo*, with a spout and everything!'

I'd like to believe that during my early days in Urbana this kind of gaffe was not as frequent as I fear, but I can't be sure; what I can be sure of is that I got used to my new life much more quickly than I expected. And it was a comfortable life. My house — a two-bedroom apartment with kitchen and bathroom — was located a five-minute walk from the Foreign Languages Building, the building that was home to the Spanish Department, at 703 West Oregon, between Busey and Coler, in a zone of narrow, private, tree-lined streets. As Marcelo Cuartero had promised, I made enough money to live without privations and my duties as Spanish teacher and doctoral student left almost all my afternoons and evenings free, as well as the lengthy weekends that included Fridays, so I had lots of time to read and write, and a vast library to keep me supplied with books. Soon curiosity for what I had in front of me replaced nostalgia for what I'd left behind. I regularly wrote to my family and my friends — especially Marcos — but I didn't feel lonely any more; in fact, I very soon discovered that, if I

13

made an effort, nothing was easier than making friends in Urbana. Like all university cities, it was a sterile, deceptive place, a human microclimate bereft of poor and old people in which each year one population composed of young people from all over the planet on their way through touched down as another took off for the world; added to the slightly worrying evidence that neither in the city nor for several hundreds of kilometres in any direction were there any distractions other than work, this circumstance facilitated social life enormously, and in fact, in contrast to the studious quiet of the rest of the week, from Friday afternoon to Sunday night Urbana turned into a seething cauldron of house parties that no one seemed to want to miss and to which everyone seemed to be invited.

However, I didn't meet Rodney Falk at any of those many house parties, but in the office we shared for a semester on the fourth floor of the Foreign Languages Building. I'll never know if they assigned me that office by chance or because no one else wanted to share with Rodney (I'm inclined to suspect the latter is more likely than the former), but what I do know is that, if they hadn't assigned me that office, Rodney and I would probably never have become friends and everything would have been different and my life wouldn't be like it is and the memory of Rodney would have been wiped from my mind the way the memories of most of the people I knew in Urbana have faded away with the years. Or perhaps not as much, perhaps I exaggerate. After all, the truth is, although nothing could

14

be further from his intentions, Rodney did not go unnoticed amid the rigorous uniformity that reigned in the department and to which everyone adhered without complaint, as if it were a tacit but palpable rule of intellectual immunization paradoxically bound to instigate competence among the members of that community proud of their strict meritocratic observance. Rodney transgressed the rule because he was quite a bit older than the rest of the Spanish assistants, almost none of whom were over thirty, but also because he never attended meetings, cocktail parties or get-togethers organized by the department, which everyone blamed, as I soon found out, on his reserved and eccentric, not to mention surly, nature, which contributed to him being surrounded by a disparaging myth that included his having obtained his position as a Spanish lecturer thanks to being a veteran of the Vietnam War. I remember at a reception put on by the department for the new teaching assistants, the night before classes began, someone commented on his habitual absence, which immediately provoked, among the little circle of colleagues around me, a cascade of vicious conjecture about what it was that Rodney must teach his students, because no one had ever heard him speak Spanish.

'Damn!' said Laura Burns, as she burst into the chorus. 'What worries me isn't that Rodney doesn't know a fucking word of Spanish, but that one of these days he's going to show up here with a Kalashnikov and blow us all away.'

I still hadn't forgotten this comment, which had been greeted with riotous laughter all round, when the next day I

15

finally met Rodney. That morning, the first of term, I arrived at the department very early, and when I opened the office door the first thing I saw was Rodney sitting at his desk, reading; the second was that he raised his eyes from the book, looked at me, stood up without a word. There was an irrational instant of panic provoked by Laura Burns' sharp remark (which suddenly no longer seemed like a sharp remark and also no longer struck me as funny) and by the size of that big, strong, reportedly unbalanced guy who was advancing towards me; but I didn't run away: I apprehensively shook the hand he held out to me and tried to smile.

'My name's Rodney Falk,' he said, looking me in the eye with disconcerting intensity and making a noise that sounded like a martial click of the heels. 'And you?'

I told him my name. Rodney asked me if I was Spanish. I told him I was.

'I've never been to Spain,' he declared. 'But one day I'd like to see it. Have you read Hemingway?'

I'd barely read Hemingway, or I'd read him carelessly, and my notion of the American writer fitted into a pitiful snapshot of a washed-up, swaggering, alcoholic old man, friend to flamenco dancers and bull fighters, who spread a postcard image of the oldest and most unbearable stereotypes of Spain through his outmoded works.

'Yes,' I answered, relieved at that hint of a literary conversation and, since I must have seen another magnificent opportunity to make very clear to my colleagues my unimpeachable cosmopolitan calling, which I'd already thought to proclaim with my homophobic comment about Almodóvar's films, I added: 'Frankly, I think he's shit.'

The reaction of my new officemate was more expeditious than that of Vieri and Solaún a few nights before: without any gesture of disapproval or agreement, as if I'd suddenly disappeared from view, Rodney turned around and left me standing there mid-sentence; then he sat back down, picked up his book and immersed himself in it again.

That morning there was nothing more and, if we discount the initial surprise or panic and Ernest Hemingway, the ritual of the days that followed came to be more or less identical. Despite always arriving at the office as soon as they opened the Foreign Languages Building, Rodney was always there before me and, after an obligatory greeting that in his case was more like a grunt, our mornings were spent coming and going from classrooms, and also sitting each at his desk, reading and preparing classes (Rodney mostly reading and me mostly preparing classes), but always firmly immured in a silence that I only timidly tried to break on a couple of occasions, until I came to understand that Rodney had absolutely no interest in talking to me. It was during those days that, keeping a surreptitious eye on him from my desk or in the corridors of the department, I began to get used to his presence. At first glance Rodney had the ingenuous, indifferent, anachronistic look of those hippies from the sixties who hadn't wanted or been able or known how to adapt themselves to the cheerful cynicism of the eighties, as if they'd been willingly or forcibly swept aside into a ditch so as not to interfere with the triumphant march of history. His clothing, however, was not out of keeping with the informal egalitarianism that reigned in the university: he always wore running shoes, faded jeans and baggy checked shirts, although in winter – in the polar winter of Urbana – he changed his shoes for military boots and bundled up in thick woollen sweaters, a sheepskin coat and fur cap. He was tall, heavy set and rather ungainly; he always walked with his eyes glued to the floor and sort of lurching, leaning to the right, with one shoulder higher than the other, which endowed his gait with the swaying instability of a pachyderm on the point of collapse. He had long, thick, reddish hair, and a robust, wide face, with slightly ruddy skin and features that seemed sculpted into his cranium: firm chin, prominent cheekbones, steep nose and a mocking or contemptuous mouth, which when open revealed two rows of uneven, almost ochre-coloured, quite deteriorated teeth. One of his eyes was abnormally sensitive to light, which obliged him to protect it from the sun with a black fabric patch held in place by a band around his head, making him look like an ex-combatant, an appearance his lurching walk and broken-down frame did nothing to contradict. Undoubtedly because of this ocular lesion his eyes appeared not to be of the same colour at first glance, although if you looked closely you'd see it was just that one was a slightly lighter brown, almost honey-coloured, and the other a darker brown, almost black.

Furthermore, I also soon noticed that Rodney had no friends in the department and that, except for Dan Gleylock – an old linguistics professor in whose office I saw him talking once or twice, coffee in hand – with the rest of the members of the faculty he maintained a relationship that didn't even reach the level of superficial cordiality that simple politeness imposes.

Nothing suggested my case would be any different. In fact, it's almost certain the relationship between Rodney and me would never have overcome the phase of autism we'd mutually confined ourselves to had it not been for the involuntary collaboration of John Borgheson. The first Friday after the beginning of classes Borgheson invited me to lunch along with a young Italian with the languid air of a dandy, called Giuseppe Rota, who was a visiting professor at the university that semester. The lunch was in two parts. During the first, Rota spoke non-stop, while Borgheson remained immersed in a meditative or embarrassed silence; during the second they swapped roles – Borgheson spoke and Rota remained silent, as if what was being aired there had nothing whatsoever to do with him – and only then did I understand the reason for the invitation. Borgheson explained that Rota had been contracted by the university to give an introductory course in Catalan literature; up to that moment, however, only three people had enrolled, which was a serious problem since university regulations obliged the department to cancel any course with less than a minimum of four students registered to take

19

it. When he got to this point, the tone of Borgheson's speech went from explanatory to vehement, as if he was trying to mask with emphasis the embarrassment he felt at having to discuss the matter. Because what Borgheson was begging of me, with the silent consent of Rota – and, to be on the safe side, flattering my vanity with the argument that, given my knowledge of the material and the requisite elementary level of the course, it wouldn't be very useful for me – was that I enroll in it, with the implication that he'd consider this small sacrifice a personal favour and also that the course wouldn't require of me any more effort than attending the lectures. Of course, I immediately agreed to Borgheson's request, thrilled to be able to return a small portion of the kindness he'd shown me, but what I could never have foreseen – nor could Borgheson have warned me – was quite what that trivial decision would entail.

I began to suspect the following Tuesday, late in the afternoon, when I walked into the room where the first Catalan literature class was to take place and saw the three who were soon to be my classmates sitting around a table. One was a sinister-looking guy, dressed entirely in black, with his red dyed hair in a mohican; the second was a small, gaunt, fidgety Chinese guy; the third was Rodney. The three of them smiled at me in silence and, after making sure I hadn't mistaken the room, I said hello and sat down; a moment later Rota showed up and the class began. Well, began in a manner of speaking. Actually, that class never finished beginning, simply because it was an unfeasible class. The reason is that, as we immediately realized to our astonishment, there was no common language among the five of us in the class: Rota, who spoke both Spanish and Catalan well, didn't speak a word of English, and the sinister-looking American, who soon told us that he wanted to learn Catalan because he was studying Romance languages, only spoke broken French, like Rodney, who also spoke Spanish; as for the Chinese guy, whose name was Wong and who was studying directing in the Department of Theatre, aside from Chinese he only knew English (much later I found out that his desire to learn Catalan stemmed from the fact that he had a Catalan boyfriend). It didn't take us long to realize that, given the circumstances, I was the only possible instrument of communication among the members of that improvised ecumenical assembly, so after Rota, sweating and upset, had tried in vain to make himself understood by all the means within his grasp, including hand signals, I offered to translate his words from Catalan into English, which was the only language all the interested parties understood, except for Rota himself. As well as being ridiculous, the procedure was exasperatingly slow, though somehow or other, it allowed us to ride out not just that introductory class, but, as incredible as it might seem, the whole semester, though not without large doses of generous hypocrisy and smiles on everyone's part. But naturally, that first day we all came out depressed and dumbfounded, so at first I could only interpret Rodney's comment as sarcasm when, after leaving the classroom together and walking in silence through the corridors of the Foreign Languages Building, we were on the point of separating at the door.

'I've never learned so many things in a single class,' was Rodney's comment. As I said: at first I thought he was joking; then I thought he wasn't referring to what I thought he was referring to and I looked him in the eye and thought he wasn't joking; then I thought he was joking again and then I didn't know what to think. Rodney added, 'I didn't know you spoke Catalan.'

'I live in Catalonia.'

'Does everyone who lives in Catalonia speak Catalan?'

'Not everyone, no.'

Rodney stopped, looked at me with a mixture of interest and wariness, asked, 'Have you read Mercè Rodoreda?'

I said yes.

'Do you like her?'

As I'd learned my lesson by now and wanted to get along with the person I had to share an office with, I said yes. Rodney gestured in a strange way that I didn't know how to interpret, and for a moment I thought of Almodóvar and Hemingway and I thought I'd made another mistake, that maybe admirers of Hemingway could only detest Rodoreda just as admirers of Rodoreda could do nothing but detest Hemingway. Before I could qualify or retract the lie I'd just inflicted on him, Rodney reassured me.

'I love her stuff,' he said. 'I've read her in Spanish

translation, of course, but I want to learn Catalan so I can read her in the original.'

'Well, you've come to the right place,' I couldn't help but say.

'What?'

'Nothing.'

I was about to say goodbye when Rodney unexpectedly said, 'Do you want to go get a Coke?'

We went to Treno's, a bar on the corner of Goodwin and West Oregon, halfway between my house and the faculty. It was a place staffed by students, with wooden tables and walls panelled with wood too, with a big unlit fireplace and a big picture window looking out onto Goodwin. We sat beside the fireplace and ordered a Coke for Rodney, a beer for me and a bowl of popcorn to share. We talked. Rodney told me he lived in Rantoul, a small city near Urbana, and that this was the third year he'd taught Spanish at the university.

'I like it,' he added.

'Really?' I asked.

'Yeah,' he answered. 'I like teaching, I like my colleagues in the department, I like the university.' He must have seen something strange in my expression, because he asked, 'Does that surprise you?'

'No,' I lied.

Rodney offered me a light and as I lit my cigarette I looked at his Zippo: it was old and must once have been silver-plated, but now it was a rusty yellow; on the upper part, in capital letters, was the word Vietnam, and underneath some numbers (68–69) and two words: Chu Lai; on the lower part there was a dog sitting and smiling and under him a phrase: 'Fuck it. I got my orders.' Rodney noticed me looking at the lighter, because as he put it away he said, 'It's the only good thing I brought back from that fucking war.'

I was going to ask him to tell me about Vietnam when he abruptly asked me to tell him about myself. I did. I talked, I think, about Gerona, Barcelona, my first impressions of Urbana, and he interrupted me to ask me how I'd ended up there. This time I didn't lie, but I didn't tell him the truth either, at least, not the whole truth.

'Urbana is a good place to live,' Rodney declared sententiously when I'd finished speaking; then, mysteriously, he added: 'It's like nothing.'

I asked him what that meant.

'It means it's a good place to work,' is all he answered. While I thought of the reasons Marcelo Cuartero had given me to go to Urbana, Rodney started talking about Mercè Rodoreda. He'd read two of her novels (*La Plaça del Diamant* and *Broken Mirror*); I'd only read the second, but I assured him with the aplomb of an infallible reader that the two books he'd read were the best things Rodoreda had written. Then Rodney made a suggestion: he said that every Tuesday and every Thursday, after Rota's class (or after Rota's class translated by me), we could go to Treno's so I could teach him to speak Catalan; in exchange he was ready to pay me whatever we agreed. He said it in a very serious

24

tone of voice, but strangely I felt like he'd just told me a slightly macabre joke that I hadn't been able to figure out or (stranger still) as if he were challenging me to a duel. I could not yet have known that this was Rodney's normal tone of voice, so, although I wasn't even sure if I could teach someone Catalan, more out of pride than curiosity, I answered, 'I'll settle for you paying for my beers.'

That's how Rodney and I became friends. That very Thursday we went back to Treno's, and from the following week on, as we'd agreed, we got together every Tuesday and every Thursday, at the end of the official Catalan class. We'd get there just after six, we'd sit at the table by the fireplace, we'd order Coke (for him), beer (for me) and popcorn (for both of us) and keep talking until they closed the place around nine. Especially during the first weeks, we tried to devote as much of the time as possible to my instructing Rodney in the rudiments of Catalan, but little by little laziness or boredom overcame us and the duty of learning gave way to the pleasure of conversation. Not that we didn't also talk in the free time we had in the office, but we did so in a distracted or discontinuous way, in between the hustle and bustle of other activities, as if that was not the place to continue the conversations we had in Treno's; at least maybe that's how Rodney saw it; or maybe for some reason he wanted to keep people in the department from finding out about our friendship. The thing is that as soon as I began to have dealings with him outside the office I guessed that, despite the fact that they both shared a similar battered physical appearance and the same lost air, as if they'd just been woken up and their eyes were still veiled with the cobwebs of sleep, there was a fundamental discrepancy, although indefinable to me, between the Rodney I knew and the one my colleagues in the department knew, but what I couldn't in any way have guessed at that time is that the discrepancy was linked to the very essence of Rodney's personality, to a neurological centre that he kept hidden and to which no one then – in a certain sense not even he – had access.

I don't have an accurate recollection of those evenings in Treno's, but some memories from them are extremely vivid. I remember, for example, the increasingly charged atmosphere of the bar as the evening wore on and the place filled with students reading or writing or talking. I remember the young, round, smiling face of the waitress who usually served us, and a bad copy of a Modigliani portrait that hung on a wall, just to the right of the bar. I remember Rodney smoothing down his messy hair every once in a while and leaning back uncomfortably in his chair, and stretching his legs, which barely fitted beneath the table, out towards the fireplace. I remember the music that came out of the speakers, very faint, almost like a distorted echo of other music, and I remember that music making me feel as if I weren't in a bar in a city in the Midwest at the end of the eighties but rather at the end of the seventies in a bar in Gerona, because it was the music of the bars of my teenage years in Gerona (like Led Zeppelin, ZZ Top, Frank Zappa).

I remember a strange detail very well: the last song they played every night, like a discreet warning to the regulars that the bar was going to close, was 'It's Alright, Ma (I'm Only Bleeding)', an old Bob Dylan song that Rodney loved because, just as ZZ Top brought back the limitless despair of my adolescence, it brought back the joy of his hippy youth, it brought it back even though it was such a sad song that spoke of disillusioned words like bullets barked and of graveyards stuffed with false gods and lonely people who cry and fear and live in a vault knowing everything's a lie and who've understood they know too soon there is no sense in even trying to understand, brought back that joy perhaps because it contained a line that I haven't been able to forget either: 'That he not busy being born is busy dying.' I remember other things too. I remember Rodney spoke with a strange icy passion, smoking constantly and gesturing a lot and animated by a kind of permanent euphoria, and that although he never (or almost never) laughed, he never gave the impression of being entirely serious. I remember that we never (or almost never) spoke of the university and that, despite the fact that Rodney never (or almost never) spoke of personal things, he never (or almost never) gave the impression he was talking about anything other than himself, and I'm sure I did not even once hear him pronounce the word Vietnam. On more than one occasion, though, we talked about politics; or, more precisely, it was Rodney who talked about politics. But it wasn't until well into the autumn that I understood that, if

27

we didn't talk about politics more often, it wasn't because it wasn't of interest to Rodney, but rather because I didn't understand a single thing about politics (and much less about US politics, which for Rodney was the only real, or at least the only relevant politics), which, to tell the truth, didn't seem to matter that much to my friend either. Every time the subject came up he gave me the impression of talking more to himself or to an abstract interlocutor than to me; one might say he was driven by a sort of furious impulse to vent, by a resentful and hopeless vehemence against the politicians of his country – whom he considered without exception a pack of liars and filibusterers – against the big corporations that held the real political power and against the media, which according to him spread the lies of politicians and corporations with impunity.

But what I mostly remember about those evenings in Treno's is that we talked almost exclusively about books. Naturally, I might be exaggerating, it might not be true and it might be that the future alters the past and that subsequent events may have distorted my memory and that in Treno's Rodney and I didn't talk almost exclusively about books, but what I remember is that we talked almost exclusively about books; in any case, what I am sure of is that I soon realized Rodney was the best-read friend I'd ever had. Although for some reason I took a while to confess that I wanted to be a writer and that there in Urbana I'd begun to write a novel, from the start I talked to him about the North American writers I was then reading: about Saul Bellow,

Philip Roth, Bernard Malamud, John Updike, Flannery O'Connor. To my surprise (and delight), Rodney had read them all; I should make clear that it wasn't that he said he'd read them, rather that from the comments he made to damp down or stoke my reckless enthusiasm (more often the former than the latter), I could tell he'd read them. Without a doubt it was Rodney who I first heard mention, during those evenings in Treno's, some of the writers I've since then always associated with Urbana: Stanley Elkin, Donald Barthelme, Robert Coover, John Hawkes, William Gaddis, Richard Brautigan, Harry Mathews. We also talked once in a while about Rodoreda, who before Rota's impossible classes was the only Catalan author my friend knew, as well as certain Latin American writers he liked, and I think Rodney showed on more than one occasion, or pretended to show, some interest in Spanish literature, although I soon realized that, in contrast to Borgheson's followers, he knew little of it and liked it less. What Rodney really liked, what fascinated him, was classic American literature. My ignorance of the subject was absolute, so it took me a little while to understand that, like any good reader, Rodney's tastes and opinions on the matter were saturated in prejudices; the fact is they were unequivocal: he adored Thoreau, Emerson, Hawthorne and Twain, considered Fenimore Cooper a fraud, Poe a minor author, Melville a moralist of unbearable solemnity and James an affected, snobbish and overvalued narrator; he respected Faulkner and Thomas Wolfe, and thought there was no better writer in the whole century than

29

Scott Fitzgerald, but only Hemingway, Hemingway of all people, was the object of his unconditional devotion. Unconditional, but not uncritical: many a time I heard him scoff at the errors, banality, schmaltz and shortcomings that afflicted Hemingway's novels, but, thanks to an unexpected dodge in the line of argument that was like a sleight of hand, those blunders always ended up turning into essential seasonings of his greatness in Rodney's eyes. 'Lots of people have written better novels than Hemingway,' he told me the first time we talked about him, as if he'd forgotten the illiterate opinion I'd blurted out the day we met. 'But no one has written better short stories than Hemingway and no one can outdo a page of Hemingway. Besides,' he concluded without a smile, before I could finish blushing, 'if you pay close attention he's a very useful idiot detector: idiots never like Hemingway.' Even though it may well have been, I didn't take this last phrase as a personal allusion; I didn't get angry, although I could have. But, whether he was right or not, with time I've come to think that, more than an admired writer, Hemingway was for Rodney a dark or perhaps radiant symbol the extent of which not even he could entirely perceive.

I said earlier that only well into autumn did I understand that Rodney's interest in politics was not merely conversational, but very serious, although also a bit excessive or at least – to put it a more conventional way – unconventional. Actually I didn't begin to sense this until one Sunday at the beginning of October when a colleague from the department called Rodrigo Ginés invited me to lunch at his house, to talk about the issue of *Línea Plural* that was supposed to come out the following semester. Ginés, who'd arrived in Urbana at the same time as me and would end up becoming one of my best friends there, was Chilean, a writer and a cellist; he was also an assistant professor of Spanish. Many years before he'd been a professor at the Austral University of Chile, but after the fall of Salvador Allende the dictatorship had dismissed him and forced him to earn his living with other jobs, among them that of cellist in the National Symphony Orchestra. He was roughly the same age as Rodney and had a wife and two children in Santiago, and the melancholy air of an orphaned Indian, with a moustache and goatee, that in no way betrayed his bleak sense of humour, his compulsive sociability or his fondness for wine and good food. That Sunday, as well as Felipe Vieri and Frank Solaún, the editors of the journal and unconditional Almodóvar fans, several assistant professors came to his house, including Laura Burns and an Austrian called Gudrun with whom our host was going out at the time. We ate roast chicken with *mole* sauce that Ginés had made, and sat round the table long after the meal discussing the contents of the journal. We talked about poems, stories, articles, about the need to find some new contributors, and when we were discussing this last point I brought up Rodney's name, with the suggestion that we could ask him to write something for the next issue; I was about to sing the praises of my friend's intellectual virtues when I noticed that all the rest of the guests were staring at me as if I'd just announced the imminent landing in Urbana of a spacecraft crewed by little green men with antennae. I shut up; there was an uncomfortable silence. That was when, as if surprised to find a suitable instrument in his hands to assure the success of the meeting, Ginés interrupted to tell a story. I can't guarantee that all its details are true, I'm just telling it the way he told it. It seems that the Tuesday of that same week, as he made his way earlier than usual to his first class of the day, my Chilean friend had seen a dusty Buick stopping abruptly in the middle of Lincoln Avenue, beside a lamppost, right at the intersection with Green Street. Ginés thought the car had broken down and kept walking towards the crossroads, but recognized he was mistaken when he saw the driver get out and, instead of going to look at the engine or check the state of the tires, opened the back door, took out a bucket and brush and a poster and stuck the poster on the lamppost. The driver was sporting a patch over his right eye and Ginés quickly recognized it was Rodney. According to Ginés, up till that day they hadn't exchanged a single word, and perhaps for that reason he stopped a few metres from the car, watching Rodney finish pasting up the poster, confused and intrigued, not knowing whether to go over to him or take off walking down Green and leave as if he hadn't seen a thing, and he was still wondering when Rodney finished smoothing the poster onto the lamppost, turned around and saw him. Then Ginés had no option but to approach. He went over and, although

32

he knew Rodney didn't have any trouble with his car, asked him if he had any trouble with his car. Rodney looked at him with his uncovered eye, smiled crookedly and assured him he didn't; then he pointed to the poster freshly pasted to the lamppost. Since he hardly understood any English, Ginés didn't understand any of what was written on it, but Rodney told him that the poster was calling for a general strike against General Electric in the name of the Socialist Workers' Party or some faction of the Socialist Workers' Party, Ginés didn't quite remember.

'Against General Electric,' Ginés repeated, interrupting his tale. 'Shit! And I didn't even know there still was a Socialist Workers' Party in this country!'

Ginés explained that he stood staring at Rodney not knowing what to say at that moment and Rodney stood staring at him not knowing what to say. A few endless seconds passed, during which, according to him, he felt successively like laughing and crying, and then, as the silence went on and he waited for Rodney to say something or for something to occur to him to say, the image of General Pinochet's face appeared in his mind, that immobile face with its invisible gaze behind those perpetual sunglasses, sitting in a box in the Military School Theatre in Santiago, while he and his colleagues in the Symphony Orchestra played the *Adagio & Allegro* by Saint-Saëns or Dvořák's *Rondo capriccioso*, either of the two pieces but never any other, and almost unwittingly tried to imagine what General Pinochet would have thought or said to

Rodney in a situation like that, thought about the budget of the Chilean State that Pinochet administered and also thought, with a satisfaction that he still didn't entirely understand, that, compared with the president of General Electric, Pinochet was like the foreman of an asbestos factory whose workers wouldn't outnumber the members of the Socialist Workers' Party (or the faction of the Socialist Workers' Party) Rodney belonged to or supported. Finally it was Rodney who broke the spell. 'Well,' he said. 'I'm done now. Do you want a lift to the faculty?'

'That was it,' Ginés concluded in his Chilean tone, finishing off his wine and opening his eyes wide and his hands in a perplexed gesture. 'He gave me a lift to the faculty and there we parted. But I spent the whole day with the strangest feeling, as if that morning I'd mistakenly snuck into a Dadaist play in which I unintentionally ended up playing the lead part.'

Knowing Ginés as I eventually came to know him, I'm sure he didn't relate this anecdote with the intention of preventing Rodney from contributing to the journal, but the fact is that Rodney's name was never mentioned again during that or any other *Línea Plural* meeting. Apart from that, I'll also say that in Rodney's company I, too, sometimes felt like I had wandered into a play or a joke (sometimes a disturbing or even sinister joke) that didn't fit into any known genre or aesthetic and that meant nothing, but that concerned me so intimately it was as if someone had written it deliberately for me. Other times the impression was the opposite: that it wasn't me but Rodney who was acting in a play – which at times promised to reveal areas of my friend's personality impervious to the almost involuntary scrutiny to which I subjected it during our conversations in Treno's – the real significance of which I touched and was about to grasp but in the end slipped through my fingers like water, just as if Rodney's transparent veneer hid nothing but a background that was also transparent. I can't omit here an episode that happened not long after we began to be friends, because in light of certain events that I found out about much later it acquires an ambiguous but eloquent resonance.

Some Friday evenings I'd go swimming at an indoor pool belonging to the university that was located about a twenty-minute walk from my house. I'd swim for an hour or an hour and a half, sometimes even two, sit in the sauna for a while, have a shower and go home exhausted and happy and with the feeling of having eliminated all the superfluous material accumulated during the week. One of those Fridays, just as I came out of the sports centre, I saw Rodney. He was across the street, sitting on a concrete bench, facing a wide, treeless expanse of grass on the other side of a flimsy wire fence, with his arms crossed, the patch over his eye and his legs crossed as well, as if idly drinking in the last rays of the evening sun. Seeing him there surprised me and pleased me: it surprised me because I knew Rodney didn't have any classes on Friday afternoons and I also thought I knew that my friend didn't stay in

Urbana any more than strictly necessary and, except for the two days of our literary chats in Treno's, he returned to Rantoul as soon as he finished his academic obligations; it pleased me because there's nothing I'd rather do after exercise than have a beer and a cigarette and talk for a while. But, as I got closer to Rodney and past a hedge that had blocked my view of the lawn, I realized my friend was not sunning himself, but watching a group of children who were playing in front of him. There were four of them and they were eight or nine, maybe ten years old, they were wearing jeans and T-shirts and baseball caps and they were throwing and catching a Frisbee that went back and forth between them spinning and gliding like a flying saucer; I imagined their parents wouldn't be too far away, but from where I was, on the opposite sidewalk, I couldn't make them out. And then, when I was going to cross the street and say hello to Rodney, I stopped. I don't really know why I did, but I think it was because I noticed something strange in my friend, something that struck me as dissuasive or perhaps threatening, a frozen stiffness in his posture, a painful, almost unbearable tension, in the way he was sitting and watching the children play. I was twenty or thirty metres from him, so I couldn't see his face clearly, or I could only see his profile. Immobile, I remember that I thought: he wants to laugh so badly he can't laugh. Then I thought: no, he's crying and he'll keep crying and won't stop crying, if he ever does stop crying, until the children have gone. Then I thought: no, he wants to cry so badly that he can't cry. Then I thought: no, he's afraid, with a fear as sharp as a razor blade, a fear that cuts and bleeds and reeks and that I cannot understand. Then I thought: no, he's mad, completely mad, so mad that he's able to fool us and pretend to be sane. I was still thinking that when one of the children threw the Frisbee too hard and it flew over the fence and landed softly a few metres from Rodney. My friend didn't move, as if he hadn't noticed the disc (which was of course impossible), the boy came over to the fence, pointed to it and said something to Rodney, who finally got up from the bench, picked up the Frisbee and, instead of returning it to its owners, went back to the fence and crouched down so he was the same height as the child, who after some hesitation came over to him. Now the two were face to face, looking at each other through the diamonds of the wire fence, or rather, Rodney was looking at the boy and the boy was looking alternately at Rodney and at the ground. For a minute or two, during which the other children stayed at a distance, watching their playmate but without making up their minds to approach, Rodney and the boy talked; or rather; it was just Rodney who talked. The boy did other things: nodded, smiled, shook his head, nodded again; at a certain moment, after looking Rodney in the eye, the boy's stance changed: he seemed incredulous or frightened or even (for a fleeting instant) gripped by panic, he seemed to want to back away from the fence, but Rodney kept him there by holding onto his wrist and telling him something he must have hoped would be calming; then the boy began

37

to struggle and I had the impression that he was about to shout or burst into tears, but Rodney didn't let him go, he kept talking to him in a confidential and almost urgent, vehement way, and then, in a second, I was afraid too, I thought something might happen, I didn't know exactly what, I wondered if I should intervene, shout and tell Rodney to let go of the boy, let him go. The next second I calmed down: suddenly the boy seemed to relax, nodded again, smiled again, first timidly and then openly, at which moment Rodney let go of him and the boy said several words in a row, which I didn't understand although I could see his mouth and I tried to read his lips. Straight away Rodney stood up without hurrying and threw the disc, which glided and fell far from where the boy's friends were waiting. The boy, to my surprise, did not go immediately back to them, but stood for a while longer by the fence, indecisively, talking calmly to Rodney, and only left there after his friends had shouted to him several times that they had to go. Rodney watched the boys running away across the grass, and, instead of turning around and leaving as well, went back to sit on the bench, crossed his legs again, folded his arms again and stayed there immobile, facing the setting sun, and I didn't dare approach him and pretend I hadn't seen anything and suggest we go for a beer and a bit of a chat, and not only because I hadn't understood the scene and I would have felt uncomfortable or perturbed, but also because I was suddenly sure that at that moment my friend wanted above all to be alone, that he wasn't going to move from that bench for a long time, that he was going to let the light fade away and night fall and dawn arrive without doing anything except maybe weep or laugh silently, nothing other than looking at that expanse of grass like an enormous empty hangar that little by little the darkness would take over and on which he would probably see (but this I didn't know or imagine until much later) some indecipherable shadows dancing that only had any significance for him, though it was a dreadful significance.

Rodney was like that. Or at least that was what Rodney was like in Urbana seventeen years ago, during the months that I was his friend. Like that and at times much more irritating, more disconcerting too. Or at least much more disconcerting and irritating to me. I remember, for example, the day I told him I wanted to be a writer. As with the friends from *Línea Plural*, in whose pages I published nothing except reviews and articles, I had not confessed it to Rodney out of cowardice or modesty (or a mixture of the two), but by that evening in late November I'd spent a month and a half investing all the free time my classes left me in writing a novel I would never finish, so I must have felt less insecure than usual, and at some point I told him that I was writing a novel. I told him eagerly, as if I were revealing a great secret, but, contrary to my expectations, Rodney didn't react with enthusiasm or show interest in the news; far from it: for an instant his expression seemed to darken and, with an air of boredom or disappointment, turned away towards Treno's big picture window, at that hour dappled with night-time lights; seconds later he recovered his usual cheerful, sleepy air, and looked at me with curiosity, but didn't say anything. The silence embarrassed me, made me feel ridiculous; embarrassment quickly gave way to resentment. To get out of that spot I must have asked him if he wasn't surprised by what I'd just said, because Rodney answered:

'No. Why would it surprise me?'

'Because not everyone writes novels,' I said.

Now Rodney smiled.

'That's true,' he said. 'Not even you.'

'What do you mean?' I asked.

'That you don't write novels, you're trying to write one, which is quite different. You'd do well not to confuse the two. Besides,' he added with no attempt to soften the harshness of his previous comment, 'no normal person reads as many novels as you do if not to end up writing them.'

'You haven't written any,' I objected.

'I'm not a normal person,' he answered.

I wanted to ask him why he wasn't a normal person, but I couldn't, because Rodney quickly changed the subject.

This interrupted conversation left me with such an unpleasant aftertaste that I cancelled our get-togethers in Treno's with the false excuse of being overwhelmed with work, but the following week we talked about the novel again and were reconciled, or rather we were reconciled and then we talked about the novel again. It wasn't in Treno's, nor in our office, but after a party at Wong's house. It happened like this. One day, as the Catalan class finished, Wong asked for the floor with a certain solemnity in order to explain that his end of term project in the Department of Theatre consisted in the staging of a one-act play and, with ceremonious humility, he assured us that it would be an honour for him if we would attend the dress rehearsal of the play, which would take place at his house that Friday evening, and tell him what we thought of it. Of course, I didn't have the slightest intention of turning up, but upon returning from the pool on Friday night, with an immense weekend devoid of activities stretching out before me, I must have thought that any excuse was a good one to avoid working and went to Wong's house. He received me with a great show of gratitude and surprise, and deferentially led me up to an attic room at one end of which was a clear space occupied only by a table and two chairs in front of which, on the floor, several spectators were already seated, among them the sinister-looking American from the Catalan literature class. Slightly embarrassed, as if I'd been caught out, I said hello, then I sat down beside him and we talked until Wong decided that no one else would show up and ordered the play to begin. What we watched was a work by Harold Pinter called *Betrayal* performed by acting students from the university; I don't remember the plot, but I do remember there were only four characters, that the chronology was reversed (it began at the end and ended at the beginning) and that it took place over several years and in several different locations, including a hotel room in Venice. Well into the play the doorbell rang. The performance did not pause, Wong got up quietly, went to open the door and immediately returned with Rodney, who, bending over so as not to bump his head on the sloping ceiling, came to sit down beside me.

'What are you doing here?' I whispered to him.

'And you?' he answered, with a wink.

When the play finished we applauded enthusiastically and, after taking the stage to greet the audience in the company of his actors, with several bows prepared for the occasion, Wong announced that some light refreshments awaited us on the floor below. Rodney and I went down the attic stairs along with the sinister-looking American, who praised Wong's production and compared it to another he'd seen years before in Chicago. In the living room was a table covered with a paper tablecloth and heaped with sandwiches, canapés and large bottles; the guests swarmed around it eagerly, starting to drink and eat without waiting until the host and actors joined us. Following their example, I poured myself a glass of beer; following my example, Rodney poured himself a glass of Coke and began to eat a sandwich. Frugal or without appetite, the sinister-looking American chatted, cigarette in hand, with a very thin, very tall girl, whose underprivileged student look perfectly complemented my classmate's punk look. Rodney took advantage of his absence to talk.

'What did you think?' he asked.

'Of the play?'

He nodded as he chewed. I shrugged.

'Good,' I said. 'Pretty good.'

Rodney's expression demanded an explanation.

'Well,' I admitted, 'the truth is I'm not sure I understood it all.'

'I, on the other hand, am sure I didn't understand any of it,' Rodney said after emitting a grunt and swallowing his mouthful with a gulp of Coke. 'But I fear that's not Wong's fault but Pinter's. I can't remember where I read how he discovered his writing method. The guy was with his wife and he said to her: "Darling, I've got quite a few good scenes written, but they've got nothing to do with each other. What should I do?" And his wife answered: "Don't worry: you just put them all together, the critics will take care of explaining what they mean." And it worked: the proof is that there's not a single line of Pinter the critics don't understand perfectly.'

I laughed, but I didn't make any comment on Rodney's comment, because at that moment Wong and the actors appeared in the living room. There was an outbreak of applause, which didn't take off, and then I went over to Wong to congratulate him. We talked about the play for a while; then he introduced me one by one to the actors, and finally to his Catalan boyfriend, a blond, haughty, chubby-cheeked computer science student who, despite the displays of affection Wong lavished on him, gave the impression of

43

doing his utmost to hide the nature of their relationship from me. Rodney didn't approach us; he didn't even say hello to Wong; he wasn't talking to anybody either. He was leaning against the frame of the door to the kitchen, perfectly still, with a half-smile on his face and a drink in his hand, just as though he was watching another production. I kept an eye on him surreptitiously, making sure I didn't meet his gaze: there he was, alone and as if invisible to all in the middle of the hubbub of the party. He didn't look uncomfortable; on the contrary: he seemed to be really enjoying the music and laughter and conversations that bubbled up around him, he seemed to be getting up the courage to break his self-imposed isolation and join in with any of the circles that were constantly forming and dissolving, but most of all (this occurred to me as I watched him watch a couple trying out a few dance steps at a clear end of the living room) he seemed like a child lost among adults or an adult lost among children or an animal lost in a herd of animals of a different species. Then I stopped spying on him and started to talk to one of the actresses, a quite good-looking blonde girl with freckles who told me how difficult Pinter was to perform; I told her how difficult Pinter was to understand, about Pinter's writing method, about Pinter's wife, about Pinter's critics; the girl looked at me very closely, unsure whether to get angry, feel flattered or laugh. When I looked around for Rodney again I didn't see him; I looked all round the living room: nothing. Then I went over to Wong and asked if he'd seen him.

44

'He just left,' he answered, pointing at the door with an offended gesture, 'without saying anything to me about the play. Without saying goodbye. That guy is obviously nuts, unless he's a complete bastard.'

I peered out a window that looked onto the street and saw him. He was standing on the porch steps, tall, bulky, vulnerable and hesitant, his aquiline profile barely standing out against the wan light of the street lamps while he turned up the collar of his sheepskin coat and adjusted his fur cap and stood very still, looking at the darkness of the night and the big snowflakes falling in front of him, covering the garden and road in a dull brightness. For a second I remembered him sitting on the bench and watching the children playing Frisbee and I thought he was crying, or rather, I was sure he was crying, but the next second what I thought was that actually he was just looking at the night in a very strange way, as if he could see things in it that I couldn't see, as if he were looking at an enormous insect or a distorting mirror, and then I thought no, actually he was looking at the night as if he were walking along a narrow pass beside a very dark abyss and no one had as much vertigo or as much fear as he did, and suddenly, while I was thinking that, I noticed all the resentment I'd been harbouring against Rodney during the week had evaporated, who knows whether because at that moment I thought I glimpsed the reason he never attended faculty meetings or parties and had, nevertheless, attended that one.

I grabbed my coat, said a rushed goodbye to Wong and

went out to find Rodney. I found him when he was opening his car door; he didn't seem especially glad to see me. I asked him where he was going; he answered home. I thought of Wong and said:

'You could at least have said goodbye, no?'

He didn't say anything, he pointed to his car and asked:

'Do you want a lift?'

I answered that my house was only a fifteen-minute walk from there and that I preferred to walk; then I asked him if he wanted to walk with me for a while. Rodney shrugged his shoulders, closed the car door and began walking alongside me, at first without saying anything and then talking with sudden animation, though I don't remember what about. What I do remember is that we walked along Race and that when we reached Silver Creek — an old brick mill converted into a chic restaurant — after a silence Rodney stopped.

'What's it about?' he asked out of the blue.

I immediately knew what he was talking about. I looked at him: the fur hat and raised lapels of his coat almost entirely hid his face; in his eyes there was no trace of tears, in fact I thought he might be smiling.

'What's what about?' I said.

'The novel,' he answered.

'Oh, that,' I said with a gesture that was at once self-satisfied and easygoing, as if Rodney's inexplicable indifference towards that matter hadn't been the reason I'd cancelled our get-togethers in Treno's. 'Well, I'm not really sure yet . . .'

46

'I like it,' Rodney interrupted me.

'What do you like?' I asked in astonishment.

'That you don't know what the novel's about yet,' he answered. 'If you know beforehand, that's bad: you'll just say what you already know, which is what we all know. On the other hand, if you don't yet know what you want to say but you're crazy enough or desperate enough or brave enough to keep writing, you might end up saying something that you didn't even know you knew and that only you can come to know, and *that* might be of interest.' As usual I didn't know whether Rodney was talking seriously or joking, but on that occasion I didn't understand a single one of his words. Rodney must have noticed, because, starting to walk again, he concluded: 'What I mean is that someone who always knows where they're going never gets anywhere, and you only know what you're trying to say once you've said it.'

That night we parted next to the Courier Café, very close to my house, and the following week we started getting together at Treno's again. After that we often talked about my novel; in fact, and although we certainly talked about other things, that's almost all I remember us talking about. They were slightly strange conversations, often confusing, in a certain sense always stimulating but only in a certain sense. Rodney, for example, wasn't interested in talking about the plot of my book, which was what I was most worried about, but rather who expounded the plot. 'Stories don't exist,' he once told me. 'What does exist is

47

who tells them. If you know who it is, there's a story, if you don't know who it is, there's no story.' 'Then I've already got mine,' I told him. I explained that the only thing I was clear about in my novel was precisely the identity of the narrator: a guy exactly like me who found himself in the exact same situation as I did. 'Then the narrator is yourself?' Rodney postulated. 'No way,' I said, content at being the one to confound him for a change. 'He's exactly like me, but it's not me.' Overdosing on Flaubert and Eliot's objectivism, I argued that the narrator of my novel couldn't be me because in that case I'd be obliged to talk about myself, which was not only a form of exhibitionism or immodesty, but also a literary error, because authentic literature never revealed the personality of the author, but rather hid it. 'That's true,' agreed Rodney. 'But talking a lot about oneself is the best way of hiding.' Rodney didn't seem too interested in what I was telling or proposed to tell in my book; what did interest him was what I wasn't going to tell. 'In a novel what is not told is always more relevant than what is told,' he said another time. 'I mean that silences are more eloquent than words, and all narrative art consists of knowing when to shut up: that's why the best way to tell a story is not to tell it.' I listened to Rodney enthralled, almost as if he were an alchemist and each phrase he pronounced the necessary ingredient for an infallible potion, but it's probable that these discussions about my future frustrated novel – which in the long run would be decisive for me and that, though neither of us could have predicted it, were also going to be practically the last Rodney and I would have – contributed in the short run to confusing me, because the truth was that almost every week the direction of my book changed completely. I've already said that back then I was very young and lacking in experience and judgement, which are as useful to life as to literature and that explains why in those conversations about literature I paid inordinate attention to anodyne observations Rodney made and barely registered others that sooner or later would prove very useful; I could be mistaken, but I now tend to believe, although it's paradoxical – or precisely because it is – that what allowed me to survive Rodney's often delirious avalanche of lucidity without suffering irreparable damage was precisely my incapacity to distinguish the essential from the superfluous and the sensible from the senseless.

Finally, one morning at the beginning of December I handed Rodney the first pages of my novel, and the next day, when I arrived at the office, I asked him if he'd read them; he said we'd talk about the matter in Treno's, after Rota's class. I was impatient to know Rodney's opinion, but that afternoon the class was so exhausting that when we got to Treno's my impatience had passed or I'd forgotten about the novel, and the only thing I wanted was to have a beer and forget about Rota and the sinister-looking American, who during an endless hour had tortured me by obliging me to translate from Catalan to English and from English to Catalan a grotesque discussion about the similarities that linked a poem by J.V. Foix and another by Arnaut Daniel.

So it's natural that when, after the second beer and without advance warning, Rodney asked me if I was sure I wanted to be a writer, I should have answered:

'Anything but a translator.' We laughed, or at least I laughed, but as I did I remembered another pending discussion, that about the first pages of my novel and, like a careless prolonging of the previous joke, I asked: 'Was it that bad?'

'Not bad,' Rodney answered. 'Dreadful.'

The comment was like a kick in the gut. I reacted quickly: I tried to explain that what he'd read was only a first draft, I tried to defend the approach of the novel I had in mind; in vain: Rodney took the pages of the novel out of the pocket of his coat, unfolded them and proceeded to pulverize the contents. He did it dispassionately, like a coroner performing an autopsy, which hurt even more; but what hurt most of all was that deep down I knew my friend was right. Depressed and furious, with all the bitterness accumulating while Rodney spoke, I asked him whether what I should do according to him was stop writing.

'I didn't say that,' he corrected me, impassively. 'What you should or shouldn't do is up to you. There's no writer who didn't start off writing garbage like this or worse, because to be a decent writer you don't even need talent: a little effort is enough. Besides, talent isn't something you have, it's something you conquer.'

'So why did you ask me if I was sure I wanted to be a writer?' I asked.

'Because you could just end up managing it.'

'And where's the problem?'

'It's a bitch of a job.'

'No worse than being a translator, I suppose. Not to mention a miner.'

'Don't be so sure,' he said with an uncertain gesture. 'I don't know, maybe only someone who can't be anything else should be a writer.'

I laughed as if trying to imitate the ferocious laughter of a kamikaze, or as if I were taking revenge.

'Come on, Rodney: don't tell me now you're going to reveal yourself as a fucking romantic. Or sentimental. Or a coward. I'm not the slightest bit afraid of failure.'

'Of course not,' he said. 'Because you don't have the slightest idea what it means. But who said anything about failure? I was talking about success.'

'Oh, so that's it,' I said. 'Now I understand. The catastrophe of success. That's what it was. But that's not an idea, man: that's just a cliché.'

'Could be,' he said, and then, as if he were laughing at me or scolding me but didn't want me to suspect either of them, he added: 'But ideas don't become clichéd because they're false, but because they're true, or at least contain a substantial part of truth. And when you get bored of truth and start saying original things in order to try to sound interesting, you end up saying nothing but nonsense. In the best cases original and even interesting nonsense, but nonsense.'

I didn't know how to answer and took a sip of beer. Noticing that sarcasm alleviated the outrage of my disappointment, I said: 'Well, at least after what you've read you'll admit that I'm immune to success.'

'Don't be too sure about that either,' Rodney replied. 'Maybe nobody's immune to success; maybe it's enough to be able to endure failure to get caught up by success. And then there's no escape. It's over. Finito. Kaput. Look at Scott, Hemingway: both of them were in love with success, and it killed them both, and long before they were buried. Especially poor Scott, who was the weaker and the most talented one and that's why the disaster caught him sooner and he didn't have time to notice that success is lethal, shameless, an unmitigated disaster, an endless humiliation. He liked it so much that when he got it he didn't even realize, although he kidded himself with protests of pride and demonstrations of cynicism, that actually he'd done nothing but search for it, and now that he had it in his hands it was useless to him and he could do nothing with it but let it corrupt him. And it corrupted him. It corrupted him till the end. You know what Oscar Wilde said: "There are only two tragedies in life: one is not getting what one wants, and the other is getting it."' Rodney laughed; I didn't. 'Anyway, what I mean is that no one dies for having failed, but it's impossible to survive success with dignity. No one says this, not even Oscar Wilde, because it's obvious or because it's very embarrassing, but that's the way it is. So, if you insist on being a writer, put off success as long as you can.'

While listening to Rodney I inevitably remembered my friend Marcos and our dreams of triumph and the master-pieces with which we thought we'd get our revenge on the world, and most of all I remembered one time, some years before, when Marcos told me that an insufferable classmate at the Faculty of Fine Arts had told him that the ideal condition for an artist is failure, and that he'd replied with a quote from the French writer Jules Renard: 'Yes, I know. All great men were ignored in their lifetimes; but I'm not a great man, so I'd prefer immediate renown.' I also thought Rodney was talking as if he knew what success and failure were, when actually he didn't know either one (or he didn't know them except by way of books or any more than me, who barely knew), and that actually his words were just the words of a loser soaked in the hypocritical and sickly mythology of failure that ruled a country hysterically obsessed with success. I thought all this and was about to say it to him, but I didn't say anything. What I did, after a silence, was mock Rodney's jeremiad.

'Fucked if you fail, fucked if you succeed,' I said. 'Great prospects.'

My friend didn't even smile.

'It's a really fucked-up job,' he said. 'But not because of that. Or not only because of that.'

'That seems minor to you?'

'Yeah,' he said, and then asked: 'What's a writer?'

'What do you think?' I lost patience. 'A guy who can string words together one after the other and is able to do so with flair.'

'Exactly,' Rodney approved. 'But it's also a guy who considers extremely complicated problems and who, instead of resolving them or trying to resolve them, like any sensible person, makes them even more complicated. That is: he's a nutcase who looks at reality, and sometimes sees it.'

'Everyone sees reality,' I objected, 'even if they're not nuts.'

'That's where you're mistaken,' Rodney said. 'Everybody looks at reality, but few people see it. The artist isn't the one who makes the invisible visible: that really is romanticism, although not the worst kind; the artist is the one who makes visible what's already visible and everybody looks at and nobody can or nobody knows how or nobody wants to see. Probably nobody wants to see. It's too unpleasant, often appalling, and you really have to have balls to see it without closing your eyes or running away, because whoever sees it is destroyed or goes crazy. Unless, of course, he has a shield to protect himself or he can do something with what he sees.' Rodney paused then went on: 'I mean normal people suffer or enjoy reality, but they're powerless to do anything with it, while the writer can, because his job consists of turning reality into meaning, even if it's an illusory meaning; that is, he can turn it into beauty and that beauty or that meaning are his shield. That's why I say that the writer is a nutcase who has the obligation or the dubious privilege of seeing reality, and that's why, when a writer stops writing, he ends up killing himself, because he hasn't been able to kick the habit of seeing reality but he no longer has his shield to protect himself from it. That's why Hemingway killed himself. And that's why once you're a writer you can't stop being one, unless you decide to risk your neck. Like I said: a really fucked-up job.'

That conversation could have turned out very badly – in fact it had all the signs of turning out very badly – but I don't know why it turned out better than any other, as Rodney and I left Treno's laughing our heads off and I was feeling more his friend than ever and wanting more than ever to become a real writer. Shortly after that the winter holidays began and, almost overnight, Urbana emptied: the students fled en masse to their homes, the streets, buildings and businesses of the campus were deserted and a strange sidereal (or maybe maritime) silence took over the city, as if it had suddenly turned into a planet spinning far from its orbit or into a gleaming ocean liner miraculously run aground in the endless snows of Illinois. The last time we were together at Treno's Rodney invited me to spend Christmas Day at his house in Rantoul. I declined the invitation: I explained that for a while Rodrigo Ginés and I had been planning a road trip through the Midwest, along with Gudrun and an American friend of Gudrun's I'd slept with a couple of times (Barbara, she was called); I also said that, if he gave me his phone number in Rantoul, when I got back I'd give him a call so we could see each other before classes began again.

'Don't worry,' said Rodney, 'I'll call you.'

And so we said goodbye, and less than a week later I set off travelling with Rodrigo, Barbara and Gudrun. We'd planned to be away from Urbana for two weeks, but in fact we didn't get back for almost a month. We travelled in Barbara's car, at first following a vaguely fixed plan, but then allowing whim or chance to guide us, and in this way, often driving all day and sleeping in highway motels and cheap little hotels, first we went south, through St Louis, Memphis and Jackson, until we got to New Orleans; we stayed there for several days, after which we began our return, making a detour through the east, up through Meridian, Tuscaloosa and Nashville till we got to Cincinnati and then to Indianapolis, from where we came home drenched in the light and the cold and the highways and sound and immensity and snow and the bars and the people and the plains and the filth and the skies and the sadness and the towns and cities of the Midwest. It was a huge and happy trip, during which I made the irrevocable decision to pay attention to Rodney, throw the novel I'd been working on for months in the garbage and start writing another one immediately. So the first thing I did when I got back to Urbana was to go look for Rodney. In the phone book there was only one Falk – Falk, Dr Robert – resident in Rantoul and, since I knew that Rodney lived with his father, I supposed it must be Rodney's father. I dialled the number several times, but no one answered. For his part, and contrary to what he'd promised, Rodney didn't get in touch with me either during the rest of the holidays.

Classes resumed at the end of January, and the first day, opening the door to my office, sure I was finally going to see Rodney again, I almost crashed head first into a chubby, little, albino-looking guy I'd never seen before. Naturally, I thought I'd opened the door to the wrong office and quickly apologized, but before I could shut the door the guy held out his hand and in a laboured Spanish told me I hadn't been mistaken; he then pronounced his name and announced he was the new assistant professor of Spanish. Perplexed, I shook his hand, mumbled something, introduced myself; then we chatted for a moment, I don't know what about, and only at the end did I resolve to ask him about Rodney. He told me he didn't know anything, except that he'd been hired to replace him. Before my first class that day I inquired in the offices: they didn't know anything there either. Finally it was the secretary of the department head who, the next day, gave me news of my friend. It seems just a few days before the end of the vacation a relative had called to say Rodney wouldn't be returning to work, leaving the head of the department furious and having to look as fast as possible for someone to replace him. I asked the secretary if she knew what had happened to Rodney; she said no. I asked if the boss knew; she said no and advised me not to even consider asking him. I asked if she had Rodney's phone number; she said no.

'I don't and neither does anyone else in the department,' she said, and then I realized that she was just as furious with Rodney as her boss; however, before I left she broke down in the face of my insistence and added reluctantly: 'But I have his address.'

A few days later I asked Barbara if I could borrow her car and went to Rantoul. It was a bright afternoon at the beginning of February. I drove out of Urbana along Broadway and Cunningham Avenue, went north on a highway that advanced between corn fields buried in snow, glistening in the sun, scattered with pine trees, maples, metal silos and isolated little houses, and twenty-five minutes later, after passing an army air base, I arrived at Rantoul, a small working-class city (really it was more like a large town) that gave Urbana a certain metropolitan air in comparison. On the outskirts, at the intersection of two streets – Liberty Drive and Century Boulevard – there was a gas station. I stopped and asked a man in overalls for Belle Avenue, which was the street where, according to the department head's secretary, Rodney lived; he gave me some directions and I continued on towards the centre. I was soon lost. It had started to get dark; the city seemed deserted. I stopped the car at a corner, just where a sign proclaimed Sangamon Avenue. In front of me were train tracks and beyond them the city dissolved into a wooded darkness, to my left the street was soon cut off, to my right, three hundred or so metres away, blinked a neon sign. I turned right and headed towards the sign: BUD'S BAR, it said. I parked the car in the middle of a string of cars and went in.

In the bar a smoky, jovial, Saturday-night atmosphere prevailed. There were lots of people: boys playing pool, women putting coins in the slot machines, men drinking beer and watching a basketball game on a giant television screen; a jukebox spread country music all through the place. I went over to the bar, behind which three waiters – two very young and the other somewhat older – wandered around a low table covered in bottles and, while waiting for someone to serve me, I looked at the photos of baseball stars and the big portrait of John Wayne dressed as a cowboy, with a dark red bandana knotted at his throat, which hung on the back wall. Finally one of the waiters, the oldest of the three, came over with a hurried air, but before he could ask me what I wanted to drink I told him I was looking for Belle Avenue, 25 Belle Avenue.

As if he were mocking me, the bartender asked:

'You want to see the doctor?'

'I want to see Rodney Falk,' I answered.

I must have said it too loud, because two men who were leaning on the bar nearby turned around to look at me. The waiter's expression had changed: now the mockery had turned to a mixture of surprise and interest; he leaned on the bar too, as if my answer had dispelled his hurry. He was a man of about forty, compact and dark, stony-faced, slanting eyes and boxer's nose; he was wearing a sweaty Red Sox cap, a few locks of greasy hair poked out from under it at his temples and the nape of his neck.

'You know Rodney?' he asked.

'Yeah,' I answered. 'We work together in Urbana.'

'At the university?'

59

'At the university.'

'I see,' he nodded thoughtfully. Then he added: 'Rodney's not home.'

'Ah,' I said, and was about to ask where he was or how he knew he wasn't home, but by then I must've started feeling uneasy, because I didn't. 'Well, it doesn't matter.' I repeated: 'Could you tell me where 25 Belle Avenue is?'

'Of course,' he smiled. 'But wouldn't you like to have a beer first?'

At that moment I noticed that the men sitting at the bar were still scrutinizing me, and absurdly imagined that everyone in the bar was waiting for my reply; a cold froth suddenly gathered in my stomach, as if I'd just entered a dream or a danger zone that I had to escape from as soon as possible. That's what I was thinking at that moment: of getting out of that bar as soon as possible. So I said: 'No, thanks.'

Just as the waiter had indicated, Rodney's house was barely five hundred metres from Bud's Bar, as soon as I turned the corner onto Belle Avenue. It was an older, bigger and more solid house than the ones lined up next to it; except for the slate grey gable roof, the rest of the building was painted white: as well as a narrow attic, it had two floors, a porch at the top of some brown steps and a front lawn buried in snow, with two bushy maples and a pole with the American flag waving gently in the breeze of twilight. I parked the car and rang the bell. No one answered and I rang again. I was just about to peer in through one of the downstairs windows when the door opened and on the threshold appeared a man with completely white hair, about seventy years old, wearing a very thick blue dressing gown and a pair of slippers of the same colour, holding the door knob in one hand and a book in the other; in the half-light of the hallway, behind him, I glimpsed a coat stand, a mirror with a wooden frame, the base of a carpeted stairway leading up to the darkness of the second floor. Except for his heavy build and the colour of his eyes, the man hardly resembled Rodney, but I immediately guessed it was his father. I smiled and, flustered, greeted him and asked for Rodney. He suddenly adopted a defensive attitude and, with intemperate severity, asked me who I was. I told him. Only then did he seem to relax a little.

'Rodney talked about you,' he said, without the little light of mistrust in his eyes going out. 'You're the writer, aren't you?'

He said this with absolutely no irony and, as had happened almost a year earlier with Marcelo Cuartero in El Yate, I felt my cheeks burn: it was the second time in my life that someone had called me a writer, and I was overwhelmed by an inextricable mix of embarrassment and pride, and also a wave of affection for Rodney. I didn't say anything, but, since the man didn't seem prepared to invite me in or break the silence, for something to say I asked if he was Rodney's father. He said yes. Then I asked for Rodney again and he answered that he didn't know where he was.

'He left a couple of weeks ago and he hasn't come back,' he said.

'Has something happened to him?' I asked.

'Why should something happen to him?' he answered.

Then I told him what they'd told me at the department.

'That's true,' the man said. 'It was me who advised them Rodney wouldn't be teaching again. I hope he hasn't caused them any problems.'

'Not at all,' I lied, thinking about the department head and his secretary.

'I'm glad,' said Rodney's father. 'Well,' he then added, beginning to close the door. 'Excuse me, but I have things to do and . . .'

'Wait a second,' I interrupted him, not knowing how I was going to go on, then went on: 'I'd like you to tell Rodney that I was here.'

'Don't worry. I'll tell him.'

'Do you know when he'll be back?'

Instead of answering, Rodney's father sighed, and immediately, as if his eyesight wasn't good enough to make me out clearly in the growing darkness of dusk, he let go of the door knob and flipped a switch: a white light suddenly swept the twilight off the porch.

'Tell me something,' he said then, blinking. 'What have you come here for?'

'I told you already,' I answered. 'I'm a friend of Rodney's. I wanted to know why he hadn't come back to Urbana. I wanted to know if something had happened to him. I wanted to see him.'

Now the man scrutinized me closely, as if till then he hadn't really seen me or as if my answer had disappointed him, maybe surprised him; unexpectedly, a moment later he smiled, a smile at once hard and almost affectionate, which covered his face in wrinkles, and in which, nevertheless, I recognized for the first time a distant echo of Rodney's features.

'Do you really think that Rodney and you were friends?' he asked.

'I don't understand,' I answered.

He sighed again and wanted to know how old I was. I told him.

'You're very young,' he said. 'Tell me something else: did Rodney ever talk to you about Vietnam?' He answered his own question. 'No, of course not. How could he talk to you about Vietnam? You wouldn't have understood a thing. He didn't even talk to me about that, or only at the beginning. He did to his mother, until she died. And to his wife, until she couldn't take any more. Did you know Rodney was married? No, you didn't know that either. You don't know anything about Rodney. Nothing. How could he be your friend? Rodney doesn't have friends. He can't have any. You understand, don't you?'

As he spoke, Rodney's father had been gradually raising his voice, charging himself with reason, getting furious, the words converted into fuel for his rage, and for a moment I

feared he was going to slam the door in my face or burst
into tears. He didn't slam the door in my face, he didn't
burst into tears. He stood in silence, suddenly decrepit, a
little out of breath, looking with the book in his hand at the
night that was falling over Belle Avenue, badly illuminated
by yellowish street lamps that gave off a dim light. I too
stayed silent, feeling very small and very fragile before that
enraged old man, and feeling most of all that I should never
have gone to Rantoul to look for Rodney. Then it was as if
the man had read my mind, because, sounding upset, he
said:

'I'm sorry. I shouldn't have spoken to you like that.'

'Don't worry,' I reassured him.

'Rodney will come back,' he declared, not looking me in
the eye. 'I don't know when he'll come back, but he'll come
back. Or that's what I think.' He hesitated for a moment and
then went on: 'For years he didn't spend much time at
home, he wandered around, he wasn't well. But lately
everything had changed, and he was very comfortable
at the university. Did you know he was comfortable at
the university?' I nodded. 'He was very comfortable, he
was, but it couldn't last: too good to be true. That's why
what had to happen happened.' He put his free hand back on
the door knob; he looked at me again: I don't know what
was in his eyes, I don't know what I saw in them (it wasn't
suspicion any more, nor was it gratitude), I don't even
know how to describe what I felt looking at him, but what I
do know is that it was very similar to fear. 'And that's all,'

he concluded. 'Believe me I'm very grateful you took the trouble to come out here, and forgive my bad manners. You're a good person and you'll be able to understand; besides, Rodney appreciated you. But listen to me: go back to Urbana, work hard, behave as best you can and forget about Rodney. That's my advice. In any case, if you can't or don't want to forget about Rodney, the best thing you can do is pray for him.'

That night I returned to Urbana confused and maybe a little scared, as if I'd just committed a mistake that would have unforeseeable consequences, feeling lonelier than ever in Urbana and feeling as well, for the first time since my arrival there, that I shouldn't stay much longer in that country that wasn't mine and whose impossible idiosyncrasies I'd never be able to decipher, prepared in any case to forget forever my mistaken visit to Rantoul and follow Rodney's father's advice to the letter. I didn't manage this last part, of course, or at least not entirely, and not only because I'd forgotten how to pray a long time before, but also because very soon I discovered that Rodney had been too important to me to get rid of him just like that, and because all of Urbana conspired to keep his memory alive. It's true that, in the weeks that followed and in all the rest of the time I spent in Urbana, hardly anyone in the department ever mentioned his name again, and even when I happened to meet Dan Gleylock in the faculty corridors I never made up my mind to ask if he had any news of him. But it's also true that every time I passed Treno's, and I passed it daily, I thought of Rodney, and that just at that time I began reading some of his favourite authors and I couldn't open a page of Emerson or Hawthorne or Twain – not to mention Hemingway – without thinking immediately of him, just as I couldn't write a line of the novel I'd started to write without feeling him vigilantly breathing over my shoulder. So, although Rodney had vanished into thin air, in fact he was more present than ever in my life, exactly as if he'd turned into a ghost or a zombie. Be that as it may, the fact is that not a lot of time passed before I convinced myself I'd never hear Rodney spoken of again.

Of course I was wrong. One night at the beginning of April or the end of March, just after Spring Break – the North American equivalent of *Semana Santa* – someone called me at home. I remember I was just finishing a short story by Hemingway called 'A Clean, Well-Lighted Place' when the phone rang; I also remember I picked it up thinking of that sorrowful story and especially of the sorrowful, nihilistic prayer it contained – 'Our nada who art in nada, nada be thy name thy kingdom nada thy will be nada in nada as it is in nada' – it was Rodney's father. I still hadn't recovered from the surprise when, after confessing he'd got my number from the department, he began to apologize for the way he'd treated me on my visit to Rantoul. I interrupted him; I told him he had nothing to apologize for, I asked him if he had any news from Rodney. He answered that he'd called from somewhere in New Mexico a few days ago, that they'd talked for a while and that he was well, although for the moment it wasn't likely he'd be coming home.

'But that's not why I called,' he immediately made clear. 'I'm calling because I'd like to talk to you. Would you have any time to spare for me?'

'Of course,' I said. 'What about?'

Rodney's father seemed doubtful for a moment and then he said: 'The truth is I'd rather talk about it in person. Face to face. If it's not too much trouble.'

I told him it was no trouble.

'Would you mind coming to my house?' he asked.

'No,' I said and, although I meant to go in any case, because by then I'd forgotten the sensation of anxiety that had seized me after my first visit to Rantoul, I added: 'But you could at least tell me what you want to talk about.'

'It's nothing important,' he said. 'I'd just like to tell you a story. I think it might interest you. How does Saturday afternoon suit you?'

STARS AND STRIPES

SIXTEEN YEARS HAVE NOW gone by since that spring afternoon I spent in Rantoul, but, perhaps because during all that
time I've known that sooner or later I'd have to tell it, that I
couldn't not tell it, I still remember quite accurately the
story Rodney's father told me in the course of those hours. I
have a much less precise memory, on the other hand, of the
circumstances surrounding them.

I arrived in Rantoul shortly after midday and found the
house with no trouble. As soon as I rang the bell, Rodney's
father opened the door and invited me into the living room, a
spacious, bright and cosy room, with a fireplace and a leather
sofa and two wingback chairs at one end, and at the other,
beside the window that faced Belle Avenue, an oak table and
chairs, walls lined to the ceiling with perfectly ordered books
and floor covered with thick burgundy-coloured rugs that
hushed footsteps. The truth is, after our unexpected phone
conversation, I had almost anticipated that from the start
Rodney's father would display a cordiality unheralded by our
first encounter, but what I could in no way have predicted is
that the diminished and intimidating man who, in dressing

71

gown and slippers, had dispatched me without a second thought just a few months earlier would now receive me dressed with a sober elegance more suitable to a venerable Boston Brahmin than a retired, country doctor in the Midwest, apparently converted into one of those false elderly men who strive to exhibit, beneath the unwelcome certainty of their many years, the vitality and poise of someone who has not yet resigned himself to enjoying only the scraps of old age. However, as he came out with the story I had gone to hear, that deceptive façade began to crumble and reveal its flaws, damp stains and deep fissures, and by the middle of his story Rodney's father was no longer talking with the exuberant energy he'd started with – when he spoke as if possessed by a long-deferred urgency, or rather as if his life depended on the act of talking and my listening to him, insistently looking me in the eye just as if he sought there an impossible confirmation of his tale – because by that point his words no longer quivered with the slightest vital impulse, but only the venomous and inflexible memory of a man consumed by regret and devastated by misfortune, and the grey light that entered through the window wrapping the living room in shadows had erased from his face all traces of his distant youth, leaving a bare preview of his skull. I remember that at one point I began to hear the pattering of rain on the porch roof, a pattering that almost immediately turned into a jubilant spring downpour that obliged us to turn on a floor lamp because by then it was almost night and we'd been sitting for many hours face to face, sunken in the two wingback chairs, he talking and me

72

listening, with the ashtray overflowing with cigarette butts and on the table an empty coffee pot and two empty cups and a pile of much-handled letters that carried US Army postmarks, letters from Saigon and Da Nang and Xuan Loc and Quang Ngai, from various parts of the Batagan peninsula, letters that spanned a period of more than two years and carried the signatures of his two sons, Rodney and also Bob, but mostly Rodney's. They were very numerous, and were ordered chronologically and kept in three black cardboard document cases with elastic closures, each of which had a handwritten label with the name Rodney and the name Bob, the word Vietnam and the dates of the first and last letter it contained. Rodney's father seemed to know them off by heart, or at least to have read them dozens of times, and during that afternoon he read me some fragments. That didn't surprise me; what did surprise me – what left me literally dumbfounded – was that at the end of my visit he insisted I take them with me. 'I don't want them any more,' he said before I took my leave, handing me the three document cases. 'Please, keep them and do with them as you see fit.' It was an absurd request, whichever way you look at it, but precisely because it was absurd I couldn't or didn't know how to refuse. Or perhaps, after all, it wasn't so absurd. The fact is, during these sixteen years I haven't given up trying to explain it to myself: I've thought he entrusted his sons' letters to me because he knew he didn't have much time left and he didn't want them ending up in the hands of someone who was unaware of their significance and who might just get rid of them; I've thought he entrusted the letters to me because doing so amounted to a symbolic and hopeless attempt to forever free himself of the story of the disaster they contained and that transferring them to me would make me the repository of the tale or even responsible for it, or because in doing so he wanted to compel me to share with him the burden of his guilt. I've thought all these things and many more besides, but of course I still don't know for certain why he entrusted me with those letters and now I'll never know; perhaps he didn't even know himself. It doesn't matter: the fact is he entrusted them to me and now I have them before me, while I write. During these sixteen years I've read them many times. Bob's are few and brief, absent-mindedly kind, as if the war entirely absorbed his energy and his intelligence and made everything alien to it seem banal or illusory; Rodney's, on the other hand, are frequent and voluminous, and in their craftsmanship one notices an evolution that is undoubtedly a mirror of the evolution that Rodney himself experienced during the years he spent in Vietnam: at the beginning they are careful and nuanced, careful not to let reality show through more than by way of a sophisticated rhetoric of reticence, made of silences, allusions, metaphors and implications, and at the end torrential and unbridled, often verging on delirium, just as if the uncontainable whirlwind of the war had burst a dam through the cracks of which had spilled a senseless avalanche of clear-sightedness.

What follows is Rodney's story, or, at least, his story as his father told me that afternoon and as I remember it, and as it appears in his letters and in Bob's letters. There are no fundamental discrepancies between those two sources, and although I've checked some names, some places and some dates, I don't know which parts of this story correspond to the truth of the story and which parts to attribute to the imagination, bad memory or bad conscience of the narrators: what I'm telling is just what they told (and what I deduced or imagined from what they told), not what really happened. I should add that, at twenty-five, when I heard Rodney's story that afternoon from his father, I knew nothing or almost nothing about the Vietnam War, which was then (I suspect) no more than a confusing background noise on the television news of my adolescence and an annoying obsession of certain Hollywood film makers, and also that, despite having been living in the United States for almost a year, I couldn't even imagine that although it had officially ended over a decade earlier, in the minds of many Americans it was still as vivid as on 29 March 1973, the day on which, after the deaths of almost sixty thousand of their compatriots – the vast majority of them boys around twenty years of age – and having completely devastated the invaded country, dropping more than eight times as many bombs on it as on all of Europe during the entire Second World War, the United States Army finally left Vietnam.

Rodney had been born forty-one years before in Rantoul. His father came from Houlton, in the state of Maine, in the northeast of the country, way up near the Canadian border. He'd studied in Augusta, where his family had moved after his grandfather was ruined in the economic crisis of 1929, and then in New York. After graduating from medical school at Columbia in 1943, he enlisted in the army as a private, and during the next two years fought in North Africa, France and Germany. He was not a religious man (or he wasn't until very late in life), but he'd been raised with that strict sense of justice and ethical probity that seems to be the patrimony of Protestant families, and he felt a private satisfaction at having fought for the triumph of liberty and that, thanks to his sacrifice and that of many other young Americans like him, the United States had saved the world from the wicked abjection of fascism; he was also convinced that, having risen in arms to guarantee freedom, his country could not shy away, whether out of complacency or cowardice, from the moral commitment it had contracted with the rest of the world, could not leave abandoned in the hands of terror, injustice or slavery anyone who requested its help to liberate them from oppression. He returned from Europe in 1945. That same year he began to practise medicine in the public hospitals of the Midwest, first in St Paul, Minnesota, and then in Oak Park, a suburb of Chicago, until, for reasons he didn't want to explain and I didn't want to inquire into (but which, he implied or I deduced, undoubtedly had something to do with his idealism or his candour and with his absolute disillusionment with the way public medicine was run), he put down roots definitively in Rantoul, which was strange and even enigmatic, because it's impossible to imagine a destination less brilliant for a cosmopolitan and ambitious young doctor like him. There, in Rantoul, he married a girl from a very humble background he'd met in Chicago; there, that same year, Rodney was born; Bob was born the following year.

From the beginning Rodney and Bob were two thoroughly opposite boys; the passing of time did nothing but accentuate this opposition. Both had inherited their father's physical fortitude and iron constitution, but only Bob felt comfortable with them and was able to take advantage of them, while for Rodney they seemed little less than an unhappy accident of nature, a personal circumstance that it was necessary to battle against as naturally or with the same resignation with which one battles against a congenital illness. As a child Rodney was extroverted to the point of naïveté, vehement, spontaneous and affectionate, and this straightforward temperament, on top of his love of reading and his brilliance at school, turned him into his father's undisguised favourite. On the other hand – and possibly to reap the benefits of their progenitor's guilty conscience over his open preference for Rodney – Bob's relations with the family evolved into a reserved and defensive, often tyrannical, moodiness abounding in reckonings, stipulations and caution, which at the beginning was maybe only a way of demanding the attention he was denied, but which insidiously became a strategy destined to hide personal and intellectual deficiencies that, with or without reason, made him feel inferior to his brother, which in time would end up turning him into one of those classic younger sons who, because they gather up the family ruses the first-born squanders, always seem much more mature than him, and often are. Nevertheless, these imbalances and dissimilarities never translated into hostility between the two brothers, because Bob was too busy accumulating rancour towards his father to feel any towards Rodney, and because Rodney, who hadn't the slightest motive for antagonism towards Bob and who was aware of needing his brother's physical competence and vital shrewdness much more than his brother needed his affection or intelligence, knew how to constantly make amends in their shared games, their shared love of hunting, fishing and baseball, their shared outings and friendships. So, by one of those unstable balancing acts upon which the most solid and lasting friendships are based, the disparity between Rodney and Bob ended up constituting the best guarantee of a fraternal complicity that nothing seemed able to break.

Not even the war. In the middle of 1967 Bob enlisted voluntarily in the Marine Corps, and a few months later arrived in Saigon as part of the First Infantry Division. The decision to sign up was entirely unexpected, and Rodney's father didn't rule out various different but complementary reasons that might explain it: his incapacity to face up to the demands of a degree in medicine that, out of pride rather than inclination – to demonstrate to himself he could be as good as his father – he'd begun to study for the previous year, and the insatiable eagerness to garner his family's admiration by that unexpected act of bravery. If that was the case — and in Rodney's father's judgement nothing seemed to lead one to suspect it was not — Bob's decision had been a good one, because as soon as he heard of it, his father could not help feeling secretly proud of him: like so many other Americans, Rodney's father then considered the Vietnam War a just war, and with that impetuous decision his son wasn't doing anything but continuing in southeast Asia the work he'd started in Europe twenty-four years earlier, freeing a distant and defenceless country from an ignominious tyranny. Perhaps because he knew him better than his parents did, Bob's decision didn't surprise Rodney, but it did horrify him and, given that he was the only member of the family to know of it before it was made, he did all he could to dissuade him from his determination and, once he'd done it, to persuade him to undo it. He wasn't able to. At that time Rodney was in Chicago, despite his father's veiled but firm initial opposition, studying philosophy and literature, and his opinion on the war differed starkly from that of his brother and his father, who attributed his first-born's position to the influence of the dissolute, anti-war atmosphere that prevailed at Northwestern University, as it did on so many campuses across the length and breadth of the United States. The fact is, however, that by the time Bob enlisted in the army, Rodney had quite a clear idea of what was going on in South Vietnam as well as in North Vietnam: he didn't just follow the vicissitudes of the war closely in the American and French newspapers, but also, as well as a complete history of Vietnam, he'd read everything he could get his hands on about the subject, including the analyses of Mary McCarthy, Philippe Devillers and Jean Lacouture and the books of Harrison Salisbury, Staughton Lynd and Tom Hayden, and he'd arrived at the conclusion, much less impulsive or more reasoned than that of many of his classmates, that the declared motivations of his country's intervention in Vietnam were false or spurious, its aim confusing and in the end unjust, and its methods of an atrociously disproportionate brutality. So Rodney began to participate very early on in all sorts of activities protesting against the war, during one of which he met Julia Flores, a Mexican girl from Oaxaca, a mathematics student at North-western, cheerful and uninhibited, who integrated him fully in the pacifist movement and initiated him in love and marijuana and sprinkled his rudimentary Spanish with swearwords.

One afternoon in the summer he graduated from uni-versity, while spending some time with his family in Rantoul, Rodney received his draft notice from the army. He undoubtedly expected it, but that wouldn't have made it alarm him any less. He didn't say anything to his parents; nor did he seek refuge with Julia or the advice of any of his comrades in the peace movement. Rodney knew he couldn't put forward any real excuses to evade that order, so it's possible he spent the days that followed torn between the fear of deserting, taking the path to exile in Canada that so many young men of his age had taken then, and the fear of going to a remote and hateful war against a martyred country, a war he knew for certain that he – unlike his brother Bob, who he rightly considered a man of action and incalculable cunning – could not survive. One of those days of pressing doubts a letter from Bob arrived at the house and, as usual, his father read it aloud at the dinner table, peppering the reading with proud elucidation that was like a rebuke, or that in his fearful nervousness his son interpreted as a rebuke. The thing is that, in the middle of one of his father's comments, Rodney interrupted him, the interruption degenerated into an argument and the argument into one of those fights in which the two contenders, because they know each other better than anybody, know better than anybody where to wound to make the other bleed most. In this one there was no blood – at least no physical blood, no blood not merely metaphorical – but there were accusations, insults and slamming doors, and the next morning, before anyone had woken up, Rodney took his father's car and disappeared and, when he returned home after three days without a word, he called his father and mother together and unceremoniously announced, giving them no chance to reply, that in two months' time he was enlisting in the army. Almost twenty years after that fateful August day, sitting across from me in the same wingback chair where he had heard Rodney's words of no return, while he held a cup of cold coffee and searched my eyes for the relief of a glimmer of exoneration, Rodney's father was still wondering where his son had been and what he'd done during those three days of flight, and was still also wondering, as he'd done over and over again for the last twenty years, why Rodney had not deserted and had ended up complying with the order to go to Vietnam. In all that time he'd been unable to find a satisfactory answer to the first question; not so the second. 'People tend to believe that many explanations are less convincing than one alone,' Rodney's father told me. 'But the truth is there's more than one reason for almost everything.' According to Rodney's father, he would not have joined the army if he could have legally got out of it, but he didn't feel able to deliberately contravene the law – although he considered it unjust – and much less to humiliate himself by asking his father to pull some professional strings to get one of his colleagues to agree to commit fraud by inventing some reason for a medical exemption. On the other hand, refusing to go to war in the name of his pacifist convictions would have cost Rodney two years in prison, and the option of exile in Canada wasn't without risks either, among them that of not being able to return to his country for many years. 'Besides,' Rodney's father went on, 'deep down he was still a boy with his head full of adventure novels and John Wayne movies: he knew his father had fought a war, that his grandfather had fought a war, that war was what men did, that only in war does a man prove he's a man.' So Rodney's father guessed that in some hidden corner of his son's mind, fed by the notions of bravery, manliness and rectitude he'd inculcated in him, and in the struggle with his own nascent ideas of a young man just out of adolescence, he still cherished, a secret but powerful, heroic and romantic concept of war as an essential fact of a man's life, which explained the conviction, matured over twenty years, that if his son had betrayed his anti-war views, swallowed his fear and obeyed the order to go to Vietnam it had really been out of shame, because he knew if he hadn't, he'd never be able to face the simple folk of his country again, because he'd never be able to face his brother or his mother again, but most of all – above all else – because he'd never be able to face him again. 'So it was me who sent Rodney to Vietnam,' Rodney's father said. 'Just as I'd done to Bob.'

Before he went to Vietnam Rodney spent an initial period of training ('basic training', they called it) at Fort Jackson, South Carolina, and a second period ('advanced training', they called it) at Fort Polk, Louisiana. His first letters date from that time. 'The first thing you notice upon arrival here,' Rodney writes from Fort Jackson, 'is that reality has receded to a primitive stage, because in this place only rank and violence hold sway: the strong survive, the weak do not. As soon as I came through the door they insulted me, shaved my head, put me in new clothes, took away my identity, so no one needed to tell me that if I wanted to get out of this alive, I had to try to blend into the background, dissolve into the crowd, and I also had to be more brutal than the rest of my comrades. The second thing you notice is something even more elemental. I already knew that perfect happiness does not exist, but here I've learned that perfect unhappiness doesn't exist either, because even the slightest breath is an infinite source of happiness.' Rodney lost ten kilos in his first three weeks at Fort Jackson. There and at Fort Polk, there were two feelings dominant in Rodney's mind: strangeness and fear. The majority of his comrades, eighteen- and nineteen-year-old boys mostly, were younger than him: some of them were delinquents whom the judge had given a choice of prison or the army; others were unfortunates who, since they didn't know what to do with their lives, had rightly imagined that the army would give them a sense of mission and meaning; the immense majority were uneducated workers who adapted to the rigours of military life with less difficulty than did he, who, despite being used to outdoor life and having a long familiarity with firearms, had led too comfortable an existence up till then to survive undamaged the roughness of the army. But there was also the fear: not fear as a state of mind, but as a physical sensation, cold, humiliating and sticky, which had hardly any resemblance to what he'd called fear until then, not fear of a distant enemy, still invisible and abstract, but fear of his commanders, his comrades, loneliness and himself: a fear that, contradictory though it may seem, didn't keep him from loving them all. There's a letter from Xuan Loc dated 30 January 1969, when Rodney had been in Vietnam for almost a year, in which he tells in detail an anecdote from those months of instruction, as if he'd needed a whole year to digest it, or to resolve to tell it. A few days before his

84

departure for Vietnam they called him and his comrades all together in the functions room in Fort Polk for a last-minute talk by a captain and a sergeant recently returned from the front on techniques of evasion and survival in the jungle. While the captain – a man with an impassive smile and cultivated manners – was speaking, the sergeant held a perfectly white, soft and nervous rabbit, with astonished childlike eyes, that captured the attention of all the soldiers with its inopportune presence. At a certain moment, the rabbit squirmed out of the sergeant's hands and ran away; the captain stopped talking, and a jubilation took over the hall while the rabbit scurried among the desks, until some-one finally caught the animal and handed it back to the sergeant. Then the captain took it and, before the ruckus had entirely died down and a brutal silence filled the hall, in a couple of seconds, the smile never leaving his lips and barely getting a drop of blood on himself, broke its neck, tore it to pieces, ripped out its entrails and threw them over the soldiers.

A few days after witnessing this spectacle, intended as a foretaste or a warning, Rodney landed at the Ton Son Nhut military airport in Saigon, after a Braniff Airlines flight that lasted almost thirty hours, during which uniformed stew-ardesses fattened them up with hot dogs. That happened at the beginning of 1968, just when the Tet Offensive was starting and in the city – then converted into a garbage dump of dead flowers, paper and spent firecracker casings from the recently concluded festival, blown about by a damp and pestilent wind that reeked of urine and human excrement – fear was palpable everywhere, like an epidemic. That was the first thing Rodney noticed when he got to Vietnam: the fear, again the fear. The second thing he noticed was the strangeness. But in this case the reason for the strangeness was different: the Vietnam he'd shaped in his mind hadn't the slightest similarity with the real Vietnam; in fact, you could say they were two different countries, and the surprising thing was that the Vietnam imagined from the United States seemed much more real than the real Vietnam and, in consequence, he felt much less alien to that one than to this one. The result of this paradox was another paradox: despite still despising what the United States was doing to Vietnam (what he was contributing to the United States doing to Vietnam), in Vietnam he felt much more American than he did in the United States, and that, despite the respect and admiration the Vietnamese soon inspired in him, he felt much further away from them there than he had in his own country. Rodney assumed that the cause of this incoherence was his absolute incapacity to communicate with the few Vietnamese people he had any contact with, and not only because some of them didn't know his language, but because even those who did know it overwhelmed him with their exoticism, their lack of irony, their incredible capacity for self-denial, their incredible and permanent serenity, their exaggerated courtesy (which wasn't difficult to confuse with a servility that inspired fear) and with their dull credulity, to the point that, at least during the first days of his time in Saigon, he often couldn't dispel the suspicion that these small men with oriental features who looked, without exception, ten years younger than they actually were and who, no matter how old they might be, didn't go bald or even grey were, also without exception, more succinct or less complicated than he, a suspicion that, despite being genuine, filled him with a vague sense of guilt. These initial impressions undoubtedly changed with time (although his letters barely register the change, surely because, by the time it happened, Rodney already had other preoccupations), but Rodney didn't take long to notice that the combined force of Vietnam and the army also robbed him of complexity, and this, which he recognized as a mutilation of his personality, secretly provided him with a source of relief: being a soldier practically destroyed any degree of personal autonomy, but that prohibition of deciding for himself, that subjugation to strict military hierarchy, humiliating and brutalizing as it was, operated at the same time as an anaesthetic that earned him an unknown and abject happiness that was no less real for being abject, because at that moment he discovered in his own flesh that freedom is richer than slavery, but also much more painful, and that at least there, in Vietnam, what he wanted least was to suffer.

So Rodney's first months in Vietnam weren't too hard. Luck contributed to that. Unlike his brother, posted to a combat battalion as soon as he arrived, by some chance he never fully understood (and that in time he ended up attributing to a bureaucratic error) Rodney was assigned to a subordinate post in a unit with headquarters in the capital, in charge of providing the troops with entertainment. The war was reassuringly far away from there, and besides, the work was not unpleasant: he spent most of his time in an air-conditioned office, and when he was obliged to go out it was only to accompany singers, movie stars and comedians from the airport to their hotel, make sure they had everything they needed or drive them to the place they'd be performing. It was a privileged job in the rearguard, with no greater risk than that of living in Saigon; the problem was that even living in Saigon then constituted a considerable risk. Rodney had occasion to see that for himself just a month after arriving in the city. The following is the story just as he told it in one of his letters.

One afternoon, after work, Rodney went into a bar near the bus stop where he caught his lift every day out to the army base where he slept. In the bar there were just two groups of soldiers sitting at tables and a noncommissioned officer from the Green Berets drinking by himself at one end of the bar; Rodney leaned his elbow on the bar at the other end, ordered a beer and drank it. When he asked how much he owed, the waitress – a young Vietnamese woman, with delicate features and evasive eyes – told him that it was already paid for and pointed to the NCO, who without turning to look at him raised a lethargic hand in greeting; Rodney thanked him from afar and left. After that he got into the habit of having a beer in that bar every evening. At first the ritual was always the same: he went in, sat at the bar, drank his beer, exchanging smiles and the odd Vietnamese word with the waitress, then he paid and left, but after four or five visits he managed to overcome the mistrust of the waitress, who turned out to speak elementary but sufficient English and who from then on began to spend her free moments chatting with him. Until one fine day all that ended. It was a Friday evening, and, as on every Friday evening, soldiers packed into the bar to celebrate the beginning of the weekend with their first drinking binge and the waitresses couldn't cope with all their orders. Rodney was about to pay for his drink and leave when he felt a clap on the shoulder. It was the NCO from the Green Berets. He said hello with exaggerated enthusiasm and offered to buy him a drink, which Rodney felt obliged to accept; he shouted for a beer for Rodney and a double whisky for himself. They talked. As they did so, Rodney took a good look at the NCO: he was short, solid and wiry, his face racked with lines, he had violent, sort of disoriented eyes, and he reeked of alcohol. It wasn't easy to understand his words, but Rodney deduced from them that he was from a small town in Arizona, had been in Vietnam for more than a year and that he only had a few days left before he went home; for his part he told him he'd only been in Saigon for a few weeks and told him about the work he was doing. After the first whisky came the second, and then the third. When the NCO was going to order the fourth Rodney announced he was leaving: it was the third time he'd done so, but on

89

that occasion he felt a hand like a claw grip his arm. 'Relax, recruit,' said the NCO, and Rodney noted beneath that vaguely friendly form of address a vibration like the blade of a newly-whetted knife. 'It's the last one.' And he ordered the whisky. While he was waiting to be served he asked Rodney an unintelligible question. 'I said what do you think we've come here to do?' the NCO repeated in his increasingly slurred voice. 'To this bar?' asked Rodney. 'To this country,' the NCO clarified. It wasn't the first time he'd been asked that question since he'd been in Saigon and he already knew the regulation reply, especially the regulation reply to give an NCO. He recited it. The NCO laughed as if he was belching, and before returning to the conversation, asked again for his whisky, which hadn't arrived. 'Not even you believe that. Or maybe you believe we're going to save these people from communism with this bunch of drunks?' he asked, indicating the bar full of soldiers with an affected and mocking gesture. 'I'm going to tell you something: these people don't want us to save them. I'm going to tell you something else: the only thing we've come here to do is to kill gooks. See that girl?' he went on to say, pointing at a waitress walking towards them weighed down with a tray full of drinks and negotiating with great difficulty the superabundance of customers. 'I asked her for a whisky half an hour ago, but she hasn't brought it. You know why? No, of course you don't . . . But I'm going to tell you. She hasn't brought it because she hates me. It's that simple. She hates me. She hates you too. If she could she'd kill you, just like me. And now I'm going to give you some advice. Some friendly advice. I advise you to kill her before she can kill you.' Rodney couldn't say anything, because at that moment the waitress passed in front of them and the NCO tripped her so she ended up sprawled on the floor amid a crash of broken glass. Rodney bent down instinctively to help the waitress up and help pick up the mess. 'What the hell are you doing?' he heard the NCO say. 'Damn it, let her deal with it herself.' Rodney ignored him, and then felt a light kick in the ribs, almost a shove. 'I told you to leave it, recruit!' repeated the NCO, this time shouting. Rodney stood up and said without thinking, as if talking to himself: 'You shouldn't have done that.' He immediately regretted his words. For two seconds the NCO looked at him with curiosity; then he roared with laughter. 'What did you say?' Rodney noticed the bar had gone quiet and that he was the target of every gaze; the waitress with evasive eyes was watching him, unblinking, from behind the bar. Rodney heard himself say: 'I said you shouldn't have tripped the girl.' The slap caught him on the temple; then he heard the NCO shout at him, insult him, mock him, hit him again. Rodney endured the humiliation without moving. 'Aren't you going to defend yourself, recruit?' the NCO shouted. 'No,' answered Rodney, feeling the fury rise in his throat. 'Why not?' the NCO shouted again. 'What are you? A fag or a fucking pacifist?' 'I'm a recruit,' answered Rodney. 'And you're an NCO, and you're also drunk.' Then the NCO slowly removed his stripes without taking his eyes off

Rodney, and then, as if his voice was emerging from the depths of a cavern, said: 'Defend yourself now, you fucking coward.' The fight lasted barely a few seconds, because a swarm of soldiers broke in between the two adversaries straight away. Otherwise, Rodney didn't come off too badly in the skirmish, and for the next few days waited with resignation to be put on report for having punched an officer, but to his surprise it never happened. He didn't return to the bar for a while, and when he did the manager told him his friend didn't work there any more and that he had the impression she'd left Saigon. He forgot the episode. He tried to forget the waitress. But a few weeks after that visit to the bar he saw her again. That afternoon Rodney was waiting at the bus stop, surrounded by soldiers like himself preparing to return to base, when one of the teenage beggars who often milled around there insisted so much on shining his boots that he finally let him do it. There he was, with one foot on the shoeshine case, when he raised his eyes and to his delight caught sight of the girl: she was across the street, looking at him. At first he thought she was happy to see him too, because she was smiling at him or he thought she was smiling at him, but he soon noticed that it was a strange smile, and his delight turned into alarm when he saw that actually the girl was motioning him urgently to come over there. He left the bootblack and started walking quickly towards where the girl was, but as he was crossing the street he saw the bootblack run past him, and at that moment the explosion went off. Rodney fell to the ground

92

in the middle of the roar, was stunned or unconscious for an instant or two, and when he came to, a catastrophic chaos reigned in the street and the bus stop had become a jumble of wreckage and death. Only hours later did Rodney find out that five American soldiers had lost their lives in the attack, and that the charge had been hidden in the shoeshine case where moments before the explosion he had been resting his foot. As for the bootblack and the waitress, he never saw them again, and Rodney came to the inevitable conclusion that the waitress who had saved his life and the bootblack who'd been about to snatch it away had been two of the perpetrators of the massacre.

During all the time he spent in Saigon that was possibly the only occasion on which he felt the nearness of death, and the fact that he'd escaped it providentially did nothing but reinforce his baseless conviction that while he stayed there he wasn't in danger, that he was going to survive, that soon he'd be back home and then it would be as if he'd never been in that war.

The one who really was in the war was Bob. Since his arrival in Vietnam Rodney received frequent news from him and, every time Bob came to Saigon on leave, he went to great pains to receive him in style: he lavished black-market gifts on him, took him drinking to the terrace of the Continental, to dinner at Givral's, a small restaurant with air conditioning on the corner of Le Toi and Tu Do, and then to exclusive places in the city centre — including, as Bob incomprehensibly took it upon himself to specify in several of his letters, the Hung Dao Hotel, a famous and popular three-storey brothel located on Tu Do street, not far from Givral's — places where the drinks and conversation would often go on into the blazing dawns of Lam Son Square. Rodney devoted himself entirely to his brother during those visits, but, when the two of them said goodbye after a week of daily binges, he was never left feeling satisfied that he'd helped Bob forget for a time the harshness of the war; he was always overcome by a vague unease that left embers of sorrow in his stomach as if he'd passed those fraternal days of laughs, confidences, alcohol and staying up all night trying to make amends for a sin he hadn't committed or didn't remember having committed, but that stung him as if it were real. At the end of May the brothers saw each other in Hué, where Rodney had gone in an advisory capacity with a famous country singer and his troupe of go-go girls. By then Bob had only a month till his discharge; a while before he'd discarded the idea, which he'd nurtured for a time and even announced to his parents in a letter, of re-enlisting in the army, and at that moment he was elated, eager to return home. Back in Saigon, Rodney wrote a letter home telling of his encounter with Bob and describing his brother bursting with optimism, but two weeks later, when he arrived at the office one morning, the captain he served under called him into his office and, after a preamble as solemn as it was confusing, told him that during a routine reconnaissance mission, on a path that emerged from the jungle into a village near the Laos border,

Bob or someone walking beside Bob had stepped on a 150-pound mine, and the only thing that remained of his brother's body and those of the four of his comrades who had had the misfortune to be with him at that moment were the bloody tatters of uniforms they'd been able to collect from the area surrounding the 30-foot-wide crater the explosion had left. Bob's death changed everything. Or at least that's what Rodney's father thought; it's also borne out by events. Because, not long after his brother died, Rodney renounced in writing the possibility of considering his military service finished and going home – a possibility he could have been legally entitled to thanks to Bob's death – and submitted a request to join a combat unit. None of his letters give the reasons for this decision, and his father did not know the real motives that induced him to make it; undoubtedly they were linked to his brother's death, but it could also be that it was an unpremeditated or instinctive decision, and that Rodney himself did not know the reasons. In any case the fact is that his letters from that point on became more frequent, longer and darker. Thanks to them, Rodney's father began to understand or imagine (as perhaps anyone who had received them would have) that this was a different sort of war from the one he had fought in, and maybe from all other wars: he understood or he imagined that in this war there was an absolute lack of order or meaning or structure, that those who were fighting had no defined sense of purpose or direction and therefore never achieved objectives, or won or lost anything, nor was there any progress they could measure, nor even the slightest possibility, not even of glory, but of dignity for anyone fighting in it. 'A war in which all the pain of all wars prevailed, but where there was no place for the slightest possibility of redemption or greatness or decency that was befitting to all wars,' Rodney's father said to me. His son would have approved of the sentence. In a letter from the beginning of October 1968, where the somewhat obsessive and hallucinatory tone of his later missives is already perceptible, he writes: 'The atrocious thing about this war is that it's not a war. Here the enemy is nobody, because it could be anybody, and they're nowhere, because they're everywhere: inside and out, up and down, in front and behind. They're nobody, but they exist. In other wars you tried to defeat them; not in this one: in this one you try to kill them, even though we all know that by killing them we won't defeat them. It's not worth kidding yourself: this is a war of extermination, so the more things we kill – people or animals or plants, it's all the same – the better. We'll devastate the country: we won't leave anything. And still, we won't win the war, simply because this war cannot be won or no one but Charlie can win it: he's willing to kill and to die, while the only thing that we want is for the twelve months we have to spend here to go by as fast as possible so we can go home. In the meantime we kill and we die. Of course we all make an effort to pretend we understand something, that we know why we're here and killing and maybe dying, but we do it only so we

96

don't go completely crazy. Because here we're all crazy, crazy and lonely and without any possibility of advancing or retreating, without any possibility of loss or gain, as if we were going endlessly round and round an invisible circle at the bottom of an empty well, where the sun never reaches. I'm writing in the dark. I'm not afraid. But sometimes it scares me to think I'm on the verge of discovering who I am, that I'll come around a bend on a path some day and see a soldier, and it will be me.'

In the letters from those first months that he spent away from the deceptive security of Saigon Rodney never mentioned Bob, but he did record in detail the novelties that abounded in his new life. His battalion was stationed in a base near Da Nang, but that was just the resting place, because they spent most of the time operating out in the region, by day squelching through the rice paddies and scouring the jungle inch by inch, asphyxiated by the heat and humidity and mosquitoes, enduring biblical downpours, covered in mud up to their eyebrows, devoured by leeches, eating canned food, always sweating, exhausted, their bodies aching all over, stinking after entire weeks without a wash, oblivious to any effort other than that of staying alive, while more than once – after walking for hours and hours armed to the teeth, carrying backpacks and conscientiously making sure of every spot they placed their feet to avoid the mines planted along the jungle paths – they surprised themselves by hoping shots would just start to be fired, if only to break the exhausting monotony of those interminable days when the boredom was often more enervating than the proximity of danger. That was during the day. During the night – after each of them had dug their sniper pits in the red twilight of the paddies, while the moon rose majestically on the horizon – the routine changed, but not always for the better: sometimes they had no choice but to try to get some sleep while rocked by the shelling of artillery, the roar of helicopters landing or shots from M-16s; other times they had to go out on patrol, and they did so holding hands, or clutching the uniform of the comrade in front of them, like children terrified of getting lost in the dark; there was also guard duty, eternal shifts when every sound in the jungle was threatening and during which they had to struggle tooth and nail against sleepiness and against the unsleeping ghosts of their dead comrades. Because it was in those days that Rodney came to know what it meant to feel death breathing down his neck daily. 'I once read a phrase by Pascal where he said that no one is entirely saddened by a friend's misfortune,' Rodney writes two months after his arrival in Da Nang. 'When I read that it struck me as mean and false; now I know it to be true. What makes it true is that "entirely". Since I've been here I've seen several friends die: their deaths have horrified me, infuriated me, made me cry, but I'd be lying if I said I hadn't felt an obscene relief, for the simple reason that the dead man was not me. Or to put it another way: the horror lies in the war, but long before it already lay within us.' These words might partially explain why in his letters of those days Rodney speaks only of his living comrades – never of the dead – and of his living commanding officers – never of the dead; I've often wondered if it also explains why they're full of stories, as if for some reason Rodney might not have wanted to say directly what the stories were able to say in their lateral or elliptical way. They are stories that had happened to him, or to someone close to him, or that he'd simply been told; I reject the hypothesis that some of them might be invented. I'll just tell the one about Captain Vinh, because I have a feeling it might have been the one that most affected Rodney.

Captain Vinh was an officer in the South Vietnamese army who was assigned as guide and interpreter to the unit my friend served in. He was a gaunt, cordial thirty-year-old with whom, according to Rodney's letter that tells the story, he'd spoken more than once as they got their strength back bolting down their field rations or smoked a cigarette while resting on a march. 'Don't go near him,' a long-serving member of his company said after seeing him chatting amicably with the captain one afternoon. 'That guy's a fucking traitor.' And he told Rodney the following anecdote. One time they captured three Vietcong guerrilla fighters, and an intelligence officer put the three of them in a helicopter and asked the captain and four soldiers, among them the old hand, to come with him. The helicopter took off and, when it was at a considerable altitude, the officer began interrogating the prisoners. The first refused to talk, and without the least hesitation the officer ordered the soldiers to throw him out of the helicopter into the void; they obeyed. The same thing happened with the next prisoner. The third one didn't have to be interrogated: crying and begging for mercy, he started talking so fast and desperately that Captain Vinh barely had time to translate his words, but when he finished his confession he met the same fate as his comrades. 'We went up in the helicopter with three guys and landed with none,' the veteran said. 'But no one asked any questions. As for the captain, he's garbage. He's seen what we're doing to his people and he keeps helping us. I don't know how they allow him to carry on here,' he complained. 'Sooner or later he'll betray us.' Not much later Rodney would have cause to remember the long-serving soldier's prediction. It all began the morning his company turned up at a village that had been occupied by the Vietcong the night before. The aim of the Vietcong's incursion had been to recruit soldiers, and to that end the guerrillas requested the help of the village leader, who seemed reluctant to cooperate with them. The guerrillas' response was so sudden and devastating that when the man tried to make amends it was already too late: they grabbed his two daughters, six and eight years old, raped them, tortured them, slit their throats and threw their mutilated bodies down the well to contaminate the village's only source of drinking water. Rodney's whole company took in the story in silence, except for Captain Vinh, who was literally sickened by it. 'My daughters,' he moaned over and over again to whomever would listen, to no one. 'They're the same age, those girls were the same ages as my daughters.' Two months later, the same day he arrived back in Da Nang after a week's leave in Tokyo, Rodney had to help with the evacuation of the thirteen dead and fifty-nine wounded of a combat company, which that very morning had been the victim of an ambush in the jungle. The event made a deep impression on him, but the impression turned into cold fury when he discovered that the rapid investigation that followed had concluded that the butchery could only have been the result of a tip-off and the perpetrator of that tip-off could only have been Captain Vinh. In his letter Rodney affirms that, when he found out about the officer's treachery, if he'd been able to he would certainly have killed 'that murderous rat with whom I'd shared food, tobacco and conversation,' but now it wasn't necessary, because the interpreter had been handed over to the South Vietnamese army, who had executed him without delay; Rodney added that he was glad of the news. The next letter Rodney's parents received was just a note: in it their son records succinctly that the same intelligence officers who had revealed Captain Vinh's treachery had just arrived at the conclusion that the officer had given the Vietcong communists the tip-off because they'd kidnapped his two daughters and threatened to kill them unless he collaborated.

After receiving that briefest of notes his parents had no news from Rodney for almost a month and, when the correspondence resumed, gradually and insidiously they

101

were overtaken by the sensation that it wasn't their son who was writing to them, but someone else who had usurped his name and handwriting. It was a strange sensation, Rodney's father told me, as if whoever was writing was Rodney but wasn't him at the same time or, stranger still, as if whoever was writing was too much Rodney (Rodney in a chemically pure state, extract of Rodney) to really be Rodney. I've read and reread those letters and, ambiguous or confused though it may be, the observation seems accurate, because in these pages, undoubtedly written in torrents, it's obvious that Rodney's writing has entered into a dubious, shimmering territory, where, although it's not difficult to identify my friend's voice in the distance, it's impossible not to perceive a powerful diapason of delirium that, without making it entirely unrecognizable, at least makes it disturbingly alien to Rodney, among other things because he doesn't always avoid the temptations of truculence, solemnity or simple affectation. I'll add that, in my opinion, the fact that Rodney wrote these letters from the hospital where he was recuperating from the ravages of the incident accounts in part for their anomalous character, but it's not enough to quash the disquieting sensation reading them brings. 'The incident': that's how Rodney's father referred to it during the afternoon I spent at his house, because it seems that's how Rodney referred to it the one time his father questioned him about it in vain. The incident. It happened during the month he had no news from his son and all Rodney's father had been able to find out over the years from various sources was that Rodney's company had taken part in some sort of raid on a village called My Khe, in the province of Quang Ngai, which had ended the lives of more than fifty victims; he had also managed to find out that, as a result of the incident or as a consequence of it, and despite having suffered no physical injury, Rodney had spent three weeks hospitalized in Saigon, and a long time later, when he was back home, he'd had to testify in a case against the lieutenant who'd been in command of his company, and who was finally acquitted of all the charges brought against him. That was all Rodney's father had managed to find out about the incident in all those years. As for his son, he never alluded to the matter other than in passing and in the most superficial way possible and only when he had no other choice but to do so, and in his letters after he got out of hospital, and the ones he wrote while he was still there, he doesn't even mention it.

The truth is that those were all completely different letters to the ones he'd written up till then, and in time his father ended up attributing this change – maybe because he needed to attribute it to some tangible reason – to Rodney's excessive reliance on marijuana and alcohol since his first months at the front. In his earlier letters Rodney tends mostly to note down events and in general avoid abstract reflections; now events and people have disappeared and barely anything is left but thoughts, singular thoughts of a vehemence that horrified his father, and that soon led him to the unhappy conclusion that his son was irremediably losing his mind. 'Now I know the truth of war,' Rodney writes, for example, in one of his letters. 'The truth of this war and of any other war, the truth of all wars, the truth that you know as well as I do and that anybody who's been to war knows, because deep, deep down this war is no different from but rather identical to all other wars and deep, deep down the truth of war is always the same. Everybody here knows this truth, it's just that nobody has the guts to admit it. They all lie. So do I. I mean I lied too until I stopped lying, until I got sick of lying, until the lie sickened me more than death: the lie is filthy, death is clean. And that is precisely the truth that everybody here knows (that anybody who's ever been to war knows) and nobody wants to admit. That all this is beautiful: that war is beautiful, that combat is beautiful, that death is beautiful. I'm not referring to the beauty of the moon rising like a silver coin in the stifling night of the rice paddies, or to the threads of blood the tracer bullets draw in the darkness, or to the miraculous instant of silence that sometimes cuts through the constant racket of the jungle at dusk, or to those extreme moments in which you seem to cancel yourself out along with your fear and anguish and solitude and shame, which fuse with the shame and solitude and anguish and fear of those at your side, and then your identity happily evaporates and you're nobody any more. No, it's not just that. Most of all it's the joy of killing, not just because while others die you stay alive, but also because no pleasure can compare with the pleasure of killing, no feeling can compare with the powerful feeling of killing, of taking away absolutely everything from somebody, and, because it's another human being absolutely identical to you, you feel something then that you couldn't even have imagined it was possible to feel, a feeling similar to what we must feel when we're born and that we've forgotten, or what God felt when he created us or what it must feel like to give birth, yes, that's exactly what you feel when you kill, don't you think, Dad, the feeling that you're finally doing something important, something truly essential, something you've unknowingly spent your whole life preparing for and that, if you couldn't have done it, would inevitably have turned you into debris, into a man without truth, without coherence or substance, because to kill is so beautiful it completes us, obliges you to arrive at parts of yourself you never even discerned, it's like discovering yourself, discovering immense continents of unknown flora and fauna where you'd imagined there was nothing but colonized land, and that's why now, after having known the transparent beauty of death, the limitless and gleaming beauty of death, I feel as if I were bigger, as if I'd stretched and lengthened and extended far beyond my previous boundaries, so paltry, and that's why I also think everybody should have the right to kill, to stretch and lengthen and extend themselves as far as they can, to attain those faces of ecstasy or beatitude I've seen on people who kill, to know yourself thoroughly or as far as war will allow, and war lets you go very far and very fast, farther and faster still, faster, faster, faster, there are moments when everything suddenly speeds up and there's a blaze, a maelstrom and a loss, the devastating certainty that if we were able to travel faster than the speed of light we'd see the future. That's what I've discovered. That's what I now know. What all of us who are here know, and what all those who were here and aren't any more knew, and also the deluded or valiant ones who never were here but it's as if they had been, because they saw all this long before it existed. Everybody knows it, everybody. But what disgusts me is not that this is true, but that nobody tells the truth, and I'm at the point of asking myself why nobody does and something occurs to me that had never occurred to me, and it's that perhaps nobody says it, not out of cowardice, but simply because it sounds false or absurd or monstrous, because nobody who doesn't know the truth beforehand is qualified to accept it, because nobody who hasn't been here is going to accept what any foot soldier here knows, and it's that things that make sense are not true. They're just sawn-off truths, wishful thinking: truth is always absurd. And worst of all, only when you know this, when you learn what you can only learn here, when you finally accept the truth, only then can you be happy. I'll put it another way: before, I hated war and hated life and most of all I hated myself; now I love life and war and most of all I love myself. Now I'm happy.'

I could gather a handful of analogous passages extracted from the letters Rodney wrote in that time: all in a similar tone, all equally dark, immoral or abstruse. It's true that one is assaulted by the temptation to recognize in these crazy words something like an X-ray of Rodney's mind at that point in his life, and even read into them many more things than Rodney perhaps meant to include. I shall resist the temptation, I shall avoid interpretations.

As soon as he was discharged from the hospital, Rodney rejoined his company, and two months later, when he had only a few days left until his obligatory stay in Vietnam was up, thanks to an acquaintance who got him into the American embassy in Saigon, he phoned his parents for the first time and told them he wasn't coming home. He'd resolved to re-enlist in the army. Maybe because they immediately grasped that the decision was irrevocable, Rodney's parents didn't try to get him to reconsider, but only tried to understand. They couldn't. Nevertheless, after a long conversation choked with entreaties and sobs, they were eventually left clinging to the precarious hope that their son hadn't lost his mind, but the war had simply changed him into another person, he was no longer the boy they'd begotten and raised and that's why he could no longer imagine himself back home as if nothing had happened, because even the prospect of returning to his student life (prolonging it by doing a doctorate, as he had originally intended) or looking for work in a high school or, much less, having a long spell of rest to recover the provincial placidness of Rantoul, now seemed ridiculous or impossible to him, and overwhelmed him with a panic they just could not understand. So Rodney stayed another six months in Vietnam. His father knew almost nothing about what happened to his son during that time, when Rodney's correspondence with his family stopped altogether, no news arrived from him except for a few telegrams in which, with military concision, he informed them that he was fine. The only thing Rodney's father could find out later was that his son was then fighting in an elite anti-guerrilla unit known as Tiger Force, part of the 101st Airborne Division's first battalion, and it's beyond doubt that during those six months Rodney engaged in combat much more often than he had done up till then, because when at the end of 1969 he finally flew back home he did so with his chest emblazoned with medals – a Silver Star for bravery and a Purple Heart figured among them – and a hip injury that would stay with him for life, condemning him to walk forever with a stumbling, unsteady, defeated gait.

The homecoming was catastrophic. Rodney's father remembered his son's arrival in Chicago all too well. For two weeks he and Julia Flores, who barely knew each other, had been phoning back and forth to finalize the preparations, but when the great day arrived everything went wrong from the start: the Greyhound bus he and his wife took from Rantoul to Chicago arrived almost two hours late because of a traffic accident; Julia was waiting for them there, got them into her car and drove as fast as possible towards O'Hare Airport, but there was a traffic jam on the way as well, so by the time they got to the terminal an hour had already gone by since Rodney's flight had landed. They asked here and there, and finally, after going around and around and making many inquiries, they had to go and find Rodney in a police station. They found him there alone and shaken, but he didn't offer any explanation, not that day or ever and, so as not to further ruin the reunion, they preferred not to ask the police for one. Only several months later did Rodney's father get a precise idea of what happened that morning in the airport. It was after the court case against Rodney – as a result of which he was sentenced to a fine, which his family paid – a case that Rodney forbade his father and mother from attending and the contents and development of which they didn't find out about until a secret interview with their son's defence lawyer. The lawyer, a well-known left-winger called Daniel Pludovsky, who had accepted the case because he was a friend of a friend of Rodney's father and who from the beginning of the conversation made an effort to calm him by trying to play down the episode, received him in his office on Wabash Street and started by telling him that Rodney had made the three-day return trip from Vietnam with a black soldier (first from Saigon to Tokyo in an Air Force C-41, then from the Philippines to San Francisco in a World Airways jet, and finally from there to Chicago) and that, disembarking in Chicago and finding no one waiting for them, the pair decided to go and have breakfast in a cafeteria. The terminal was unusually busy and a festive atmosphere prevailed, or at least that was the first, bewildering and happy impression the two recent arrivals had, until at a certain point, as they dragged their kit bags down a crowded corridor, a girl broke away from a group of students, came up to Rodney, who was the only one of the two veterans still in uniform, and asked him if he was coming from Vietnam. Surprised by the absence of his parents and Julia, who had promised to be waiting for him at the airport, Rodney might have imagined that the girl had been sent by them, so he stopped and smiled and cheerfully said yes. Then the girl spat in his face. Looking at her uncomprehendingly, Rodney asked the girl why she'd done that, but, since she didn't answer, after a moment's hesitation he wiped the saliva off his face and carried on walking. The students followed them chanting anti-war slogans, laughing, shouting things they didn't understand and insulting them. Until Rodney couldn't take any more, turned around and confronted them; the black soldier grabbed his arm and begged him not to pay any attention to them, but Rodney pulled away and, while the students kept on with their chants and their shouts, he tried to talk to them, tried to reason with them, but finally gave up, said they hadn't done anything to them and asked them to leave them alone. They were about to go on when an abusive or defiant comment, hurled by a guy with very long hair, was heard above the commotion of the students, and Rodney was instantly on top of the guy and started beating him up and would have killed him if not for the last-minute intervention of the airport police. 'And that was it,' Pludovsky told Rodney's father, leaning back in his armchair with a cigarette in hand and an undisguised air of satisfac-

110

tion, downplaying it with the tone of someone who's just told a tale of amusing childish mischief. Rodney's father did not smile, said nothing, just remained silent for a few moments and then, without looking up, asked the lawyer to tell him what it was the boy had said to Rodney. 'Oh, that.' Pludovsky tried to smile. 'Well, the truth is I don't remember exactly.' 'Of course you remember,' Rodney's father said without a doubt. 'And I want you to tell me.' Suddenly uncomfortable, Pludovsky sighed, put out his cigarette, folded his hands on top of his large oak desk. 'As you wish,' he said with annoyance, as if he'd just lost a case at the last minute in the stupidest way imaginable. 'What the boy said was: "Look what cowards they are, these baby-killers".'

By the time Rodney's father left the lawyer's office he already understood that the altercation at O'Hare had just been one reflection of what had happened in the last few months and a foreshadowing of what was going to happen in the future. He was not wrong. Because Rodney's life never again resembled the one he'd been forced to leave behind a year and a half earlier to go to Vietnam. The day of his arrival in Rantoul his old friends had organized a homecoming party; his mother convinced him to go, but, although he left the house dressed for the occasion and with the car keys in hand and returned in the early hours, the next morning his parents found out that he hadn't even shown up at the party, and in the following days discovered from neighbours and friends that he'd spent that night

111

talking on the phone from a booth near the train station and driving around town in his father's Ford. A few months later he and Julia got married and went to live in a suburb of Minneapolis where she was teaching in a secondary school. The union lasted barely two years; in fact, it took her much less time to realize that the marriage was impossible, just as any other Rodney might have attempted then would have been. Physically, he had returned from Vietnam, but actually it was as if he were still there, or as if he'd brought Vietnam home with him. Worse still: while he was in Vietnam Rodney never stopped talking about Vietnam in the letters he wrote to his parents, to Julia, to his friends; now he ceased entirely to do so, and not, perhaps, because he didn't want to – the truth was most likely the opposite: there was probably nothing in the world he wanted as much – but because he couldn't, who knows whether because he harboured the certainty that no one was in a position to understand what he had to tell, or because he thought he shouldn't do so, as if he'd seen or experienced something that those who knew him should remain unaware of. What's certainly clear is that, if while he was in Vietnam he didn't think about anything but the United States, now that he was in the United States he didn't think about anything but Vietnam. It's possible that he often felt nostalgia for the war, that he thought he should never have come home and that he should have died over there, fighting shoulder to shoulder with his comrades. It's possible that he often felt, compared to the life of a cornered rat he now led in the

United States, life in Vietnam was more serious, more real, more worth living. It's possible that he realized he could never return to the country he'd left to go to Vietnam, and not only because it didn't exist any more and was now another, but also because he was no longer the same person who'd left it. It's possible that he might very soon have accepted that no one comes back from Vietnam: that, once you've been there, return is impossible. And it's almost surely the case that, like so many other Vietnam veterans, he felt mocked, because as soon as he set foot back on American soil he knew the whole country spurned him or, at best, wished to hide him as if his very presence was an embarrassment, an insult or an accusation. Rodney could not have expected to be received as a hero (because he wasn't one and because he was not unaware that the defeated were never received as heroes, even if they were), but neither could he have expected that the same country that had demanded he ignore his own conscience, not desert to Canada, fulfil his duty as an American and go to a despicable, faraway war, should now shrink from his presence as though he were a criminal or had the plague. His presence and that of so many veterans like him, who, if they were guilty of something, were guilty because of the brutal circumstances of a war they'd been pushed into and the country that had forced them to fight. Or at least that's what Rodney must have thought then, just like so many other Vietnam veterans when they went home. As for his former anti-war activism, Rodney undoubtedly now had many more reasons than in his student years to consider the war a deception orchestrated by politicians' fanaticism and irresponsibility, stoked by the fraudulent use of the rhetoric of old-fashioned American values, but it's also indisputable – or at least it was for Rodney's father – that the fact of being for or against the war had been reduced to an almost banal matter in his eyes, relegated to the background by the lacerating disgrace of the United States having sent thousands and thousands of boys to the slaughter and then abandoned them to their fate in a lost little corner of the globe, sick, exhausted and crazed, drunk on desire and impotence, fighting to the death against their own shadows in the swamps of a country reduced to ashes.

But all this is nothing but conjecture: it's reasonable to imagine that, for a long time after his return from Vietnam, Rodney might have thought or felt like that; it's not impossible to imagine that he might have thought or felt the exact opposite. Facts, however, are facts; I'll stick to them. In the first months he spent back in the United States Rodney barely left his house (neither his family home in Rantoul nor the one he shared with Julia in Minneapolis), and when he began to go out it was only to get involved in fights almost invariably provoked by his irrepressible tendency to interpret any mention of Vietnam or his time in Vietnam, no matter how trivial or innocuous, as a personal affront. He lost his Chicago friends and his Rantoul ones, and he cut off all connections to his old comrades from Vietnam, maybe because, voluntarily or involuntarily, he wished to hide the fact that he was an ex-combatant, which would explain the fact that for a long time he categorically refused to go for help or company to the offices of the Veterans' Association. Despite Julia's unceasing efforts, shortly after their wedding the marriage had deteriorated irreversibly. As for his family, he only kept in touch with his mother, while for years he avoided his father's company and conversation. He drank and smoked a lot, whisky and beer, tobacco and marijuana, and often fell into slumps that would plunge him into deep depressions lasting weeks or months and oblige him to stuff himself with pills. He never hunted or fished again. He never mentioned his brother Bob again. He lived in a continual state of anxiety. For almost a year and a half, he suffered from a relentless insomnia, and only managed to overcome it when he went to the movies with Julia, who held his hand and felt him gradually abandon himself in the murmuring darkness of the cinema and finally immerse himself in sleep as if it were the depths of a lake. During the day he never sat with his back to a window, and he was obsessed with keeping all the blinds in the house closed. He spent his nights giving vent to his anxiety in the hallways and, before finally getting futilely into bed, he would begin a nightly ritual that involved inspecting each and every one of the doors and windows of the house, making sure there was no obstacle that might hinder his escape and that everything he needed to defend himself was at hand, as well as mentally running through the appropriate modus operandi in the implausible case of an emergency. With time he managed to fall asleep in his own bed, but he was frequently assaulted by nightmares, and an inoffensive noise in the yard would be enough to wake him and cause him to rush outside to find out what had made the noise. When he and Julia divorced he moved back to his parents' house in Rantoul, and in the years that followed crossed the country from sea to sea several times: he'd suddenly pack his bags one day, load up the car and leave without any warning or fixed destination, and after one or two or three or four months he'd come home without the slightest explanation, as if he'd been out for a stroll around the neighbourhood. He survived two suicide attempts, as a result of the second he eventually agreed to be admitted to the Chicago VA Medical Centre. He didn't take long to start looking for a job, but he did in finding one, because, although being an ex-combatant entitled him to certain privileges, for a long time he considered it humiliating to take advantage of them, and each time he went to an interview he returned home seized by an uncontrollable rage, convinced that prospective employers began to see him as a two-headed monster as soon as they found out he was a war veteran. The first job he got was an easy and not badly paid administrative position in a jam factory, but he barely lasted a few months in it, more or less like the ones that followed. Later he tried giving language classes in Rantoul or around Rantoul, and also tried to take up his studies again, enrolling in a master's course in philosophy at Northwestern. It was all futile.

When Rodney returned from Vietnam converted into a broken-down shadow of the brilliant, hard-working and sensible young man he'd once been, his father was sure that time would eventually restore his lost nature, but eight years had gone by since his return and Rodney was still immersed in an impenetrable fog, transformed into a ghost or a zombie; in Rantoul he spent whole days lying in bed, reading novels and smoking marijuana and watching old movies on television, and when he went out it was only to drive for hours on highways that led nowhere or to drink alone in the bars around town. It was as if he was hermetically sealed inside a steel bubble, but the strange thing (or what his father found strange) is that he didn't seem to experience that situation of neglect and absolute solitude as an affliction, but rather as the triumphant fruit of a precise calculation, like the ideal antidote to his exorbitant suspicion of other people and his no less exorbitant suspicion of himself. And so at some point Rodney's parents ended up accepting, with a resignation not devoid of relief, that Vietnam had changed their son forever and that he would never go back to being who he used to be.

Suddenly everything changed. A year and a half before Rodney began giving classes at Urbana, his mother died of stomach cancer. Her suffering was long but not terrible, and Rodney endured it without frights or dramatics, giving up from one day to the next his vague, lazy habits to take care of his dying mother, who during all those years of convalescence from the war had been his sole and silent moral

117

support; the afternoon they buried her no one saw him shed a single tear. Nevertheless, days later, returning from a house call, Rodney's father found his son leaning on the kitchen table, lit up by the bright midday sun that was pouring in through the window, crying his eyes out. He couldn't remember having seen Rodney cry since he was a boy, but he didn't say a thing: he left his things in the hall, went back to the kitchen, made two cups of camomile tea, one for his son, the other for himself, sat down at the table, held his son's big, rough, veiny hand, and stayed beside him for a long time, in silence, sipping his camomile tea and then Rodney's as well, without letting go of his hand, listening to him cry as if he'd stored up an inexhaustible reserve of tears during all those years and he wasn't ever going to stop crying. For a long time father and son had been living in the same house hardly ever speaking to each other, but that evening Rodney began to talk, and it was only then that his father had a blinding glimpse of the vertigo of remorse his son had been living in for all those years, because he came to understand that Rodney didn't only feel he was to blame for the deaths of his brother and his mother and an indefinable number of people, but also for not having had the courage to obey his conscience and having yielded to the order to go to war, for having abandoned his comrades there, for having witnessed the unmitigated horror of Vietnam and for having survived it. The conversation ended in the early hours, and the next day, when they woke up, Rodney asked to borrow his father's car and went to Chicago. The trip was repeated the following week and the one after that, and Rodney's visits to the capital soon became a weekly ritual. At first he'd go and come back on the same day, leaving very early in the morning and getting home at night, but as time went by he began to spend two or sometimes three days away from Rantoul. In order not to spoil the improvement in relations with his son since the death of his wife, Rodney's father didn't make enquiries, but merely lent him the car and asked when he thought he might be back. But one evening, on his return from one of those journeys, Rodney told him: told him that he went each week to the Chicago headquarters of the Vietnam Veterans' Association — the same place where he'd been admitted twice in the past and treated with Largactil injections — where he received the help of a psychiatrist who specialized in war-induced disturbances and where he got together with other veterans with whom he collaborated in the organization of public functions, demonstrations and conferences, as well as the production of a magazine in which for several years he published articles on film and literature and furious denunciations of the culpable frivolity of his country's politicians and their servile compliance with the dictates of big corporations. The news didn't surprise Rodney's father, who by then had been noticing for a while the changes his son had undergone in just a few months, and not just in relation to him; Rodney had stopped drinking and smoking marijuana, had started to share in the running of the house, to eradicate his eccentric habits and recover

119

some of his old friends. Gradually that transformation became more solid and more visible because Rodney soon accepted a job keeping the books for a restaurant in Urbana, began to work as a volunteer for a small independent trade union and to frequent the local chapter of the Association of Veterans of Foreign Wars. It was as if Rodney's entire life had hit crisis point with the death of his mother: as if, thanks to his trips to Chicago and the help of the Veterans' Association, the bubble he'd spent more than fifteen years suffocating inside had begun to disintegrate and he was overcoming the shame of being a former Vietnam combatant or finding some form of pride in the fact of being a survivor of that phantasmagoric war. So, by the time he got his job as a Spanish teacher at Urbana, Rodney led such an orderly and industrious life that there was no reason to suspect he hadn't left behind once and for all the infinite consequences of his stint in Vietnam.

But he hadn't left them behind. Rodney's father realized it one night over the Christmas holidays in 1988, a few months before he told me his son's story in his house in Rantoul, just a few days after Rodney and I had said goodbye at the door of Treno's with the finally frustrated promise that we'd see each other again as soon as I got back from my road trip through the Midwest in the company of Barbara, Gudrun and Rodrigo Ginés. That evening a man had telephoned the house asking for his son. Rodney was out, so his father asked who was calling. 'Tommy Birban,' said the man. Rodney's father had never heard that sur-

120

name, but the fact didn't surprise him, because since Rodney had broken out of the confinement of his bubble it was not unusual for strangers to call the house. The man said he was a friend of Rodney's, promised to call back in a while and left a phone number in case Rodney wanted to call him first. When Rodney got home that night, his father handed him a piece of paper with his friend's phone number on it; his son's reaction surprised him: slightly pale, taking the paper he was handing him, he asked if he was sure that was the name of the stranger and, although he assured him it was, he made him repeat it several times, to convince himself his father hadn't been mistaken. 'Is something up?' Rodney's father asked. Rodney didn't answer or answered with a gesture both discouraging and disparaging. But later, when they were having dinner, the telephone rang again, and before his father could get up to answer it Rodney stopped him sharply with a shout. The two men sat and looked at each other: that was when Rodney's father knew something was wrong. The telephone kept ringing, until it finally stopped. 'Maybe it was someone else,' said Rodney's father. Rodney said nothing. 'He's going to call again, isn't he?' Rodney's father asked after a while. This time Rodney nodded. 'I don't want to talk to him,' he said. 'Tell him I'm not here. Or better yet, tell him I'm away and you don't know when I'll be back. Yeah: tell him that.' That night Rodney's father didn't risk any more questions, because he knew his son was not going to answer, and he spent the whole next day waiting for Tommy Birban's call. Of course,

121

the call came, and Rodney's father picked up the receiver quickly and did what his son had asked him to do. 'Yesterday you didn't tell me Rodney was away,' Tommy Birban said suspiciously. 'I don't remember what I said yesterday,' he answered. Then he improvised: 'But it would be better if you didn't call here again. Rodney has gone away and I don't know where he is or when he'll be back.' He was just about to hang up when Tommy Birban's voice on the other end of the line stopped sounding threatening and began to sound imploring, like a perfectly articulated sob: 'You're Rodney's father, right?' He didn't have time to answer. 'I know Rodney's living with you, they told me at the Chicago Veterans' Association, they gave me your number. I want to ask you a favour. If you do me this favour I promise I won't call again, but you have to do this for me. Tell Rodney I'm not going to ask anything of him, not even that we see each other. The only thing I want is to talk to him for a while, tell him I only want to talk to him for a while, tell him I need to talk to him. That's all. But tell him, please. Will you tell him?' Rodney's father didn't know how to refuse, but the fact that his son received the message without batting an eyelid or making the slightest comment allowed him to kid himself that this episode he couldn't understand and didn't want to understand had concluded without any grave consequences. Predictably, a few days later Tommy Birban called again. Rodney was no longer answering the phone, so it was Rodney's father who picked it up. He and Tommy Birban argued for a few seconds fiercely, and he was about to hang up when his son asked him to hand him the phone; with some hesitation, and warning him with a look that there was still time to avoid the mistake, he handed it over. The two old friends talked for a long time, but he wouldn't allow himself to listen to the conversation, of which he only caught a few unconnected snippets. That night Rodney couldn't get to sleep, and the next morning Tommy Birban called again and the two talked again for several hours. This ominous ritual went on for over a week, and the morning of New Year's Day Rodney's father heard a noise downstairs, got up, went out onto the porch and saw his son putting the last piece of luggage in the trunk of the Buick. The scene didn't surprise him; actually, he was almost expecting it. Rodney closed the trunk and came up the steps to the porch. 'I'm off,' he said. 'I was going to come up to say goodbye.' His father knew he was lying, but he nodded. He looked at the snow-covered street, the sky almost white, the grey light; he looked at his son, tall and broken in front of him, and felt the world was an empty place, inhabited only by the two of them. He was about to tell him. 'Where are you going?' he was about to ask. 'Don't you know the world is an empty place?' but he didn't say that. What he said was: 'Isn't it about time you forgot all that?' 'I've already forgotten, Dad,' answered Rodney. 'It's all that that hasn't forgotten me.' 'And that's the last thing I heard him say,' Rodney's father concluded, sunken in his wingback chair, as exhausted as if he hadn't dedicated that endless afternoon in his house in Rantoul to reconstructing his son's story for me, but rather trying to scale an impassable mountain weighed down with useless equipment. 'Then we hugged and he left. The rest you know.'

That's how Rodney's father finished telling his story. Neither of us had anything to add, but I stayed a little longer with him, and for an indeterminate space of time, which I wouldn't know whether to calculate in minutes or hours, we sat facing one another, keeping up a faint imitation conversation, as if we shared a shameful secret or the responsibility for a crime, or as if we were looking for excuses so I wouldn't have to face the road back to Urbana alone and he the springtime loneliness of that big house with nobody in it, and when, past midnight, I finally decided to leave, I was sure I'd always remember the story Rodney's father had told me and that I was no longer the same person who that afternoon, many hours earlier, had arrived in Rantoul. 'You're too young to think of having children,' Rodney's father said to me as we parted, and I haven't forgotten. 'Don't have any, because you'll regret it; although if you don't have any you'll regret that too. That's life: no matter what you do, you regret it. But let me tell you something: all love stories are absurd because love is an illness that only time can cure; but having a child is risking a love so absurd that only death can end it.'

That's what Rodney's father said to me, and I have not forgotten.

Otherwise, I never saw him again.

STONE DOOR

I RETURNED TO SPAIN a little more than a year after that spring afternoon when Rodney's father told me his son's story. During the rest of the time I spent in Urbana many things happened. I'm not going to try to tell them here, and not just because it would be tedious, but mainly because most of them don't belong in this story. Or perhaps they do and I haven't figured out how yet. It doesn't matter. I'll just say that I spent a month of the summer holiday back home in Spain; that the next term I returned to Urbana, carried on with my classes and my things, and began a doctoral thesis (which I never finished) supervised by John Borgheson; that I had friends and lovers and became better friends with the friends I already had, especially Rodrigo Ginés, Laura Burns, Felipe Vieri; that I was busy being born and I wasn't busy dying; that during all that time I worked diligently on my novel. So diligently that by the following spring I'd finished it. I'm not sure it was a good novel, but it was my first novel, and writing it made me extremely happy, for the simple reason that I proved to myself I was capable of writing novels. I should perhaps add that it wasn't about

127

Rodney, although there was a secondary character whose physical appearance owed something to Rodney's physical appearance; it was, however, a novel about ghosts or zombies set in Urbana and the protagonist was a character exactly like me who found himself in the same circumstances as me . . . So when I left Urbana I left it with my first novel in hand, feeling very fortunate and also feeling that, although I hadn't travelled much, nor seen very much of the world, nor lived very intensely, nor accumulated very many experiences, that long spell in the United States had been my real doctorate, convinced I had nothing more to learn there and that, if I wanted to become a real writer and not a ghost or a zombie – like Rodney or like the characters in my novel and some of Urbana's inhabitants – then I had to go home immediately.

And so I did. Although I was prepared to go back at any price, the truth is the return was less uncertain than I'd foreseen, because in May, just when I was about to start packing my bags, Marcelo Cuartero phoned from Barcelona to offer me a position as associate professor at the Autonomous University. The salary was meagre, but, supplemented by the income provided by occasional freelance jobs, was enough to rent a studio apartment in the neighbourhood of Sant Antoni and to survive without too many hardships while waiting for the novel to be published. That was how I eagerly began to regain my life in Barcelona; I also, naturally, regained Marcos Luna. By then Marcos was already living with Patricia, a photographer who worked for a fashion magazine, and was making a living doing illustrations for a newspaper, had begun to exhibit with certain regularity and was making a name for himself among the painters of his generation. In fact it was Marcos who, at the end of that year, after my novel had come out with a minor publisher and been greeted by a silence barely broken by one futile and rapturously complimentary review by one of Marcelo Cuartero students (or by Marcelo Cuartero himself under a pseudonym), got me an interview with a sub-editor at his paper, who in his turn invited me to write columns and reviews for the cultural supplement. So, somehow or other, with the help of Marcos and Marcelo Cuartero I began to make my way in Barcelona while getting down to work on my second novel. A long time before I managed to finish it, however, Paula came along, which ended up disrupting everything, including the novel. Paula was blonde, shy, willowy and bright, one of those disciplined and aloof thirty-somethings whose apparent haughtiness is a transparent mask over their urgent need for affection. She'd just separated from her first husband and was working for the cultural supplement of the paper; since I hardly ever went to the offices, I didn't meet her for quite a while, but when I finally did I understood that Rodney's father was right and that falling in love is letting yourself be defeated simultaneously by absurdity and by an illness that only time can cure. What I'm trying to say is that I fell so in love with Paula that, as soon as I met her, I had the certainty that

129

those in love always have: that up till then I'd never been in love with anyone. The idyll was marvellous and exhausting, but most of all it was absurd and, since one absurdity leads to another, a few months later I moved in with Paula, then we got married and then we had a son, Gabriel. All these things happened in a very brief space of time (or in what seemed to me a very brief space of time), and before I knew it I was living in a little terraced house, with a garden and lots of sunshine, in a residential neighbourhood on the outskirts of Gerona, suddenly converted into the almost involuntary protagonist of an insipid vignette of provincial well-being that I couldn't have imagined even in my worst nightmares when I was an aspiring young writer steeped in dreams of triumph.

But, to my surprise, the decision to change cities and lifestyle turned out to be a good move. In theory we'd taken it because Gerona was a cheaper and quieter place than Barcelona, and one could get to the centre of the capital in an hour, but in practice and in time I discovered that the advantages didn't end there: since in Gerona Paula's salary from the paper was almost enough to meet all the family needs, I was soon able to give up working at the university and writing articles to devote myself entirely to writing my books; I have to add that in Gerona we could count on all kinds of help from relatives and friends with children, and that there were hardly any distractions, so our social life was non-existent. Aside from that, Paula went to Barcelona and back daily, while I took care of the house and Gabriel, which left me lots of free time for my work. The results of this framework of favourable circumstances were the happiest years of my life and four books: two novels, one collection of columns and another of essays. It's true that they all went as unnoticed as the first, but it's also true that I didn't experience that invisibility as a frustration, much less as failure. In the first place, by way of a defensive blend of humility, arrogance and cowardice, I wasn't annoyed that my books didn't receive any more attention than they did because I didn't think they deserved it and, at the same time, because I thought very few readers would be in a position to understand them, but also because I secretly feared that had they received more attention than they did, they would inevitably reveal their glaring poverty. And, in the second place, because by then I'd already understood that, if I was a writer, it was because I'd turned into a nutcase who was obliged to look at reality and sometimes see it, and, if I'd chosen that bitch of a job, perhaps it was only because I couldn't be anything other than a writer: because in a way it hadn't been me who had chosen my trade, it had been my trade that had chosen me.

Time went by. I began to forget Urbana. I couldn't forget, however (or at least not entirely), my friends from Urbana, especially because occasionally, and with no effort on my part, I kept hearing news of them. The only one who was still there was John Borgheson, who I saw again several times, each time more venerable, more professorial and more British, on his occasional visits to Barcelona. Felipe

Vieri had finished his studies in New York, got a job as a professor at NYU and since then lived in Greenwich Village, turned into what he'd always wanted to be: a New Yorker from head to toe. Laura Burns' life was more turbulent and more varied: she'd finished her doctorate at Urbana, married a Hawaiian computer engineer, divorced him and, after traipsing around several west coast universities, had ended up in Oklahoma City, where she'd remarried, this time to a businessman who had made her give up her work at the university and forced her to live back and forth between Oklahoma and Mexico City. As for Rodrigo Ginés, he'd also finished his doctorate at Urbana and, after teaching at Purdue University for a couple of years, had returned to Chile, not to Santiago, but to Coyhaique, in the south of the country, where he'd married again and was teaching at the University of Los Lagos.

The only one I didn't know anything about for a long time was Rodney, and that was despite the fact that, every time I was in touch with anyone who had been in Urbana when I was there (or immediately before, or immediately after), I'd always ask about him eventually. But not knowing anything about Rodney didn't mean I'd forgotten him either. In fact, it would be easy to imagine now that I never stopped thinking about him in all those years; actually that's only partly true. It's true that every once in a while I wondered what had become of Rodney and his father, how long my friend had stayed away from home after his flight and how long it had been before he'd left again after his return. It's also true that on at least a couple of occasions I was attacked by a serious desire or urgency to tell his story and that, every time that happened, I dusted off the three black cardboard document cases with elastic straps that Rodney's father had given me and reread the letters they contained and the notes that I had taken as soon as I got back to Urbana of the tale he'd told me that afternoon in Rantoul, just as it's true that I did thorough research, reading everything I could get my hands on about the war in Vietnam, and that I took pages and pages of notes, drew up outlines, sketched out characters and planned scenes and dialogues, but the fact is there were always pieces left over that wouldn't fit, blind spots impossible to clear up (especially two: what had happened in My Khe, who was Tommy Birban), and maybe that's why each time I decided to start to write I soon gave up, bogged down in my inability to invest with meaning a story that deep down (or at least that's what I suspected at the time) perhaps lacked any. It was a strange feeling, as if, despite the fact that Rodney's father had made me in some way responsible for the story of his son's disaster, that story wasn't entirely mine to tell and I wasn't the one who had to tell it and therefore I lacked the courage, madness and desperation needed to tell it, or perhaps as if it was still an unfinished story, yet to arrive at the boiling point or level of maturity or coherence that makes a story no longer stubbornly resist being written. And it's also true that, just like in Urbana with my first frustrated novel, for a long time I could never sit down to write without feeling Rodney breathing down my neck, without wondering what he'd think of this sentence or that one, of this adjective or that one – as if Rodney's shadow was at once a ferocious judge and a guardian angel – and of course I was still unable to read Rodney's favourite authors – and I read a lot of them – without mentally arguing with my friend's tastes and opinions. All that is true, but it's just as true that, as time went by and the memory of Urbana began to dissolve in the distance like the feathery vapour trail of an airplane as it vanishes into a clear blue sky, the memory of Rodney dissolved with it too, so by the time my friend unexpectedly reappeared I was not only convinced I'd never write his story, but also that, unless some improbable chance came into play, I'd never see him again.

It happened three years ago, but it didn't happen by chance. A few months earlier I'd published a novel that hinged on a tiny episode of the Spanish Civil War; except for its subject matter, it wasn't a very different novel from my previous novels – although it was more complex and less timely, perhaps more eccentric – but, to everyone's surprise and with very few exceptions, the critics received it with a certain enthusiasm, and in the short space of time since its publication it had sold more copies than all my previous books put together, which to tell the truth still wasn't enough to turn it into a bestseller: at most it was a *succès d'estime*, although in any case that was more than enough to provoke happiness or even euphoria in someone like me, who by that stage had begun to fall into that habitual scepticism of those forty-something scribblers who've long since silently dumped the furious aspirations of glory they'd nourished in their youth and have resigned themselves to the golden mediocrity the future has in store for them with hardly any sadness or any more cynicism than strictly necessary to survive with some semblance of dignity.

It was at that moment of unexpected joy that Rodney reappeared. One Saturday night, when I returned from a promotional tour of several cities in Andalucía, Paula greeted me at home with the news that Rodney had been in Gerona that very day.

'Who?' I asked incredulously.

'Rodney,' Paula repeated. 'Rodney Falk. Your friend from Urbana.'

Of course, I'd often talked to Paula about Rodney, but that didn't diminish the shock of hearing that foreign and familiar name coming from the lips of my wife. Paula went on to tell me about Rodney's visit. Apparently, the doorbell had rung midway through the morning; since she wasn't expecting anyone, before opening the door she looked out through the peephole, and was so alarmed by the sight of a heavy-set stranger with his right eye covered with a veteran's cloth patch that she was tempted to keep quiet and not answer. Her curiosity, however, was stronger than her anxiety, and she ended up asking who it was. Rodney identified himself, asked for me, said who he was again, and Paula finally clicked, opened the door, told him I was away, invited him in and made some coffee. While they were drinking it, watched by Gabriel from a suspicious distance, Rodney told her he'd been travelling around Spain for a week, and had arrived in Barcelona three days ago, seen my latest book in a bookshop, bought it, read it, called the publisher's office and, after trying and trying and finally tricking one of the publicists, managed to get them to give him my address. It wasn't long before Gabriel abandoned his initial distrust and – according to Paula, maybe because he was amused by Rodney's orthopaedic Spanish, or his impossible Catalan learned from me in Urbana, or because Rodney had the shrewdness or instinct to treat him like an adult, which is the best way to win over children – hit it off immediately with my friend, so before Paula knew it Gabriel and Rodney were playing ping pong in the garden. The three of them spent the day together, wandering around the old part of the city and spending a long time in a bar on the plaza de Sant Domènec playing table football, a game Gabriel loved and Rodney had never seen, which didn't stop him, according to Paula, playing with the passion of a novice and celebrating every goal with shouts, hugging Gabriel and lifting him up in the air and kissing him. So at dusk, when Rodney announced he had to leave, Gabriel and Paula tried to persuade him to change his mind with the argument that I'd be back in just a few hours; they didn't succeed: Rodney claimed he had to catch a train that same night from Barcelona to Pamplona, where he planned to spend the San Fermín fiestas.

'He's staying here,' said Paula at the conclusion of her

136

tale, handing me a piece of paper with a name and telephone number scrawled in Rodney's pointy and unmistakable hand. 'Hotel Albret.'

That night a double uneasiness kept me awake, only half related to Rodney's visit. On the one hand, it was barely twenty-four hours since I'd slept with the local writer who'd presented my book in Málaga; it wasn't the first time in the last few months I'd been unfaithful to Paula, but after each tryst I was viciously tortured by remorse for days. But on the other hand I was also uneasy about Rodney's unexpected reappearance, his reappearance precisely at the moment I became established as a writer, perhaps as if I feared my friend had not shown up to celebrate my success, but to reveal the sham of it, humiliating me with the memory of my farcical beginnings as an aspiring writer in Urbana. I think I fell asleep that night before I extinguished the remorse, but having decided I wouldn't phone Rodney and would try to forget about his visit as soon as possible.

The next day, however, there didn't seem to be any topic of conversation in my house other than Rodney. Among other things Paula and Gabriel told me that my friend lived in Burlington, a city in the state of Vermont, that he had a wife and had just had a son, and that he worked for a real estate agency. I don't know what surprised me more: the fact that Rodney, always so reluctant to talk to me about his private life, had talked about it to Paula and Gabriel, or the no less puzzling fact that, judging from what he'd told my wife and son, Rodney now led the tranquil life of a husband and father incompatible with the man secretly corroded by his past who, though no one could have suspected it, he still had been in Urbana, just as if the time gone by since then had eventually cured his war wounds and allowed him to emerge from the interminable tunnel of misfortune through which he'd walked alone and in darkness for thirty years. On Monday Paula got the photographs that she and Gabriel had taken with Rodney developed; they were happy photos: most showed just Gabriel and Rodney (in one they're playing table football; in another they're sitting on the cathedral steps; in another they're walking along the Rambla, holding hands); but in two of them Paula appeared as well: one was taken on Les Peixeteries Velles bridge, the other at the station entrance, just before Rodney caught his train. Finally, on Tuesday morning, after having turned the matter over and over in my mind, I decided to call Rodney. It wasn't because Paula and Gabriel asked me again and again during those three days if I'd spoken to him yet, but for three distinct but complementary reasons: the first is that I realized I wanted to talk to Rodney; the second is that I came to understand that the suspicion that Rodney had come to rain on my parade was absurd and petty; the third – though not the least important – is that by then I'd spent more than half a year without writing a single line, and at some point it occurred to me that if I managed to talk to Rodney about his time in Vietnam and throw light on the blind spots of that story as I knew it from the testimony of his father and the letters Rodney and Bob had sent from the front, then maybe I'd get a complete understanding of it and be able to safely tackle the ever-postponed task of telling it.

So on Tuesday morning I phoned the Hotel Albret in Pamplona and asked for Rodney. To my surprise, the receptionist told me he wasn't staying there. Since I thought there'd been a mistake, I insisted and, after a few seconds, the receptionist told me that in fact Rodney had stayed in the hotel on Sunday night, but on Monday morning he'd suddenly cancelled his five-night reservation and left for Madrid. 'He left word that if anyone asked for him to say he'd be at the Hotel San Antonio de La Florida,' the receptionist added. I asked if they had the telephone number of the hotel; he said no. I hung up. I picked up the phone. I got the number for the Hotel San Antonio de La Florida from directory inquiries; I called and asked for Rodney. 'One moment, please.' I waited a moment, after which I again heard the voice of the receptionist. 'I'm sorry,' he said. 'Señor Falk is not in his room.' The next morning I phoned the hotel again, I asked for Rodney again. 'He just went out,' the same receptionist told me (or maybe it was another). Furious, I was about to slam down the receiver, but I stopped myself in time to ask how many days Rodney had reserved his room for. 'He'll still be here tonight,' answered the receptionist. 'But not tomorrow.' I thanked him and hung up the phone. Half an hour later, once I arrived at the conclusion that if I lost Rodney's trail I'd never find it again, I called the hotel again and reserved a room for that night. Then I called Paula at the newspaper, I told her I was going to Madrid to see Rodney, packed a change of clothes, a book and the three document cases with Rodney's and his brother's letters and left for Barcelona airport.

I landed in Madrid at six, and forty minutes later, after skirting the city along the M-30, a taxi dropped me off at the Hotel San Antonio de La Florida, in the neighbourhood of La Florida, just across the street from the Príncipe Pío railway station. It was a modest hotel, whose façade gave onto a noisy sidewalk filled with old-fashioned bars and patios. I crossed a hall and went up some carpeted steps that led to a spacious foyer; at one end was the reception, flanked by two phone booths and a plastic pyramid of tourist postcards. I registered, they gave me the key to my room, I asked for Rodney. The receptionist – a very neat, sallow-skinned, bespectacled man – consulted the registry and then a set of pigeonholes.

'Room 334,' was his answer. 'But he's not there now. Do you want me to give him a message when he comes back?'

'Tell him I'm staying in the hotel,' I answered. 'And that I'm waiting for him.'

The receptionist wrote down the message on a piece of paper and a bellhop led me to a tiny, slightly sordid room with cream-coloured walls and blood-red doors and frames. I got undressed, had a shower, got dressed again. Lying on a hard old bed covered by a bedspread with a floral print identical to the one on the drawn curtains, which spared the vision of a knot of highways and a densely treed corner of the Casa de Campo, beyond which began the outskirts of the city, expecting Rodney to knock on my door at any moment, I kept myself busy imagining our encounter. I wondered how Rodney would have changed since the last time I'd seen him, a winter night fourteen years earlier, on the snowy sidewalk in front of Treno's; I wondered if his father would have told him about my visit to Rantoul and what he'd told me about him; I wondered if he'd agree to talk to me about his years in Vietnam, to explain to me what had happened in My Khe, who Tommy Birban was; I wondered why he'd gone to Gerona to see me and what he thought of my novel. Until, consumed with impatience or tired of wondering, towards nine I went back downstairs to reception and asked the receptionist to tell Rodney when he arrived that I was waiting for him in the café.

The café was very busy. I sat at the only free table, ordered a beer and buried myself in the novel I'd brought from home. Several beers later I ordered a sandwich, and then a coffee and a double whisky. Time went by; people came and went from the place, but Rodney still didn't show up. It must have been very late by the time I ordered a second coffee, because the euphoric effect of the whisky and the first coffee had completely vanished. 'I'm sorry,' the waiter answered. 'We're just closing.' I persuaded him to serve me a coffee in a plastic cup and, carrying it, went up to the foyer, where at that moment the receptionist was attending to a pair of late arrivals. Hours earlier, when I had come down to eat, the foyer was brightly lit by a row of spotlights pointed at the ceiling, but now it had been overtaken by a darkness only lessened by the light of the reception desk and that of a couple of floor lamps whose circle of light barely managed to drag from the shadows the prints of old Madrid, the Goyaesque lithographs and the charmless still lifes that decorated the walls. I sat beneath the light of one of the lamps, my back to the big window that ran the length of the room and almost at the top of the steps that came up from the entrance, facing a wall clock that showed two o'clock; beyond, beneath another lamp, a man sat alone watching a black and white film on the television. The man soon turned off the television and took the elevator up to his room. By then the receptionist had dealt with the pair of tourists and was dozing behind the counter. I kept waiting and, pausing from my reading, disheartened by fatigue and sleepiness, wondered whether Rodney hadn't escaped again and the most sensible thing might not be to go to bed.

Shortly after that he appeared. I heard the street door open and, as I'd done each time that had happened, waited expectantly for a moment; this time I saw Rodney emerge from the shadows of the stairway and, without noticing my presence, head towards the reception desk with his quick and stumbling gait. While Rodney woke up the receptionist from his snooze, I felt my heart in my mouth: I set my book down on the coffee table beside my chair, got up and stood there, without managing to take a step or say anything, as if bewitched by the expected appearance of my friend. The receptionist's voice shattering the silence of the foyer broke the spell.

'That man is waiting for you,' he said to Rodney, pointing over his shoulder.

Rodney turned around and, after a few seconds' hesitation, began to advance towards me, peering through the semi-darkness of the room with a look more inquisitive than incredulous, as if his poor eyes couldn't quite recognize me.

'Well, well, well,' he finally croaked when he was a few steps away from me, smiling with his whole mouthful of mistreated teeth and throwing open two arms like sails. 'I can't believe it. The celebrated author in person. But what the hell are you doing here?'

He didn't give me time to answer: we hugged.

'Have you been waiting long?' he asked.

'A while,' I answered. 'Yesterday I phoned the number in Pamplona you gave Paula and they told me you were staying here. I tried to get in touch with you, but I couldn't, so this afternoon I got on a plane and came to Madrid.'

'Just to see me?' he feigned surprise, shaking me by the shoulders. 'You could have at least told me you were coming. I would have been waiting for you.'

As if he were apologizing, Rodney recounted the circumstances that had disrupted his travel arrangements. At first, he explained, his plan had been to spend the week of San Fermín in Pamplona, but when he arrived in the city last Sunday and checked into the Hotel Albret — a hotel

quite a distance from the centre, near the university clinic –
he realized he'd made a mistake and that it wasn't worth
running the risk of letting the real *Sanfermines* spoil the
radiant fictional *Sanfermines* that Hemingway had taught
him to remember. So the next day he packed his bags again,
cancelled his hotel reservation and, without allowing himself even a glimpse of the festive city, went to Madrid. That
said, Rodney began describing the circuitous itinerary of his
trip through Spain, and then talked enthusiastically about
his visit to Gerona, about Gabriel and about Paula. As he
did so I was trying to superimpose my precarious memory
of him on the reality of this man I now had before me;
despite the fourteen years that had passed since the last time
I'd seen him, the fit was almost perfect, with barely any
need for adjustments, because in all that time Rodney's
physical appearance hadn't changed much: maybe the
pounds he'd put on gave him a less stony and more
vulnerable air, maybe his features had softened a little,
maybe his body leaned a little further to the right, but he
dressed with the same militant sloppiness as ever – running
shoes, faded jeans, blue checked shirt – and his long hair,
reddish and a bit messy, the permanent restlessness of his
eyes which were almost different colours and his ungainly
heaviness still gave him that lost pachyderm air of my
memories.

At some point Rodney broke off his explanation mid-
sentence with another explanation.

'Tomorrow I'm catching the 7 a.m. train for Seville,' he

said. 'We've got the whole night ahead of us. Shall we go have a drink?'

We asked at the desk for a nearby bar where we could have a drink, but he told us that all the ones in the neighbourhood were closed by that time, and in the centre we'd only find the clubs open. Annoyed, we asked him if he could serve us something in the foyer.

'I'm sorry,' he said. 'But there is a coffee machine on the first floor.'

We went up to the first floor laughing about Madrid's non-stop nightlife which, according to Rodney, the travel guides all touted, and then returned to the hall with the concoction from the coffee machine and sat down on the sofa where I'd been waiting for him. Rodney couldn't resist the temptation of taking a quick glance at the cover of the novel lying on the table; since I noticed he made a perplexed grimace, I couldn't resist the temptation of asking him if he knew the author.

'Of course,' he answered. 'But he's too intelligent for me. Actually I'm afraid he's too intelligent to be a good novelist. He's always demonstrating how intelligent he is, instead of letting the novel be the intelligent one.' Taking a sip of coffee, he leaned back on the sofa and carried on, 'And speaking of novels, I suppose you must've started turning into a cretin or a son of a bitch by now, huh?'

I stared at him, uncomprehending.

'Don't make that face, man,' he laughed. 'It was a joke. But, really, isn't that what all successful guys end up turning into?'

'I'm not so sure,' I defended myself. 'Maybe what success

does is just bring out some people's inner cretin or son of a bitch. It's not the same. Besides, I hate to tell you but my success is so minor, it's not even enough for that.'

'Don't be so optimistic,' he insisted. 'Since I've been in Spain two or three different people have already told me about your book. *Malum signum.* By the way: did Paula tell you that even I've read it?'

I nodded and, to save myself from the humiliation of asking him what he'd thought of it, in one motion I finished off my coffee and put a cigarette between my lips. Rodney leaned over with his rusty old yellowing Zippo he'd brought back from Vietnam.

'Well, actually I think I've read them all,' he said.

I choked on the first drag.

'All of them?' I asked once I'd stopped coughing.

'I think so,' he said after lighting himself a cigarette as well. 'In fact, I think I've become a notable expert on your oeuvre. Oeuvre with a capital or small O?'

'Go to hell.'

Rodney laughed again happily. He really seemed glad that we were together again; I was too, but less so, perhaps because Rodney's provocations wouldn't allow me to entirely discard the paranoid fear that my friend had travelled all the way from the United States just to ridicule my success, or at least to take me down a peg or two. Maybe to rule out this fear once and for all, or to confirm it, since Rodney didn't seem willing to go on, I asked, 'Well, aren't you going to tell me what you thought of it?'

146

'Your latest novel?'

'My latest novel.'

'I thought it was good,' said Rodney, making an uncertain gesture of assent and looking at me with his cheerful, brown eyes. 'But, can I tell you the truth?'

'Of course,' I said, cursing the hour I'd decided to travel to Madrid in search of Rodney. 'As long as it's not too offensive.'

'Well, the truth is I liked the first one you wrote more,' he said. 'The one about Urbana, I mean. What's it called?'

'*The Tenant.*'

'Yeah, that's the one.'

'I'm so pleased,' I lied, thinking of Marcelo Cuartero or Marcelo Cuartero's student who had written about that book. 'I have a friend who thinks the same. I thought he was the only one who'd read it. In his review he more or less said there was an immense gulf in universal literature between me and Cervantes.'

Rodney let out a guffaw that revealed his whole mouthful of bad teeth.

'What I like about it is that it seems like a cerebral novel, but it's actually full of feeling,' he said afterwards. 'But this latest one seems full of feeling, but it's actually too cerebral.'

'Exactly the opposite to what the critics who didn't like it thought. They say it's sentimental.'

'You don't say? Then I'm right. These days, when some halfwit doesn't know how to attack a novel, they attack it by saying it's sentimental. The halfwits don't understand

147

that writing a novel consists of choosing the most moving words to provoke as much emotion as possible; nor do they understand that sentiments are one thing and sentimentalism something else entirely, and that sentimentalism is the failure of sentiment. And, since writers are a bunch of cowards who don't dare take issue with the halfwits in charge and who've banned sentiment and emotions, the result is all these well-mannered, cold, pale, lifeless novels that seem like they've come directly out of some avant-garde civil servant's office to please the critics . . .' Rodney took a greedy drag on his cigarette and seemed lost in thought for a few seconds. 'Listen, tell me something,' he added, then suddenly looked me in the eye. 'The nutcase professor in the novel is me, right?'

The question shouldn't have caught me off guard. I've already said that in my Urbana novel there was a semi-hopeless character whose eccentric physical appearance is based on Rodney's physical appearance, and at that moment I remembered that while I was writing the novel, I often imagined that, in the unlikely case that he read it, Rodney would unavoidably recognize himself. I suppose to gain time and find a convincing reply that, without straying from the truth, wouldn't hurt Rodney's feelings, I asked, 'What professor? What novel?'

'What novel do you think?' answered Rodney. '*The Tenant*. Is Olalde me or not?'

'Olalde is Olalde,' I improvised. 'And you're you.'

'Throw another dog that bone,' he said in Spanish, as if

148

he'd just learned the phrase and was using it for the first time. 'Don't give me that old story of novels being one thing and life another,' he went on, back in English now. 'All novels are autobiographical, my friend, even the bad ones. And as for Olalde, well, I think he's the best thing in the book. But, in truth, what I think is funniest is that you saw me like that.'

'How?' I asked, no longer trying to hide the obvious.

'As the only one who really understands what's going on.'

'And why do you think that's funny?'

'Because that's exactly how I saw myself.'

Now we both laughed, and I took advantage of the situation to change the subject. Of course, I was eager to talk to him about Vietnam and my frustrated attempts to tell his story, but because I thought it might be counterproductive to be too hasty or premature and could put him off broaching a subject he'd never wanted to talk about with me, I opted to wait, sure that the night would eventually afford me the opportunity without turning that friendly reunion into an interrogation and without Rodney conceiving the not entirely baseless suspicion that I'd only come to see him to pump him for information; so, trying to recover in the late summer night of that Madrid hotel the complicity of those winter evenings in Treno's – with the snow lashing the windows and ZZ Top or Bob Dylan coming out of the speakers – I started talking about Urbana: about John Borgheson, Giuseppe Rota, Wong, the Chinese guy and the sinister-looking American, whose name we'd both forgotten or never known, about Rodrigo Ginés, Laura Burns, Felipe Vieri and Frank Solaún. Then we talked at length about Gabriel and Paula, and I summed up my life in Urbana after he disappeared and also my life in Barcelona and Gerona after Urbana disappeared, and finally, without my asking, Rodney told me with a few extra bits what Paula had already told me: that he'd been living in Burlington, Vermont for almost ten years, that he had a son (called Dan) and a wife (called Jenny), that he was employed at a real estate agency; he also told me that in the next few days he would find out if he'd got a position as a teacher in a public school in Rantoul, something he fervently desired, because he very much wanted to go back to live in his home town. As soon as he pronounced that name I realized my opportunity had arrived.

'I know the place,' I said.

'Really?' asked Rodney.

'Yeah,' I answered. 'After you stopped teaching at Urbana I went to your house to look for you. I saw a bit of the city but I spent most of the time with your father. I thought he would have told you.'

'No,' said Rodney. 'But that's normal. It would have been strange if he had told me.'

'I hope he's well,' I said, for something to say.

Rodney didn't answer straight away; suddenly, in the yellowish light of the floor lamp, surrounded by the darkness of the foyer, he looked tired and sleepy, maybe abruptly bored, as if nothing could interest him less than

150

talking about his father. He said, 'He died three years ago.' I was about to resort to some hackneyed consolation when Rodney interrupted to save me the trouble. 'Don't worry. There's nothing to be sorry for. For years my father did nothing but torment himself. At least he doesn't any more.'

Rodney lit another cigarette. I thought he was going to change the subject, but he didn't; with some surprise I heard him carry on, 'So you went to see him.' I nodded. 'And what did you talk about?'

'The first time we didn't,' I explained, carefully choosing my words. 'He didn't want to. But after a while he phoned me and I went back to see him. Then he told me a story.'

Now Rodney looked at me with curiosity, raising his eyebrows inquisitively. Then I said, 'Wait here for a minute. I want to show you something.'

I stood up, hurried past the receptionist, who started up from his snooze, got in the elevator, went up to my room, grabbed the three black document cases, went back down to the foyer and put them on the table, in front of Rodney. With an ironic glint in his eyes and voice, my friend asked, 'What's this?'

I didn't say anything: I just pointed to the document cases. Rodney opened one of them, contemplated the pack of chronologically arranged envelopes, took one, read the address and the return address, looked at me, took the letter out of the envelope and, as he tried to decipher his own handwriting on the rough US Army paper, since the silence was lengthening I asked, 'Recognize them?'

Rodney looked at me again, this time fleetingly, and, without answering, left the letter on the table, picked another envelope, took out another letter, started to read that one too.

'My father gave them to you?' he murmured, waving the one he had in his hand. I didn't answer. 'It's strange,' he said after a couple of seconds.

'What's strange?'

'That they should be here, in Madrid,' he answered, not taking his eyes off the letters. 'That I wrote them and now I don't understand them. That my father should have given them to you.'

Slowly he put the letters back in the envelopes, put the envelopes back in the document case, asked, 'Have you read them?'

I said I had. He nodded indifferently, forgetting about the letters and sitting back again on the sofa. After another pause he asked again with apparent interest, 'What'd you think?'

'What, of this?'

'Of my father,' he corrected me.

'I don't know,' I admitted. 'I only saw him twice. I couldn't form an opinion. But I don't think he was sure of having done the right thing.'

'In relation to what?'

'In relation to you.'

'Ah.' He smiled weakly: on his face not the slightest trace was left of the vivacity that had animated it until a few minutes ago. 'You're mistaken there. Actually he was never sure of having done the right thing. Not in relation to me or in relation to anybody. That type of person never is.'

'I don't understand.'

Rodney shrugged; by way of explanation he added, 'I don't know, maybe it's true there're only two types of people: the sinners who always think they're righteous, and the righteous who always think they're sinners. At first my father was the first type, but then he turned into the champion of the second. I imagine that happens to lots of people.' He pushed a nervous hand through his messy hair and for a moment seemed on the point of laughing, but he didn't laugh. 'What I mean is that after a certain point in time my father didn't give me many chances to feel proud of him. Of course, I didn't give him many chances to feel proud of me either. So I suppose it was all a damned misunderstanding. But, well, these things happen to everybody.' He sighed, still smiling as he put out his cigarette in the overflowing ashtray. Starting to get up from the sofa, he gestured towards the clock on the wall by the stairs: it said five o'clock. 'Ah well, I'm starting to babble. This story is of no interest to anyone any more, and I'd better get a bit of sleep, don't you think?'

But I wasn't prepared to let that occasion escape. I told him to hang on a second, that the story interested me. A little surprised, Rodney questioned me silently with a sort of malicious naïveté. Then, aware it was now or never, all in one go I told him his father had summoned me to Rantoul precisely to tell me about it, I told him what his father had told me and asked him why he thought he'd done so, why he'd given me his letters and Bob's as well. Rodney listened to me attentively and settled back into his seat; after a long silence, during which his gaze was lost beyond the ring of light we'd stolen from the darkness of the room, he looked at me again and burst out laughing.

'What's so funny?' I asked.

'Either you've changed a lot or that's a rhetorical question.'

'What do you mean?'

'You know exactly what I mean,' he answered. 'What I mean is that after talking to my father you left my house convinced that what he wanted was for you to tell my story, or at least that you had to tell it. Am I wrong?'

I didn't blush; I didn't deny the truth either. Rodney moved his head from one side to the other in a gesture that resembled reproach but was actually mockery.

'The presumption,' he muttered. 'The fucking presumption of writers.' He paused and, looking me in the eye, said, 'And so?'

'And so what?'

'So why haven't you told it?'

'I tried,' I admitted. 'But I couldn't. Or rather I didn't know how.'

'Yeah,' said Rodney, as if my answer had disappointed him, and then asked, 'Tell me something? What is it that my father told you?'

'I already told you: everything.'

'What's everything?'

'What he knew, what you'd told him, what he imagined, what's in the letters,' I explained. 'He also told me there were things he didn't know. He told me about an incident in a village, for example. My Khe it was called. He didn't know what had happened there, but he explained that after that incident you spent some time in hospital, and then you re-enlisted in the army. Anyway, that's in the letters too.'

'You've read them all,' Rodney said almost as a question.

'Of course,' I said. 'Your father gave them to me to read. Besides, I've already admitted that at some point I wanted to tell your story.'

'Why?'

'For the same reason any story gets told. Because I was obsessed with it. Because I didn't understand it. Because I felt responsible for it.'

'Responsible?'

'Yeah,' I said, and, almost without realizing it, added, 'maybe a person isn't only responsible for what they do, but also for what they see or read or hear.'

As soon as I heard myself pronounce that sentence I regretted having said it. Rodney's reaction confirmed my mistake: his lips curled instantly into a cunning smile, which soon vanished, but before I could put things right my friend began to speak slowly, as if possessed by a sarcastic and controlled rage.

'Ah,' he said. 'Nice phrase. You writers sure like your pretty phrases. There's a few in your last book. Real pretty.

So pretty they almost seem true. But, of course, they're not true, they're just pretty. The funny thing is you still haven't learned that writing well is the opposite of writing pretty phrases. No pretty phrase is capable of expressing truth. Probably no phrase is capable of capturing truth, but . . .'

'I didn't say I wanted to tell the truth,' I interrupted him in irritation. 'I just said I wanted to tell your story.'

'And what difference is there between the two?' he answered, trying to catch my eye with a sad air of defiance. 'The only stories worth telling are the true ones, and if you couldn't tell my story it might not be that you're not capable of it, it might be that it can't be told.'

I held my tongue. I shouldn't have held my tongue, but I did. I should have said: 'That's a pretty phrase too, Rodney, and perhaps it's true.' I should have said: 'You're wrong, Rodney. The only stories worth telling are the ones that can't be told.' I should have said one of those two things, or perhaps both of them, but I didn't say either and I held my tongue. I was sleepy, I was hungry, I felt the night was beginning to turn to dawn, but most of all I felt the astonishment of being embroiled in that conversation that I'd never imagined I could have had with Rodney and that I thought we were only having because Rodney secretly knew he owed it to me, and maybe as well because, against all expectations, time had ended up cauterizing my friend's interminable wounds. I let a few seconds go by, lit a cigarette and after the first drag heard myself say: 'What happened in My Khe, Rodney?'

We were almost whispering, but the question resounded in the quiet of the foyer like a shot. I'd been asking myself for fourteen years, and during that time I'd found out a few things about My Khe. I knew, for example, that nowadays it was a vast tourist beach located fifteen kilometres from Quang Ngai, in the Son Tinh district, not far from the port of Sa Ky, a ribbon of land seven kilometres long, squeezed between a dark forest of poplars and the clear waters of the Kinh River, of which I'd seen many photographs that showed the same anodyne images of summery idleness as any beach in the world: women and children paddling near the calm shore, the gentle slope of very fine sand scattered with red plastic tables and chairs, a crest of rolling hills in the distance placidly cut out against a sky as blue as the sea; I also knew that thirty-two years earlier there'd been a village beside that beach and that one day in 1968 Rodney had been there. But although I had imagined many times what happened in My Khe – with my imagination by then corroded by reportage, history books, novels, documentaries and films about Vietnam – I knew nothing for certain. I thought Rodney had read my mind when he asked with a sort of resignation or indifference: 'Can't you guess?'

'More or less,' I answered, sincerely. 'But I don't know what happened.'

'You don't need to,' he assured me. 'What you imagined is what happened. What happens in all wars happened. No more, no less. My Khe is only an anecdote. Besides, in Vietnam there wasn't just one My Khe, there were many.

What happened in one happened more or less in all of them. Satisfied?'

I said nothing.

'No, of course not,' guessed Rodney, hardening his voice again, and then went on as if he didn't want me to understand what he said but rather what he meant. 'But if it means that much to you I can tell you something that'll leave you satisfied. What would you prefer? I know lots of stories. I've got an imagination too. Tell me what you need to make you think your story tallies and make yourself believe you understand it. You tell me and I'll tell you and we'll be done, okay? But before that let me warn you about something: no matter what I tell you, no matter what I invent, you're never going to understand the only thing that matters, and that's that I don't want your pity. Understand? Not yours or anybody else's. I don't need it. That's the only thing that matters, or at least it's the only thing that matters to me. You understand, right?'

I nodded, regretting having pushed the conversation to such an extreme and, as I looked away from Rodney's gaze, I noticed a bitter taste of ashes or old coins in my mouth. In the big window that overlooked Príncipe Pío station, dawn was already vying with the morning's waning darkness, unhurriedly sweeping away the room's shadows. The receptionist had stopped dozing a while ago and was scurrying about in his cubicle. I exchanged a blank look with him and, looking back at Rodney, muttered an apology. Rodney didn't give any sign of having heard

158

it, but after a long silence sighed, and at that moment I thought I guessed from a barely perceptible change in his expression what was going to happen. I wasn't wrong. With a calmed voice and a tired air he asked, 'Do you really want me to tell you?'

Knowing that I'd won, or that my friend had let me win, I didn't say anything. Then Rodney crossed his legs and, after thinking for a moment, began to tell the story. He did so in a strange way, quick, cold and precise all at the same time; I don't know if he'd told it to someone before, but while I listened I knew he'd told it to himself many times. Rodney told me that the week before the incident at My Khe, a routine patrol made up of soldiers from his company had been accosted at a crossroads by a Vietnamese teenager, who, as she went from one to the next asking for help with urgent gestures, set off a hand grenade hidden inside her clothing, and that the result of this encounter was that, along with the teenager, two members of the patrol were blown to pieces, another lost an eye and two others were injured less seriously. The episode obliged them to redouble security, injecting the company with extra nervousness, which might partly explain what happened later. And what happened was that one morning his company was sent on a reconnaissance mission to the village of My Khe with the object of making sure some information they'd received that members of the Vietcong were hiding there was false. Rodney remembered it all like it was wrapped in the fog of a dream, the Chinook they travelled in descending first over the sea and then over the sand and finally in circles over a handful of neat garden plots while the peasants ran towards the village square, seized with panic because of the peremptory voices spat out by the loudspeakers, the helicopter landing beside a graveyard and then the flash of the sun in the exemplary blue sky and the dazzle of the flowers on the windowsills and a diffuse or remote clamour of hens or children in the crystal-clear morning air as the soldiers dispersed in an impeccable geometrical formation down the deserted streets until at some moment, without really knowing how or why or who had started it, the shooting broke out, first a single shot was heard and almost immediately bursts of machine gun fire and later screams and explosions, and in just a few seconds an insane torment of fire pulverized the miraculous tranquillity of the village, and when Rodney went towards the place where he imagined the battle had started he heard at his back a confused noise of mass escape or ambush and he turned and shouted in rage and fright and opened fire, and then he kept shouting and shooting not knowing why he was shouting or where or at whom he was shooting, shooting, shooting, shooting, and shouting too, and when he stopped the only thing he saw in front of him was an unintelligible jumble of clothes and hair soaked in blood and tiny, dismembered hands and feet and lifeless or still imploring eyes, he saw something multiple, wet and slippery that quickly escaped his comprehension, he saw all the horror in the world concentrated in a few metres of death, but he couldn't bear that refulgent vision and from

160

that moment his conscience abdicated, and of what came next he had only a very vague, dreamlike memory of fires and disemboweled animals and weeping old men and corpses of women and children with their mouths open like exposed entrails. Rodney didn't remember anything more; during his months in hospital and during the rest of his time in Vietnam no one ever mentioned the incident again, and only much later, when they had a trial back in the United States, Rodney found out what his father also found out and had told me: there hadn't been any battle in My Khe, there weren't any guerrillas hiding there, none of the members of his company had even been injured, and the incident had left fifty-four Vietnamese dead, most of them women, old people and children.

When Rodney finished talking we remained still for a moment, not even daring to look at each other, as if his tale had taken us to a place where only fear was real and we were waiting for the benign apparition of a visitor who would give us back the shared safety of that squalid foyer of a Madrid hotel. The visitor did not arrive. Rodney leaned his big hands on his knees and got up from the sofa with a creaking of joints; bent over and a little unsteady, as if he were dizzy or suffering from vertigo or nausea, he took a few steps and stood looking at the street, leaning on the window frame.

'It's almost daylight,' I heard him say.

It was true: the skeletal light of dawn was inundating the room, endowing everything in it with a phantasmal or precarious reality, as if it were scenery submerged in a lake, and at the same time sharpening Rodney's profile, his silhouette standing out doubtfully against the cobalt blue of the sky; for an instant I thought that, rather than a bird of prey, it was the profile of a predator or a big cat.

'Well, that's more or less the story,' he said in a perfectly neutral tone of voice, returning to the sofa with his hands hidden in his pockets. 'Is that how you imagined it?'

I pondered my answer for a moment. My mouth didn't taste of ashes or old coins any more, but of something that very closely resembled blood but wasn't blood. I felt horror, but I didn't manage to feel pity, and at some moment I felt – hating myself for feeling it and hating Rodney for making me feel it – that all the suffering his time in Vietnam had inflicted on him was justified.

'No,' I finally answered. 'But it's not far off.'

Rodney kept talking, standing up in front of me, but I was too stunned to process his words, and after a while he took one hand out of his pocket and pointed at the clock on the wall.

'My train's leaving in just over an hour,' he said. 'I better go upstairs and get my things. Will you wait for me here?'

I said I would and stayed waiting for him in the foyer, looking through the big unsleeping window at the people going into the Príncipe Pío station and the traffic and the incipient morning activity in the neighbourhood of La Florida, watching them without seeing them because the only thing that occupied my mind was the mistaken and

162

bittersweet certainty that Rodney's entire story only just now made sense to me, an atrocious sense that nothing could soften or rectify, and ten minutes later Rodney returned weighed down with luggage and freshly showered. While he checked out of the hotel a guy went into one of the two phone booths that flanked the reception desk and, I don't know why, but as I saw him dial the number and wait for an answer, with a start I remembered a name and almost said it out loud. Without taking my eyes off the guy inside the phone booth I heard Rodney ask the receptionist how to get to Atocha station and the receptionist telling him the quickest way was to get a train from Príncipe Pío station. Then Rodney turned back to me to say goodbye, but I insisted on accompanying him to the station.

We went down to the hall and before going outside onto paseo de La Florida, Rodney put his eye patch on. We crossed the street, went inside the station, Rodney bought a ticket and we went towards the platform beneath an enormous steel framework with translucent glass like the skeleton of an enormous prehistoric animal. While we waited on the platform I asked if I could ask one more question.

'Not if it's for your book,' he answered. I tried to smile, but I couldn't. 'Take my advice and don't write it. Anyone can write a book if they put their mind to it, but not everyone can keep quiet. Besides, I already told you, that story can't be told.'

'That may be,' I admitted, though now I didn't want to

hold my tongue, 'but maybe the only stories worth telling are the ones that can't be told.'

'Another pretty phrase,' said Rodney. 'If you write the book, remember not to include it. What is it you wanted to ask me?'

Without a second's doubt I asked: 'Who is Tommy Birban?'

Rodney's face didn't change, and I didn't know how to read the look in his one eye, or maybe there was nothing to read in it. When he spoke he managed to keep his voice sounding normal.

'Where did you get that name?'

'Your father mentioned it. He said that before you left Urbana you and he spoke on the phone and that's why you left.'

'He didn't tell you anything else?'

'What else should he have told me?'

'Nothing.'

At that moment they announced over the loudspeakers the imminent arrival of the Atocha train.

'Tommy was a comrade,' said Rodney. 'He arrived in Quang Ngai when I was already a veteran, and we became friends. We left almost at the same time, and I haven't seen him since . . .' He paused. 'But you know something?'

'What?'

'When I met you, you reminded me of him. I don't know why.' With the trace of a smile on his lips Rodney waited for my reaction, but I didn't react. 'Well, I do actually. You

164

know? In war there are those who go under and those who save themselves. That's all. Tommy was one of those who go under, and you would have been too. But Tommy survived, I don't know how but he survived. Sometimes I think it would have been better for him if he hadn't . . . Anyway, that was Tommy Birban: an underdog who sunk even further to save himself.'

'That doesn't answer my question.'

'What question?'

'Why did you leave after talking to him on the phone?'

'You didn't ask me that question.'

'I'm asking you now.'

Knowing time was on his side, Rodney just answered with an impatient gesture and an evasive: 'Because Tommy wanted to get me involved in a mess.'

'What kind of mess? Was Tommy at My Khe?'

'No. He arrived long after that.'

'So?'

'So nothing. Soldier things. Believe me: if I explained it to you, you wouldn't understand. Tommy was weak and he kept obsessing over things from the war . . . Grudges, enmities, things like that. I didn't want to know about any of that stuff any more.'

'And you left just because of that?'

'Yeah. I thought I was over all that, but I wasn't. I wouldn't do it now.'

I realized Rodney was lying to me; I also understood or thought I understood that, contrary to what I'd thought in the hotel foyer only a little while earlier, the horror of My Khe didn't explain everything.

'Anyway,' said Rodney as the Atocha train stopped beside us. 'We've spent the night talking nonsense. I'll write you.' He hugged me, picked up his bags and, before climbing onto the train, added: 'Take good care of Gabriel and Paula. And take care of yourself.'

I nodded, but didn't manage to say anything, because I could only think that that was the first time in my life I'd hugged a murderer.

I went back to the hotel. When I got to my room I was sticky with sweat, so I took a shower, changed my clothes and lay down on the bed to rest a while before getting the plane back. I had a bitter taste in my mouth, a headache and a buzzing in my temples; I couldn't stop going over and over my encounter with Rodney. I regretted having gone to see him in Madrid; I regretted knowing the truth and having insisted on finding it out. Of course, before that night's conversation I imagined Rodney had killed: he'd been to war and dying and killing is what you do in wars; but what I couldn't imagine was that he'd participated in a massacre, that he'd murdered women and children. Knowing what he'd done filled me with a pitiless, unflinching aversion; having heard him tell it with the indifference with which you describe an innocuous domestic incident increased the horror to disgust. Now the misery of remorse in which Rodney had spent years bleeding seemed a benevolent punishment, and I wondered if the implausible fact that

166

he'd survived the guilt, far from being commendable, didn't increase the appalling burden of responsibility. There were, of course, explanations for what he'd told me, but none of them equal to the size of the disgrace. On the other hand, I didn't understand why, having revealed without beating about the bush what happened in My Khe, Rodney would have avoided telling me who Tommy Birban was and what he represented, unless his evasions were meant to try to hide from me a greater horror than My Khe, a horror so unjustifiable and unutterable that, to his eyes and by contrast, it turned My Khe into an utterable and justifiable horror. But what unimaginable horror of horrors could that be? A horror in any case sufficient to pulverize Rodney's mental equilibrium fourteen years before and make him leave his home and his job and resume his fugitive life as soon as Tommy Birban had reappeared. Of course it was also possible that Rodney hadn't told me the whole truth of My Khe and that Tommy Birban had arrived in Vietnam by the time it happened and was in some way linked to the massacre. And what had he meant when he said that Tommy Birban was weak and that he shouldn't have survived and that he reminded him of me? Did this mean that he'd protected Tommy Birban or he was protecting him like he'd protected me? But what had he protected Tommy Birban from, if he had protected him? And what had he protected me from?

At noon, when reception woke me up to tell me I had to check out, it took me a few seconds to accept that I was in a hotel room in Madrid and that my encounter with Rodney hadn't been a dream, or rather a nightmare. Two hours later I flew back to Barcelona, with my mind made up to forget once and for all my friend from Urbana.

I didn't manage it. Or rather: Rodney kept me from managing it. Over the following weeks I received several letters from him; at first I didn't answer them, but my silence didn't daunt him and he kept writing, and after a while I gave in to Rodney's stubbornness and to the uncomfortable evidence that our encounter in Madrid had sealed an intimacy between the two of us that I didn't want. His letters from those days were about different things: his work, his acquaintances, what he was reading, Dan and Jenny, especially about Dan and about Jenny. So I found out that the woman with whom Rodney had a son was almost my age, fifteen years younger than him, that she'd been born in Middlebury, a small town near Burlington, and that she worked as a cashier in a supermarket; in several letters he described her to me in detail, but curiously the descriptions differed, as if he had too deep a knowledge of her to be able to capture her in a bunch of improvised words. Another curious detail (or one that now seems curious to me): on at least two or three occasions Rodney again tried, as he already had in Madrid, to talk me out of my plan to tell his story; insisting so much struck me as strange, among other reasons because I judged it superfluous, and I think at some point it ended up arousing the ephemeral suspicion that deep down my friend had always wanted me to write a book about him, and that the conversation we'd had in Madrid, like all the ones we'd had in Urbana, contained a sort of coded instruction manual about how to write it, or at least about how not to write it, just as if Rodney had been training me, surreptitiously and since we met, so that one day I'd tell his story. At the beginning of August Rodney announced that he'd got the teaching job he'd been hoping for and was preparing to move with Dan and with Jenny to his old family home in Rantoul. Over the next couple of weeks Rodney almost stopped writing to me and, by the time his correspondence began to resume its previous rhythm, in the middle of September, my life had experienced a change the real extent of which I could not even have suspected then.

It was an unforeseeable change, although perhaps in a way Rodney had foreseen it. I've already said that before the summer break the reception given my novel about the Spanish Civil War, which unexpectedly became a notable critical success and a small success in terms of sales, had surpassed my rosiest expectations; nevertheless, between the end of August and the beginning of September, when the new literary season begins and the books from the previous one get confined to the oblivion of the bookshops' back shelves, the surprise struck: as if during the summer journalists had reached an agreement not to read anything but my book, suddenly they began to summon me to talk about it in newspapers and magazines, on radio and television; as if during the summer readers had reached an agreement not to read anything but my book, I suddenly started to receive jubilant news from my publisher about sales of the book skyrocketing. I'll leave out the details of the story, because they're public and more than one will still remember them; I won't leave out that in this case the image of a snowball, despite being a cliché (or precisely because it is one), is accurate: in less than a year the book had been reprinted fifteen times, had sold more than three hundred thousand copies, was being translated into twenty languages and adapted for the cinema. It was an unmitigated triumph, which no one in my situation would have dared imagine in their wildest dreams, and the result was that from one day to the next I went from being an unknown, insolvent writer, who led an isolated, provincial life, to being famous, having more money than I knew how to spend and finding myself caught up in a whirlwind of trips, awards ceremonies, launches, interviews, round tables, book fairs and literary festivals that dragged me from one place to another all over the country and to every capital on the continent. Incredulous and exultant, at first I couldn't even recognize I was spinning uncontrollably in the vortex of a demented cyclone. I sensed it was a perfectly unreal life, a farce of colossal dimensions resembling an enormous spider's web that I was secreting and weaving myself and in which I was caught, but, though it might be a deception and I an impostor, I was willing to run all the risks with the only condition being that no one snatched away the pleasure of thoroughly enjoying that hoax. Smug professionals affirm that they don't write to be read by anyone except the select minority who can appreciate their select writings, but the truth is that every writer, no matter how ambitious or hermetic, secretly yearns to have innumerable readers, and that even the most unyielding, degraded, courageous, damned poet dreams of youngsters reciting his verses in the streets. But deep down that hurricane had nothing to do with literature or readers, but rather with success and fame. We know wise men have always advised accepting success with the same indifference as failure, not boasting of victories or degrading yourself with tears in defeat, but we also know that even they (especially they) cry and degrade themselves and boast, unable to respect that magnificent ideal of impassivity, and that's why they recommend we aspire to it, because they know better than anyone that there is nothing more poisonous than success and nothing more lethal than fame.

Although at first I was barely conscious of it, success and fame began to degrade me straight away. They say that someone who rejects a compliment wants two: the one that's already been paid him and the one his false modesty extracts with the denial. I learned very soon to garner more compliments by turning them away, and to exercise modesty, which is the best way to feed vanity; I also soon learned to feign fatigue and chagrin at fame and to invent small misfortunes that would win me compassion and ward off envy. These strategies weren't always effective and, as is logical, I was often the victim of lies and slander, but the worst thing about slander and lies is they always end up contaminating us, because it's very difficult not to cede to the temptation of defending ourselves against them by turning into liars and slanderers. Nothing secretly pleased me more than rubbing shoulders with the rich, the powerful and the winners, and being seen with them. Reality seemed to offer no resistance (or it offered only a tiny resistance compared to what it used to offer), so, in a vertiginous way, everything I'd ever desired seemed now to be within reach, and bit by bit everything that used to be flavoursome began to taste insipid. That's why I drank at all hours: when I was bored, to not be bored; when I was having fun, to have more fun. It was undoubtedly the drink that finally pushed me onto a roller coaster of euphoric nights of alcohol and sex and days of apocalyptic hangovers, and which revealed guilt, not as an occasional discomfort as a result of breaking self-imposed rules, but as a drug whose dose had to be continually increased in order to keep having its narcotic effects. Maybe for that reason – and because the intoxication of success blinded me with an illusion of omnipotence, whispering in my ear that the long-awaited moment to take my revenge on reality had arrived – I suddenly turned into an indiscriminate womanizer; I still loved Paula and still felt guilty every time I cheated on her, but I couldn't stop cheating on her, nor did I want to. For the same reasons, and also because I felt celebrity had suddenly elevated me above them and I didn't need them any more, I looked down on those I'd always admired and those who'd always

172

been friendly to me, while I flattered those who used to look down on me or did look down on me, or who I'd looked down on, with the insatiable hope – because once you've got success then you only want success – of winning their approval. I remember, for example, what happened with Marcelo Cuartero. One afternoon of that frenetic autumn we were about to run into each other on a street in central Barcelona, but as we got closer I suddenly felt uncomfortable with the idea that I'd have to stop and talk to him and at the last minute I crossed the street to avoid him. Not long after that thwarted encounter someone brought up Marcelo's name in one of those impromptu groups at a literary cocktail party. I don't know what we were talking about, but the thing is at some point a reviewer who wanted to be a non-fiction writer mentioned a book of Marcelo's as an example of the kind of arid, sterile and narrow-minded non-fiction writing that triumphed in the universities, and a successful non-fiction writer who wanted to be a novelist seconded his opinion with a comment that was more bloody than sharp. That was when I joined in, sure of winning the smiling acquiescence of the little chorus.

'Sure,' I said, agreeing with the non-fiction writer's comment, despite having read Marcelo's book and having thought it brilliant. 'But the worst thing about Cuartero isn't that he's boring, or even that he thinks we should admire him for demonstrating he's read stuff no one wants to read. The worst thing is he's gaga, for fuck's sake.'

I haven't forgotten what happened in those months with

Marcos Luna either. If it's true that no one is entirely saddened by a friend's misfortune, then it's also true that no one is entirely delighted by a friend's happiness; it's possible, however, that in those days no one was closer to being entirely delighted by my happiness than Marcos Luna. Furthermore, it came at a particularly rough time for him. In September, just as my book began its climb towards fame, Marcos had surgery for a detached retina; the operation didn't go well, and two weeks later they had to do it again. He had a prolonged convalescence: Marcos spent over two months in hospital altogether, laid up with the depressing certainty that he would be half blind when he finally got out of there. But this time he was lucky, and by the time he went home he had almost entirely recovered his sight in the affected eye. During the time he spent in hospital I spoke to him several times by phone, when he called me from his bed to congratulate me each time he heard someone talking about my book or heard me talking on the radio, or each time that someone told him of my triumphs; but, trapped as I was by the proliferating obligations of success, I never found time to visit him, and when I did see him again fleetingly, in a terrace bar in Eixample, just before some publicity dinner, I almost didn't recognize him: old and shrunken, his hair thinning and almost entirely grey, he looked the very image of defeat. We didn't see each other again for a long time, but in the meantime we got into the habit (or I got into it, or imposed it) of talking almost every week by phone. We usually spoke on Saturday nights, when I'd already been drinking for many hours and, using the alibi of our old friendship, I'd call him and unburden myself of all the anguish caused by the sudden change my life had undergone, and while I was at it I flattered my pride by showing myself that success hadn't changed me and I was still friends with my old friends; I know there is a kind of inverse vanity in someone who torments himself with blame for disgraces he hasn't committed, and I don't want to make that mistake, but I can't help suspecting that those late-night alcoholic confidences functioned between Marcos and me as a periodic and subliminal reminder of my victories, and maybe they were another way of inflicting on my friend, beneath the deceitful disguise of my complaints against my privileged situation, the humiliation of my triumphs at a moment when, with his health in a bad way and his career as a painter stagnating, he was reasonably feeling the same we'd both unreasonably felt many years before when we'd shared an apartment on calle Pujol: that his life was going to hell. Maybe that explains why on one of those Saturday nights, impassioned by the hypocritical arrogance of virtue, I remembered the conversation I'd had with Rodney in Madrid.

'Success doesn't turn you into a cretin or a son of a bitch,' I said to Marcos at some point. 'But it can release the inner son of a bitch or cretin.' And then I added: 'Who knows: if it had been you, and not me, who'd been successful, maybe we wouldn't be talking right now.'

Marcos didn't hang up on me at that moment, but he did the next day, when I called him to apologize for my pettiness: he didn't accept my apology, he reminded me of my words, reproached me for them, called me a son of a bitch and a cretin, told me not to phone him again and slammed the phone down. Two days later, however, I received an email message from him asking for my forgiveness. 'If I can't even hang onto a thirty-year-old friendship, then I really am finished,' he grumbled. Marcos and I were reconciled, but a few weeks later came an episode that sums up better than any other the dimensions of my disloyalty to him. I won't go into many details, after all, the facts themselves (not what they reveal) are perhaps unimportant. It was after the launch of a book by a Mexican photographer for which I'd written the prologue. The event was some place in Barcelona (maybe it was the MACBA, maybe the Palau Robert) and Marcos was there with Patricia, his wife, who, it seems, was old friends with the photographer. During the cocktail party after the presentation, Marcos, Patricia and I were talking, but when it was over, alleging an early start the next day, my friend refused to come along to dinner, and Patricia and I couldn't convince him to change his mind. My memory of what follows is fuzzy, even more so than other nights around that time, possibly because in this case my memory has made an effort to suppress or confuse what happened. What I remember is that Patricia and I went along with a big group for supper at Casa Leopoldo; we sat together and although we'd always had a cordial but distant relationship – as if we'd both agreed that my friendship with Marcos didn't automatically make us friends – that night we sought a complicity that we'd never wished for or allowed ourselves. I think it was with the first after-dinner whisky that the desire to sleep with her crossed my mind; startled by my temerity, I tried to push the thought away immediately. I didn't manage it, or at least I didn't manage to keep it from hanging around in my head insidiously, like an obscenity that was ever less obscene and ever more plausible, while a few nighthawks carried on the festivities in the bar of the Giardinetto and I poured whiskies down my neck talking to this person and the next, but always aware that Patricia was still there. Finally, when they closed the Giardinetto in the early hours, Patricia gave me a lift to my hotel. During the journey I didn't stop talking for a second, as if looking for a formula to hold onto her, but when she stopped her car in front of the door and leaned over to kiss me on the cheek I could only think to suggest we have one last drink in my room. Patricia looked amused, almost as if I were a teenager and she an older nurse who had to take my clothes off. 'You wouldn't be insinuating anything, would you?' she laughed.

I didn't have time to feel ashamed, because before that could happen a cold fury seared my throat. 'You're not a very good whore,' I heard myself spit out. 'You spend all night leading me on and now you leave me in the lurch. Go to hell.'

I slammed the car door and, instead of going into the hotel, began to walk. I don't know how long I was walking, but by the time I got back to the hotel my fury had turned to remorse. The effect of the alcohol, however, had not yet dissipated, because the first thing I did when I got to my room was to call Marcos' house. Luckily, it was Patricia who answered. Stumbling over my words, I begged her to forgive me, pleaded with her to ignore what I'd said, claimed I'd had too much to drink, asked for her forgiveness again. With a cold voice Patricia accepted my apology, and I asked her if she was planning to tell Marcos.

'No,' she answered before hanging up. 'Now go to bed and sleep it off.'

I won't go on. I could go on, but I won't go on. I could tell more anecdotes, but I don't want to forget the bigger picture. A few days ago I read a poem Malcolm Lowry wrote after publishing the novel that brought him fame, money and prestige; it's a truculent, emphatic poem, but sometimes there's no alternative but to be truculent and emphatic, because reality, which almost never respects the laws of good taste, often abounds in truculence and emphasis. The poem goes like this:

Success is like some horrible disaster
Worse than your house burning, the sounds of ruination
As the roof tree falls following each other faster
While you stand, the helpless witness of your damnation.

Fame like a drunkard consumes the house of the soul
Exposing that you have worked for only this —

Ah, that I had never suffered this treacherous kiss
And had been left in darkness forever to founder and fail.

Many years earlier Rodney had warned me and, although at the time I interpreted his words as the inevitable moralizing discharge of a loser drenched in the sickly mythology of failure that governs a country hysterically obsessed with success, at least I should have foreseen that no one is immune to success, and that only when you have to confront it do you understand that it's not just a misunderstanding, one day's cheerful disgrace, rather it's a humiliating and disgraceful misunderstanding and disgrace; I should also have foreseen that it's impossible to survive it with dignity, because it consumes the house of the soul and because it's so beautiful that you discover that, though you kid yourself with protests of pride and cleansing demonstrations of cynicism, in reality you've done nothing but seek it, just as you discover, as soon as you have it in your hands and it's too late to turn it down, that it's only good for destroying you and everything around you. I should have foreseen it, but I didn't. The result was that I lost respect for reality; I also lost respect for literature, which was the only thing that had given reality meaning or an illusion of meaning up till then. Because what I thought I discovered then is exactly the worst thing to discover: that my real vocation wasn't writing but having written, that I wasn't a real writer, that I wasn't a writer because I couldn't be anything else, but because writing was the only instrument

I'd had at hand to aspire to success, fame and money. Now I'd achieved them: now I could stop writing. That's why, perhaps, I stopped writing; for that reason and because I was too alive to write, too keen to drain success of its last breath, and you can only write when you write as if you're dead and writing is the only way to evoke life, the last strand that unites us with it. So, after twelve years of living only to write, with the exclusive vehemence and passion of a dead man who won't be resigned to his death, I suddenly stopped writing. That was when I really began to be at risk: I found out that, just as Rodney had told me years before – when I was so young and unwary I couldn't even have dreamt that success might one day crash down on me like a burning house – the writer who stops writing ends up seeking or attracting destruction, because he's contracted the disease of looking at reality, and sometimes of seeing it, but he can no longer use it, can no longer turn it into sense or beauty, no longer has the shield of writing to protect himself from it. Then it's the end. It's over. Finito. Kaput.

The end came one Saturday in April 2002, exactly a year after the publication of my novel. By then it had been many months since I had completely stopped writing and begun to relish the jubilant toxin of triumph; by then the lies, infidelities and alcohol had completely poisoned my relationship with Paula. That night the proprietor of a literary magazine that had just awarded me a prize for the best book of the year gave a dinner in my honour at his house in the country, in a village in L'Empordà; there was a large group of people gathered there:

journalists, writers, film-makers, architects, photographers, professors, literary critics, friends of the family. I attended the engagement with Paula and Gabriel. This was unusual and I can't remember why I did: maybe because the host had assured me on the phone that it was going to be almost a family party and that other guests would also be bringing their children with them, maybe to quiet my guilty conscience for cheating on Paula so often and barely spending any time with Gabriel, maybe because I judged that this domestic image would endorse my reputation as a writer impervious to the trappings of fame, a reputation for incorruptibility and modesty that, as I discovered very early, was the ideal tool to win me the favour of the most powerful members of literary society – who are always the most candid, because they feel their status is secure – and also to protect me from the hostility that my success had elicited among those who felt neglected because of it, who felt I'd snatched it away from them. The fact of the matter is that, unusually, I attended the dinner with Gabriel and with Paula. They seated me across the table from the host, an elderly businessman with interests in Barcelona newspapers and publishing companies; Paula was beside me, and on the other side was a young radio journalist, the host's niece, who, following her uncle's instructions, made sure the whole conversation revolved around the causes of my book's un-expected success. Since the journalist practically forced all the guests to participate, there were opinions of every stripe; as for me, happily settled into my position as protagonist of the evening, I confined myself to commenting with hesitant

181

approval on everything that was said and, in a gently ironic tone, begging our host every once in a while that we change the subject, which was interpreted by all as proof of my humility, and not as a ruse designed to prevent the discussion of my merits from flagging. After dinner we had coffee and liqueurs in a large entrance hall that had been fitted out as a reception room, where the guests mingled in smaller groups that assembled and reassembled at the whims of the various conversations. It was after midnight when Paula interrupted a conversation that I, whisky in hand, was having with a screenwriter, his wife and the host's niece about the cinematic adaptation of my novel; she told me that Gabriel had fallen asleep and that she had to work the next morning.

'We're leaving,' she announced, adding without conviction: 'but you stay if you want.'

I was already probing for arguments to try to convince her we should stay a little longer when the screenwriter interjected.

'Of course,' he said, supporting Paula's insincere suggestion and pointing at his wife. 'We're driving back to Barcelona tonight. If you want we can stop in Gerona and drop you off at home.'

I looked with relief into Paula's eyes.

'You wouldn't mind?'

All eyes converged on her. I knew she minded, but she said, 'Of course not.'

I accompanied Gabriel and Paula to the car and, when Gabriel was stretched out on the back seat, exhausted, Paula closed the door and muttered, 'Next time you can go to your party by yourself.'

'Didn't you say you wouldn't mind if I stayed?'

'You're a bastard.'

We argued; I don't remember what we said, but as I watched my car disappear as fast as possible down the gravel driveway that led out of the property I thought what I'd thought so often during that time: that a moment arrives in the life of every couple when everything they say they say to hurt each other, that my marriage had turned into a refined form of torture and the sooner it ended the better for all concerned.

But I soon forgot about my fight with Paula and continued enjoying the party. It went on into the early hours, and when I got into the screenwriter's car I found myself sitting beside a very serious young woman with an intellectual air, who I'd barely noticed all night. The trip to Gerona was brief, but long enough for me to realize that the girl had had quite a bit to drink, to be sure she was flirting with me and to vaguely ascertain that she was a friend of the host's niece and worked for a local television station. When we got to the city the girl suggested we all go for one more drink at a bar that belonged to some friends of hers, and which, she said, never closed before dawn. The screenwriter and his wife declined the offer arguing that it was very late and they should keep going to Barcelona; I accepted.

We went to the bar. We drank, chatted, danced and I finished off the night in the girl's bed. When I left her house dawn was about to break. In the street the taxi I'd phoned was waiting for me; I gave the driver my address and dozed the whole way, but when the taxi stopped at the door of my house I wished I were dead: standing in front of a squad car, two Mossos d'Esquadra were waiting beside the driveway that led to the garage. I paid the taxi driver with a trembling note, and as I got out of the car I noticed the driveway, where we usually parked the car, was empty, and I knew that Paula and Gabriel weren't home.

'What's happened?' I asked as I approached the two officers.

Young, grave, almost spectral in the livid light of daybreak, they asked me if I was me. I said I was.

'What's happened?' I repeated.

One of the policemen pointed to the door of my house and asked: 'Could we speak to you inside for a moment, please?'

I opened the door for the two policemen, we sat in the dining room, I asked again what had happened. The policeman who'd spoken before was the one to answer me.

'We've come to inform you that your wife and your son have been involved in an accident,' he said.

The news didn't surprise me; with a thread of a voice I managed to ask: 'Are they injured?'

The policeman swallowed before he answered: 'They're dead.'

The policeman then took out a notebook and must have begun an antiseptic and detailed account of the circumstances of the accident, but, despite making an effort to pay attention to the explanation, the only thing I could catch were random words, incoherent or meaningless phrases. My memory of the hours that followed is even more shaky: I know I went to the hospital where they'd taken Paula and Gabriel that morning, that I didn't see or didn't want to see their bodies, that relatives and the odd friend immediately started arriving, that I made some confusing arrangement for funerals, which took place the next day, that I didn't attend them, that some newspaper included my name in the article about the accident and that my house filled up with telegrams and faxes of condolence that I didn't read or that I read as veiled accusations. In reality, there's only one thing I remember from those days with an hallucinatory clarity — my visits to the Mossos d'Esquadra headquarters. In a very short space of time I was there four times, maybe five, although now they all seem like the same one. I was received in an office by a pretty, cold, painstakingly professional uniformed sergeant, who, sitting across from me behind a very cheerful desk, with flowers and family photographs, set out for me the information the police had gathered concerning the accident, sketched diagrams and answered my questions over and over again. They were long meetings, but, despite the causes and circumstances of the accident not raising any doubts for the police (the road surface made slippery by the damp night air, maybe a tiny distraction, a curve taken a bit faster than advisable, a desperate swerve into the oncoming lane, the final horror of blinding lights in front of you), I always left them with new

185

questions, which I'd return to try to clear up at the station hours or days later. The sergeant arranged a meeting for me with the two officers who'd arrived first at the scene of the accident and been in charge of the investigation and, in the company of one of them, took me one afternoon to the exact curve where it had happened; the next morning I went back to the place alone and stayed there for a while, watching the cars go past, not thinking about anything, looking at the sky and the asphalt and the desolation of that piece of open ground swept by the north wind. I couldn't say why I acted like that, but I wouldn't rule out the idea that part of me suspected that something didn't quite tally, there were still loose ends in that story, the police were hiding something from me and, if I could discover what it was, that a door would immediately open and Paula and Gabriel would walk through it, alive and smiling, just as if it had all been a mistake or a bad joke. Until one morning, when I walked into the sergeant's office for our umpteenth interview, I found her accompanied by an older man, with a beard and civilian clothes. The sergeant introduced us and the man explained that he was a psychologist and director of an association called Bereavement Support Services (or something like that), assigned to offer help to relatives of people killed in accidents. The psychologist carried on with his presentation for a while, but I stopped listening to him; I didn't even look at him: I confined myself to looking at the sergeant, who tired of avoiding my eyes and interrupted the man.

186

'Take my advice and go with him,' she said, finally meeting my gaze, and for the first time I perceived a trace of cordiality or emotion in her voice. 'There's nothing more I can do for you.'

I left the station and never went back. That same afternoon I went to a real estate agency, rented the first apartment they offered me in Barcelona, a flat near Sagrada Familia, and, after selling the house in Gerona at a loss as quickly as possible and getting rid of all of Gabriel's and Paula's belongings, I moved into it and prepared to busy myself conscientiously with the job of dying, and not with that of being born. I discovered that Rodney's father was right and the world was an empty place; but I also discovered that in those moments solitude was less a bane for me than the only possible balm, the only possible blessing. I didn't see my family, I didn't see my friends, I didn't have a television or a radio or a telephone. Aside from that I made sure that only the absolutely indispensable people had my address, and when one of them (or someone who had located me through one of them) knocked on my door, I simply didn't answer. That happened with Marcos Luna, who for a while appeared regularly at my house and got sick of ringing the bell knowing I was inside, listening to him, until he realized that he wasn't going to get to talk to me and from then on he just left in my mailbox, every Friday at lunchtime, a cigarette packet full of freshly rolled joints. My literary agent also sent me a list of the people who called her office requesting my presence somewhere or asking after me every once in a while, although I never answered. Of course, I didn't work, but the sales of the book had provided me with enough income to live without working for years, and I didn't see any reason not to let time go by until that money ran out. My only effort consisted in not thinking, especially in not remembering. At first it had been impossible. Until I left the house I'd shared with Paula and Gabriel and went to Barcelona I couldn't stop torturing myself thinking about the accident: I wondered if Gabriel had woken up at the last moment and been aware of what was about to happen; I wondered what Paula had thought at that moment, what memory had distracted her as she drove, provoking the swerve that in its turn had provoked the accident, what would have happened if, instead of staying at the party, I'd gone home with them . . . Those who experienced the programmed brutality of the Nazi or Soviet concentration camps often say that, to bear it, they kept themselves going by remembering the happiness they'd left behind, because, remote though it may have been, they always held on to the hope that they might one day recover it; I lacked that comfort: since the dead don't come back to life, my past was irretrievable, so I applied myself conscientiously to obliterating it. Maybe that's why, as soon as I installed myself in Barcelona, I began to live by night. I sometimes spent entire weeks without leaving the house, reading detective novels in bed, living on packets of soup, tinned food, tobacco, marijuana and beer, but normally I'd spend the nights

188

outside, traipsing relentlessly all over the city, walking aimlessly, stopping now and then to have a drink and rest awhile and get my strength back before continuing my walk to nowhere until dawn, when I'd return home wrecked and throw myself into bed, desperate for rest and unable to sleep, maddened by other people's noises in the world, which incredibly kept to its imperturbable course. Insomnia turned me into a passionate theoretician of suicide, and I now think that if I didn't put it into practice it wasn't only due to cowardice or excess of imagination, but also because I feared my remorse would survive me, or more likely because I discovered that, more than to die, what I desired was never to have lived at all, and that's why sometimes I managed a clear, dreamless sleep when I imagined myself living in the pure limbo of non-existence, in the happiness before light, before words. I took to playing with death. Sometimes I'd take the car and drive obsessively and rashly for days on end, on a whim, stopping only to eat or to sleep, comforted by the permanent certainty that at any moment I could swerve or go into a skid like the one that had killed Gabriel and Paula. One night, in a brothel in Montpellier, I got involved in a meaningless argument with two individuals who ended up giving me a beating that put me in hospital, from which I emerged with my body black and blue and my nose broken. I also bought a pistol: I kept it in a drawer and took it out every once in a while, loaded it and pointed it at my forehead or under my chin or put it in my mouth and held it there, tasting the acidity of the barrel and gently caressing the trigger while sweat poured down my temples and my panting seemed to thunder in my head and fill the silence of the flat to bursting. One night I spent a long time walking along the parapet of my roof terrace, happy, naked and precariously balanced, with my mind a blank, aware only of the breeze that made my skin bristle and the lights of the city and the vertiginous precipice gaping beside me, humming a song I've now forgotten.

I spent the spring, summer and autumn in this dead-end tightrope-walking state, and it wasn't until one night at the beginning of last winter that, thanks to the providential alliance of a disagreeable incident, a chance discovery and a revived memory, I suddenly had a flicker of a hint that I wasn't condemned to endure forever the underground life I'd been leading for months. It all started in Tabú, a nightclub on the lower part of the Rambla frequented by tourists, who go there to see local porn shows at an affordable price. It's a dark and threadbare place, with a bar off at an angle to the right of the entrance and a stage surrounded by metal tables and chairs with silvery sequined lampshades suspended above them, to the left of which a curtain hides the booths reserved for paying couples. I'd already been there a couple of times, always very late, and, as I'd done on my previous visits, that night I ordered a whisky from the slight, old woman plastered in makeup who seemed to be in charge of the place and who stayed at one end of the bar, drinking and smoking and watching the show from a distance. It must have been a weekday, because although among the clients there was a conspicuous group of loud, frenzied youths fraternizing effusively with the artistes and climbing up on stage as soon as they hinted at it, the rest of the bar was almost deserted, and there were only two couples leaning on the bar not far from me: one halfway down, the other a bit further along. I'd already had my first whisky and was just about to order a second when, just as a naked woman began fellating a man dressed as a Roman soldier on stage, I felt something abnormal was going on beside me; I turned and saw that the couple halfway down the bar were arguing violently. I'm lying: I didn't see that; what I saw, in a few flashing seconds of stupefaction, was that the man and the woman were shouting at each other wildly, the man slapped the woman across the face, the woman tried unsuccessfully to retaliate in kind, and, seized by a blind fury, the man began to hit the woman, and he kept hitting her and hitting her until he knocked her to the floor, from where she tried to defend herself with tears, insults, punches and kicks. I also saw the couple that were further down the bar move away from the scene, fascinated and terrified; the volume of the music prevented the audience over by the stage from noticing the fight, and the only person who seemed determined to stop it, shouting herself hoarse behind the bar, was the old woman who ran the place. As for me, I stood stock-still, paralyzed, watching the fight with my empty whisky glass gripped tightly in my fist, until, undoubtedly alerted by the manager, two bouncers appeared, subdued the aggressor with quite a bit of difficulty and took him outside with one arm twisted up behind his back, while the manager took the girl backstage escorted by other prostitutes. It was also the manager who, once she was back in the room, took care of calming the worries of a clientele who, for the most part, had seen only a confusing glimpse of the end of the altercation, and it was also she who, after making sure the show was going on, as she passed me on her way back behind the bar, spat out without even looking at me, as if I were a regular customer and she could give vent to the accumulated tension with me: 'And you could have done something too, don't you think?'

I didn't say anything; I didn't order a second whisky; I left the place. Outside it was bone-chillingly cold. I went up the Rambla towards the plaza de Catalunya and, as soon as I saw an open bar, went in and ordered the whisky I hadn't dared order in Tabú. I downed it in a couple of hurried gulps and ordered another. Comforted by the alcohol, I reflected on what had just happened. I wondered what state the woman was in, since at the last moment she'd stopped resisting her aggressor's kicks and lay defenceless on the floor, exhausted or maybe unconscious. I told myself that, had it not been for the last-minute intervention of the two bouncers, there was nothing to indicate that the man would have stopped beating his victim until he ran out of steam or killed her. I didn't ask myself, however, what the manager of the place had asked me – why had I done nothing to stop the fight – I didn't ask myself because I knew – out of fear, maybe out of indifference, and even out of a shadow of cruelty – it's possible that some part of me had enjoyed that spectacle of pain and fury, and that same part wouldn't have minded if it had gone on. That was when, as if emerging from a centuries-old chasm, I remembered a parallel and reverse scene to the one I'd just witnessed in Tabú, a scene that happened more than thirty years before in a bar in a distant city I'd never seen. There, some place in Saigon, my friend Rodney had defended a Vietnamese waitress from the boozed-up brutality of a Green Beret NCO; he hadn't been indifferent or cruel: he'd overcome his fear and his courage hadn't failed him. Exactly what I hadn't done a few minutes earlier. More than shame for my cowardice, my cruelty and my indifference, I felt surprise at the fact of remembering Rodney at precisely that moment, when it had been almost two years since I'd forgotten him.

Hours later, going over what had happened that night, I thought that untimely memory was actually a premonition. That's what I thought then, but I could have thought it long before, just when, as I finished my whisky in that bar on the Rambla and took out my wallet to pay for it, a bunch of disorderly papers I kept in it fell out onto the floor; I bent down to pick them up: there were credit cards, my driver's licence and ID card, overdue bills, pieces of paper with scribbled phone numbers and vaguely familiar names. Among them was a folded and wrinkled photograph; I unfolded it, looked at it for a second, less than a second, recognizing it without wanting to recognize it, more incredulous than astonished; then I folded it up again quickly and put it back in my wallet with the other papers. I paid at once, went out onto the street with a sensation of vertigo or real danger, as if I were carrying a bomb in my wallet, and started walking very fast, not feeling the night's cold, not noticing the lights and people of the night, trying not to think about the photograph but knowing that image from a life I almost believed cancelled could explode before the stone door my future had become, opening a crack through which reality, future and past, would filter into the present. I went up the Rambla, crossed the plaza de Catalunya, walked up the paseo de Gràcia, turned left when I got to Diagonal and kept walking very quickly, as if I needed to exhaust myself as soon as possible or gather courage or postpone as much as possible the inevitable moment. Finally, at a corner in Balmes, in the changing light of a traffic signal, I made up my mind: I opened my wallet, took out the photo and looked at it. It was one of the pictures of Paula and Gabriel with Rodney during my friend's visit to Gerona, and also the only image of Paula and Gabriel that I had accidentally kept: I'd got rid of the rest when I moved to Barcelona. There they both were, on that forgotten piece of paper, like two ghosts who refuse to disappear, diaphanous, smiling and intact on Les Peixeteries Velles bridge; and there was Rodney, standing up straight between the two of them, with his patch over his eye and his two enormous hands resting on the shoulders of my wife and my son, like a Cyclops ready to protect them from an as yet invisible threat. I kept looking at the photograph; I won't try to describe what I was thinking: to do so would distort what I felt while I was thinking. I'll only say that I had been staring at the photo for a long time when I realized I was crying, because the tears, which were streaming down my cheeks, were soaking my flannel shirt and the collar of my coat. I was crying as if I would never stop. I was crying for Paula and for Gabriel, but perhaps most of all I was crying because up till then I hadn't cried for them, not when they died or in the months of panic, blame and reclusion that followed. I cried for them and for me; I also knew or thought I knew that I was crying for Rodney and, with a strange sense of relief – as if thinking of him was the only thing that could exempt me from having to think about Paula and Gabriel – I imagined him at that very moment in his house in Rantoul, his provincial two-storey house with an attic and a porch, a front yard with two maples on Belle Avenue, with his calm, routine work as a schoolteacher, watching his son grow up and his wife mature, redeemed from the incurable, maladjusted fate that for more than thirty years had fiercely cornered him, master of all that I'd had in the glossy and inaccessible time of the photograph that now brought it back.

I don't know how long I'd been standing beside the traffic light when I managed to put the photograph back in my wallet, crossed Balmes and, still crying (or I think so), started walking as far as Muntaner and then towards the upper part of the city. Again I tried not to think of anything, but I thought of Paula and Gabriel; doing so hurt like an amputation: to avoid the pain I forced myself to think about Rodney again. I remembered our tireless conversations at Treno's, my visit to his father in Rantoul, my ever-postponed plan to one day write his story and the conversation we had in Madrid, when I discovered with a repugnance that now struck me as repugnant that my friend had the deaths of women and children on his conscience. And at some point, among the images that crossed my disturbed mind like clouds or meteorites, I remembered Rodney at that party of Wong's, surrounded by people and yet impervious, as alone as a lost animal in the middle of a herd of animals of another species, I remember him on Wong's porch steps, that same night, tall, wrecked, vulnerable and hesitant, wrapped in his sheepskin coat and fur hat as I observed him from the window that overlooked the street and the snow fell on the road in big flakes and he looked at the night without crying (although at first I'd thought he was crying), looked at it more like he was walking along a narrow pass beside a very dark abyss and there was no one who had as much vertigo and as much fear as him. And then I suddenly understood what I hadn't understood that night so many years before, and it was that if I had left the party and had gone in search of Rodney it was because, watching him from the window, I knew he was the loneliest man in the world and that, for some unquestionable reason that was nevertheless beyond my reach, I was the only person who could keep him company, and I also understood that on this night so many years later the tables had turned. Now I was responsible for the death of a woman and a child (or I felt responsible for the death of a woman and a child), now I was the loneliest man in the world, a lost animal in the middle of a herd of animals of a different species, now it was Rodney, and perhaps only Rodney, who could keep me company, because he had travelled long before and for much longer than me the same corridor of fright and remorse along which I had been feeling my way and had found an exit: only Rodney, my fellow, my brother – a monster like me, like me a murderer – could show me a sliver of light in that tunnel of woe through which, without even having the energy to want to get out of it, I had been walking alone and in the dark since the deaths of Gabriel and Paula, just like Rodney had done for thirty years since he rounded some bend on some trail in some unnamed place in Vietnam and saw a soldier appear who was him.

That night I went home earlier than usual, lay down in bed with my eyes open and, for the first time in many months, slept for six hours straight. I had two dreams. In the first only Gabriel appeared. He was playing table football in a big, dilapidated, empty place like a garage, hitting the balls with adult, almost ferocious glee; he had no opponent or I couldn't see his opponent, and he didn't seem to hear my shouts as I tried to get his attention; until suddenly he let go of the handles and, frustrated or furious, turned towards me. 'Don't cry, Papá,' he said then, with a voice that wasn't his, or that I couldn't quite recognize. 'It didn't hurt.' The second dream was longer and more complicated, more disconnected as well. First I saw Paula and Gabriel's faces, close together, almost cheek to cheek, smiling at me in an inquisitive way as if they were on the other side of a pane of glass. Then Rodney's face joined theirs and the three began to superimpose like transparencies, blending into each other, so Gabriel's face changed until it turned into Paula's or Rodney's, and Paula's face changed until it turned into Rodney's or Gabriel's, and Rodney's face changed until it turned into Gabriel's or Paula's. At the end of the dream I saw myself arriving at Rodney's house in Rantoul, on a bright, sunny day, and discovering, with unspeakable anguish, between false smiles and suspicious looks, not his wife and son living with my friend, but Paula and Gabriel, or a woman and a boy who imitated Paula and Gabriel's voices and appearance and even their affectionate gestures but who, in some perverse way, weren't them.

The next day I was woken by anxiety. I shaved, showered, got dressed and, while I was having coffee and smoking a cigarette, I decided to write to Rodney. I remember the letter very well. I started it by apologizing for having stopped writing to him; then I asked about his life, asked after his wife and son; then I lied: I wrote about Gabriel and Paula as if they were still alive, and I also talked about myself as if for many months I hadn't been busy dying but being born, as if I hadn't turned into a ghost or a zombie and was still living and writing just as if the house of my soul had not been consumed. I immediately noticed that

198

writing to Rodney operated on me like a soothing balm and, while watching the words appear like insects on the computer screen, almost without noticing it I conceived the unarguable illusion that visiting Rodney at his house in Rantoul was the only way to break the logic of annihilation in which I found myself trapped. I had barely formulated this idea when I began putting it in writing, but, because I realized it was imperious and incredible and demanded too many explanations, I immediately deleted it, and, after thinking it over and over and going through several drafts, I ended up simply expressing my desire to return to Urbana one day and for us to see each other again there or in Rantoul, a vague enough declaration not to be out of synch with the placid and casual mood of the rest of the missive. Night had fallen by the time I finished writing it, and the next morning I sent it to Rantoul by express mail.

For a couple of weeks I waited in vain for Rodney's reply. Fearing my letter had got lost, I printed up another copy and sent it again; the result was the same. This silence was disconcerting. I didn't think it plausible that neither of the two letters had reached their destination, but I did think Rodney might have received them and, for some reason (maybe because he'd taken as ingratitude or insult my inexplicable interruption of our correspondence in the middle of the maelstrom of my success), refused to answer them; there was also the possibility that Rodney no longer lived in Rantoul, a speculation backed up by the fact that, as far as I could find out, there was no listing for a telephone number under the name of Falk in Rantoul. Either of the two hypotheses was credible, but I don't remember how I arrived at the conclusion that the second was the more reasonable, and that it was also the most worrying or least optimistic: after all, if hurt pride was the cause of Rodney's silence, then there was hope of breaking it, because it wasn't foolish to think that sooner or later it would heal; but if the cause of his silence was that Rodney hadn't received my letters because he'd moved with his family to another city (or, even worse, because he'd fled again, turned back into the chronic fugitive incapable of freeing himself from his dishonourable past), then any prospect of seeing Rodney again evaporated forever. Soon the unease turned to despondency, and the fleeting fantasy that an encounter with Rodney would have the effect of a sort of salubrious sorcery on me was suddenly revealed as a last and ridiculous decoy of my powerlessness. Once again I had nothing before me but a stone door.

I went back to my underground life; I let time pass. One Friday in February, two months, more or less, after trying to resume my correspondence with Rodney, when I opened my mailbox to retrieve the packet of joints that Marcos left for me each week I found a letter from my literary agent. Unusually, this time I opened it: my agent told me in the letter that the Spanish Embassy in Washington was proposing a promotional trip to various universities in the United States. I don't know if I've already said that these invitations to travel here and there had turned into something as routine as the administrative silence with which I answered them all. I was about to throw the letter away when I thought of Rodney; I opened Marcos' packet, took out a joint, lit it, took a couple of tokes and put the letter in my pocket. Then I went outside and started walking towards the city centre. That night I didn't do anything different from what I'd been doing for months; same on the Saturday and the Sunday night. But during the whole weekend I didn't stop thinking about the proposal, and on the Monday afternoon, after giving no sign of life for a long time, I called my agent. She still hadn't recovered from the shock of hearing from me when I gave her the additional surprise of my decision to accept the proposal for the trip to the United States with the non-negotiable condition that one of its legs include Urbana. From there everything moved very quickly: the embassy and the universities accepted my conditions, organized the trip and in the middle of April, almost fifteen years after leaving Urbana, I got back on a plane for the United States.

ALGEBRA OF THE DEAD

THE TRIP TO THE United States lasted two weeks during which I crossed the country from coast to coast, dominated at first by a state of mind that was at the very least contradictory: on the one hand I was expectant, keen not only to return to Urbana, to see Rodney again, but also – which perhaps amounted to the same thing – to emerge for a while from the filth of the underground and unburden myself of the weight of a past that didn't exist or that I could pretend did not exist once I arrived; but, on the other hand, I also felt a gnawing apprehension because for the first time in almost a year I was going to emerge from the state of hibernation in which I'd tried to protect myself from reality and I had no idea what my reaction would be when I exposed myself to it again in the flesh. So, though I soon realized I wasn't entirely unaccustomed to being out in the open, for the first few days I had a bit of a feeling of groping my way around, like someone taking a while to get used to the light after a long confinement in darkness. I left Spain on a Saturday and only arrived in Urbana seven days later, but as soon as I set foot in the United States I began to receive news of people from Urbana. The first stop was at the University of Virginia, in Charlottesville. My host, Professor Victor T. Davies, a renowned specialist in literature of the Enlightenment, came to pick me up at Dulles Airport, in Washington, and during the two-hour drive to the university we talked about acquaintances we had in common; Laura Burns turned out to be one of them. I hadn't had any news of Laura for years, nor of any of the rest of my friends from Urbana, but Davies had kept in frequent contact with her since she'd published a critical edition (which he described as excellent) of *Los eruditos a la violeta*, the book by José Cadalso; according to what Davies told me, Laura had been divorced from her second husband for several years and now taught at the University of St Louis, less than three hours' drive from Urbana.

'If I'd known you were friends, I would have told her you were coming,' Davies said ruefully.

When we got to Charlottesville I asked him for Laura's phone number and that same night I phoned her from my room in the Colonnade Club, a sumptuous eighteenth-century pavilion where official visitors to the university are put up. The call filled Laura with an exaggerated and almost contagious jubilation and, once we got beyond the first moment of astonishment and a quick exchange of information, we agreed that she'd get in touch with John Borgheson, who was now the head of the department and had organized my stay in Urbana, and in any case we'd see each other there the following Saturday.

The second city I visited was New York, where I was supposed to speak at Barnard College, an affiliate of Columbia University. The night I arrived, after the lecture, my host, a Spanish professor called Mercedes Esteban, took me out for dinner along with two other colleagues to a Mexican restaurant on 43rd Street; there, sitting at a table waiting for us was Felipe Vieri. It seems Esteban and he had met when they were both teaching at NYU and had remained close friends since then; she'd let him know about my visit, and between the two of them they'd organized that unexpected reunion. Vieri and I had stopped writing to each other many years before and, apart from the odd bit of news caught here and there (of course, echoes of my novel's success had reached Vieri's ears, too), we knew nothing about each other's lives, but during the meal my friend did what he could to fill that void. So I found out that Vieri was still teaching at NYU, still living in Greenwich Village, he'd published a novel and several non-fiction books, one of which dealt with the films of Almodóvar; for my part I lied to him the same way I'd done in the useless letter I'd sent to Rodney, just as I'd lied to Davies and Laura: I talked about Gabriel and Paula as if they were alive and about my happy life as a successful provincial writer. But what we mostly talked about was Urbana. Vieri had brought several copies of *Línea Plural* ('an elusive gem,' he joked, putting on an effeminate voice and gesture and addressing the rest of the dinner guests) and a pile of photos among which I recognized one from the meeting of contributors to the journal

207

when Rodrigo Ginés told of his Dadaist encounter with Rodney while he was sticking up Socialist Workers' Party posters against General Electric. Pointing at a guy in the photo who was looking at the camera with a radiant smile, sandwiched between Rodrigo and me, Vieri asked:

'Remember Frank Solaún?'

'Of course,' I answered. 'Whatever happened to him?'

'He died seven years ago,' said Vieri, without taking his eyes off the photo, 'of AIDS.'

I nodded, but no one said anything else and we kept on talking: of Borgheson, of Laura, of Rodrigo Ginés, of friends and acquaintances; Vieri had quite specific news of many of them, but during the dinner I didn't dare ask him about Rodney. I did later, in a bar at the corner of Broadway and 121st Street, near the Union Theological Seminary – the university dormitory where I was staying – where we were talking on our own until the early hours. Predictably, Vieri remembered Rodney very well; predictably, he hadn't heard anything about him; also predictably, he thought it strange that I, who had been his only friend in Urbana, should be asking him about Rodney.

'I'm sure they'll know something in Urbana,' he ventured.

With that hope I finally got to Urbana at midday on Saturday, arriving from Chicago. I remember as we took off from O'Hare and began to fly over the suburbs of the city – with the serrated line of the skyscrapers cut out against the vehement blue of the sky and the vivid blue of Lake Michigan – I couldn't help remembering my first trip from

Chicago to Urbana, seventeen years earlier, in the dog days of August, in a Greyhound bus, while around me an endless expanse of brown uninhabited land rolled past, just like the land that now seemed to be held almost perfectly still beneath my plane, dotted here and there with green patches and the occasional farm; I remembered that first trip and it seemed astonishing to be about to arrive in Urbana, which at that moment, just when I was going to set foot in it again after so long, suddenly seemed as illusory as an invention of desire or nostalgia. But Urbana was not an invention. In the airport John Borgheson was waiting for me, maybe a bit more bald but no more decrepit than the last time I'd seen him, years ago, in Barcelona, in any case just as affable and welcoming and more British than ever and, as he drove me to the Chancellor Hotel and I gazed at the streets of Urbana without recognizing them, he outlined the plan for my stay in the city, told me the welcome party was set for that very evening at six and he would come and pick me up at the hotel ten minutes before. In the Chancellor I took a shower and changed my clothes; then I went down to the foyer and killed time walking up and down waiting for Borgheson, until at some point I fleetingly thought I recognized someone; surprised, I backtracked, but the only thing I saw was my face reflected in a large wall mirror. Wondering how long it had been since the last time I'd looked at myself in a mirror, I stared at the image of my face in the mirror as if I were looking at a stranger, and while I was doing so I imagined I was shedding my skin, thought that this was the port in the storm, thought about the weight of the past and the filth underground and the promising clarity outside, and I also thought that, although the objective of that trip was chimerical or absurd, the fact of embarking on it was not.

Borgheson arrived at the agreed time and took me to the house of a literature professor who had insisted on organizing the party. Her name was Elizabeth Bell and she had started at Urbana about the same time I finished there, so I only vaguely remembered her; as for the rest of the guests, the majority of them were Spanish professors and teaching assistants. I didn't know a single one, until Laura Burns rushed in, blonde and beautiful, and hugged and kissed me noisily, kissed and hugged Borgheson noisily, noisily greeted the rest of the guests and immediately took over the conversation, seemingly determined to make us pay for the two-and-a-half-hour drive it had taken her to get there from St Louis with her absolute starring role. It wasn't the first time she'd made that trip: during the conversation I'd had with her on the phone from Charlottesville, Laura told me that every once in a while she went to visit Borgheson, who, as I found out that evening, had given up treating her like an exceptional student in order to treat her like an unruly stepdaughter whose madcap escapades he was slightly embarrassed to find irresistibly amusing. During dinner Laura didn't stop talking for a second, although, despite the fact that we were sitting beside each other, she didn't exchange a word with me alone or in an aside; what she did was talk to the others about me, as if she were one of those wives or mothers who, like symbiotic creatures, seem to live only through the achievements of their husbands or children. First she talked about the success of my novel, which she'd reviewed rapturously for *World Literature Today*, and later she argued with Borgheson, Elizabeth Bell and her husband – a Spanish linguist called Andrés Viñas – about the real characters hidden behind the fictional characters in *The Tenant*, the novella I'd written and set in Urbana, and at some point told us that the head of the department at the time had considered the head of the department who appeared in the book to be a depiction of him and had arranged for all the copies in the library to disappear, however, I was surprised that neither Laura nor Borgheson nor Elizabeth Bell nor Viñas mentioned Olalde, the fictitious Spanish professor whose exaggerated appearance – and perhaps not just his physical appearance – was so clearly inspired by Rodney. Then Laura seemed to tire of talking about me and started telling anecdotes at the expense of her two ex-husbands and especially at her own expense as the wife of her two ex-husbands. Not until after dinner did Laura cede the monopoly on the conversation, which inevitably drifted into an itemized list of the differences between the Urbana of fifteen years ago and the Urbana of today, and then into a frayed recounting of the disparate and eventful lives led by the professors and teaching assistants who'd been there at the same time as me. Everyone knew a story or a snippet of a story, but the one who seemed best informed was Borgheson, who was the longest-serving professor in the department after all, so when we stepped outside to smoke a cigarette along with Laura, Viñas and a teaching assistant, I asked him if he knew anything of Rodney.

'Shit, yeah,' said Laura. 'That's right: that nutcase Rodney.'

Borgheson didn't remember him, but Laura and I helped to remind him.

'Of course,' he finally said. 'Falk. Rodney Falk. The big guy who'd been in Vietnam. I'd completely forgotten him. He was from around here somewhere, Decatur or somewhere like that, wasn't he?' I didn't say anything, and Borgheson went on, 'Of course I remember. But I didn't have much to do with him. You don't mean to say you were friends?'

'We shared an office for a semester,' I answered evasively. 'Then he disappeared.'

'Oh, come on now,' Laura burst in, draping herself over my shoulder. 'But the two of you were always conspiring together in Treno's like you were in the CIA. I always wondered what you spent so much time talking about.'

'Nothing,' I said. 'Books.'

'Books?' said Laura.

'He was a strange fellow,' Borgheson intervened, addressing Viñas and the teaching assistant, who were following the conversation looking like they were actually interested. 'He looked like a typical redneck, a boor, and then he never did give the impression of having his head screwed on entirely right. But he was a very cultured guy, extremely well-read. Or at least that's what Dan Gleylock, who actually was friends with him, said. Do you remember Gleylock?'

'But how could he not remember?' Laura answered for me. 'I don't know about you, but I've never met anyone else who could speak seventeen Amerindian languages. You know, John, I always thought, if Martians landed on Earth, we'd have at least one way of making sure whether they were Martians or not: send them to Gleylock and if he doesn't understand them, they're Martians alright.'

Borgheson, Viñas and the teaching assistant laughed.

'He retired two years ago,' Borgheson continued. 'He lives in Florida now, every once in a while I get an email from him . . . As for Falk, the truth is I haven't heard a single word about him.'

The party ended about nine, but Laura and I went to have a drink by ourselves before she headed back to St Louis. She took me to The Embassy, a small bar, dark and narrow, the walls and floors covered in wood, located beside Lincoln Square, and as soon as we sat at the bar, facing a mirror that reflected the quiet atmosphere of the place, I remembered that a scene in my novel set in Urbana took place in that bar. As we ordered our drinks I told Laura.

'Obviously,' she smiled. 'Why do you think I brought you here?'

We stayed in The Embassy talking until very late. We talked a bit about everything, including, as if they were alive, about my wife and my son. But what I most remember about that conversation is the end of it, perhaps because at that moment, for the first time, I had the deceptive intuition that the past is not a stable place but changeable, permanently altered by the future, and that therefore none of what had already happened was irreversible. We'd asked for the bill when, not like someone summing up the evening but like someone offering a nonchalant comment, Laura said that success agreed with me.

'Why should it disagree with me?' I asked, and immediately, automatically said what I'd said every time, over the last two years, someone had made that same mistake: 'Successful writers say that the ideal condition for a writer is failure. Believe me: don't believe them. There's nothing better than success.'

And then, as I also always did, I quoted the French writer Jules Renard's phrase, with which Marcos had shut up a classmate at the Faculty of Fine Arts: 'Yes, I know. All great men were ignored in their lifetimes; but I'm not a great man, so I'd prefer immediate renown.'

Laura laughed.

'No doubt about it,' she said. 'It agrees with you. But whatever you say, it's rare. Look at my second husband. The fucking gringo made a mint doing what he enjoys doing, but he never stops complaining about the slavery of success, this, that and the other. Bullshit. At least those of us who fail don't waste time trying everyone else's fucking patience with our failure.'

With deliberate naïveté I asked:

'You've failed?'

Her lips curved into a scathing smile.

'Of course not,' she said in an ambiguous tone, halfway between aggressive and reassuring. 'It was just a manner of speaking. We all know only idiots fail. But tell me something: what do you call having thrown two marriages overboard, being all alone in the world, forty years old and not even having forged a decent academic career?' She paused and, since I didn't respond, went on harshly, 'Anyway, let's drop the subject . . . What are you going to do tomorrow?'

The waiter came over with the bill.

'Nothing,' I lied as I paid, shrugging my shoulders. 'Take a walk around here. See the city.'

'Good idea,' said Laura. 'You know something? I have the impression that in the two years you spent in Urbana you didn't see anything, didn't understand a thing. The truth is, kiddo, it seemed like you had blinkers on.'

Laura sat there for a moment looking at me as if she hadn't just spoken, as if she was hesitating or as if she was going to apologize for her words, but then she put her glass down on the bar, stroked my cheek, kissed me on the lips, smiled gently as she leaned back from the kiss, and repeated in a low voice:

'Not a thing.'

I sat there in silence, perplexed. Laura picked her glass up again and finished off her drink in one swallow.

'Don't worry, kid,' she said then, going back to her usual tone of voice. 'I'm not going to ask you to go to bed with me, I'm a bit grown-up now to get the brush-off from a jerk like you, but at least do me the favour of wiping that fucking stunned look off your face . . . So, shall we go?'

Laura gave me a lift to the Chancellor, and when she pulled up outside the door I suggested we have one last drink in the hotel bar; as soon as I pronounced those words I thought of Patricia, Marcos' wife, and regretted the suggestion: more than an insinuation, it seemed like a pathetic attempt at making amends, a consoling pat on the back. Laura shook her head.

'Better not,' she said, barely smiling. 'It's very late and I've still got a two-hour drive ahead of me.'

We hugged and, as we did, for an instant I felt a stab of anticipated nostalgia, because I sensed that was the last time I was going to see Laura, and I sensed that she sensed it too.

'I'm very glad to've seen you,' she said when I opened the car door. 'I'm glad you're well. Who knows: maybe I'll get to Barcelona one of these days, I'd like to meet your wife and son.'

Not yet all the way out of the car I looked her in the eye and thought of saying: 'They're both dead, Laura. I killed them.'

'Sure, Laura,' was what I actually said. 'Come whenever you want. They'd love to meet you.'

Then I closed the door and went into the hotel without turning around to watch her go.

The next day I woke up not knowing where I was, but that feeling only lasted a few seconds and, after reconciling myself to the astonishing fact that I was back in Urbana, while I was showering I decided to turn the lie I'd told Laura in The Embassy into truth and postpone until midday my visit to Rodney in Rantoul. So after having breakfast in the Chancellor I started walking downtown. It was Sunday, the streets were almost deserted and at first they all seemed vaguely familiar, but after just a few minutes I was already lost and I couldn't help but think that maybe Laura was right and I had spent those two years in Urbana with blinkers on, like a ghost or a zombie wandering among that population of ghosts and zombies. I had to stop a jogger who was listening to a Walkman to ask him to tell me how to get to campus; when I finally came out onto Green Street, by following his directions, I got my bearings. That was how, just as if I were following the shadow of the cheerful, fearsome, arrogant kamikaze I'd been in Urbana, I saw the Quad, the Foreign Languages Building, my old house at 703 West Oregon, Treno's. It was all more or less as I'd remembered it, except Treno's, converted into one of those interchangeable cafés that American snobs consider European (from Rome) and European snobs consider American (from New York), but which are impossible to find in either New York or Rome. I went in, ordered a Coke at the bar and, watching the sunny morning through the big windows that gave onto Goodwin, I drank a couple of sips. Then I paid and left.

At the front desk in the Chancellor they'd told me where there was a car rental agency that was open on Sundays. I rented a Chrysler there, checked my route with the guy behind the counter to make sure I remembered the way, and half an hour later, after following the same route I'd travelled fifteen years before to see Rodney's father (up Broadway and across Cunningham Avenue and then the highway north), I arrived in Rantoul. As soon as I got into the city I recognized the intersection of Liberty Drive and Century Boulevard, and also the gas station, which was now called Casey's General Store and had been refurbished with modern gas pumps and expanded with a supermarket and cafeteria. Since I wasn't sure of being able to find Rodney's house, I stopped the car there, went into the cafeteria and asked where Belle Avenue was; a fat waitress in a white uniform and cap shouted some directions at me without pausing from attending her customers. I went back to the car, tried to follow the waitress's directions and, just when I thought I was lost again, saw the railway tracks and suddenly knew where I was. I backed up, turned right, passed the closed door of Bud's Bar and soon I was parked in front of Rodney's house. It didn't look much different than it had fifteen years ago, although its size and the slightly faded elegance of an old country mansion contrasted even more than in my memory with the blandly functional neighbouring buildings. Rodney had no doubt renovated it for his family, because the façade and the porch looked freshly whitewashed, and so I was surprised to see that, between the pair of maples in the front yard, the stars and stripes of the American flag still waved from a small pole stuck in the lawn. I stayed in the car for a moment, with my heart pounding in my throat, trying to absorb the fact of finally being there, at the end of the road, about to see Rodney again, and after a few seconds I went up the porch steps and rang the bell. No one answered. Then I rang again, with the same result. A few metres from the door, to the right, there was a window that, as far as I remembered, looked into the living room where I had talked with Rodney's father, but I couldn't see inside the house through it because a pair of white curtains were drawn. I turned around. A 4 × 4 driven by an old man came round the corner, passed slowly in front of me and carried on towards town. I went down the porch steps and, while I lit a cigarette in the front yard, thought of knocking on the door of one of the neighbours' houses to ask after Rodney, but I discarded the idea after I noticed a woman in a housecoat scrutinizing me through a window on the other side of the street. I decided to go for a walk. I walked towards the tracks, beyond which the city seemed to disintegrate into a disorderly mix of vacant lots, tiny woods and cultivated fields, and then walked along parallel to them retracing the route I'd just travelled by car, and when I reached Bud's Bar again I saw they'd just opened: the door was still closed but there was a pick-up truck parked in front of it and, despite the vertical morning sun, illuminated ads for Miller Lite, Budweiser, Icehouse and Milwaukee Best shone feebly in the windows; above them was a big sign in support of the American soldiers fighting overseas: PRAY FOR PEACE. SUPPORT OUR TROOPS.

I went in. The place was empty. I sat on a stool, in front of the bar, and waited for someone to come and serve me. Bud's was still the charmless small town bar I remembered, with its faint smell of stables and its pool tables and jukebox and television screens all over the place, and when I saw a sluggish guy appear through the swinging door, wearing a Red Sox baseball cap, I wanted to think it was the same waiter who, fifteen years before, had told me where Rodney's house was. The man made some comment that I didn't entirely understand (something about not being able to trust people who start drinking before breakfast), and then when he was behind the bar, a little dazzled by the glare of the sun that came in through the windows at my back, he asked me what I wanted to drink. I looked at his stony face, his slanting eyes, his boxer's nose and the few locks of greasy hair poking out from under his sweaty cap; not without a certain surprise I said to myself that it was indeed the same man, fifteen years older. I ordered a beer, he served it, leaned his slaughterman's hands on the bar and before I could interrogate him about Rodney he asked:

'You're not from around here, are you?'

'No,' I answered.

'Can I ask where you're from?'

I told him.

'Shit,' he exclaimed. 'That's far away, huh?' He corrected himself: 'Well, not that far. Nowhere's that far away any more. Besides, you guys are in the war, aren't you?'

'The war?'

'God almighty, where've you been for the last year, buddy? Iraq, Madrid, haven't you heard anything about that?'

'Yes,' I said, after lighting a cigarette. 'I have heard something. But I'm not sure we're as much in the war as you guys.'

The man blinked.

'I don't understand,' he said.

Luckily at that moment a girl with circles under her eyes and a shiny silver stud in her belly button suddenly rushed into the bar. Without even saying hello the man began to reproach her for something, but the girl told him to go to hell and disappeared through the swinging door; I wondered if the girl was his daughter.

'Shit,' the owner said again, as if laughing at his own anger. 'These kids don't respect anyone any more. In our day things were different, don't you think?' And, as if the girl bursting into the bar had paradoxically improved the morning's outlook, the man added: 'Hey, would you mind if I joined you?'

I didn't need to answer. While he got himself a beer I thought he must be fifty-five or sixty years old, more or less the same age as Rodney; mentally I repeated: 'Our day?' The bartender had a sip of beer and set the bottle down on the bar; smoothing his hair under his Red Sox cap, he asked:

'What were we talking about?'

'Nothing important,' I hurried to say. 'But I wanted to ask you a question.'

'Fire away.'

'I've come to Rantoul to see a friend,' I began. 'Rodney Falk. I just called at his house but no one answered. It's been a while since I lost track of him, so I don't even know if he's still . . .'

I stopped talking: the bartender had calmly raised his hand and, making a screen to defend himself from the light, was examining me with interest.

'Hey, I know you, don't I?' he finally said.

'You know me, but you don't remember me,' I answered. 'I was here a long time ago.'

The man nodded and lowered his hand; in a few seconds the happiness had drained from his face, to be replaced by an expression that wasn't mockery, but resembled it.

'I'm afraid you've made the journey in vain,' he said.

'Rodney doesn't live here any more?'

'Rodney died four months ago,' he answered. 'Hung himself from a beam in his shed.'

I was speechless; for a second I couldn't breathe. Stunned, I looked away from the bartender and, trying to find something to focus on behind the bar, I saw the photos of baseball stars and the big portrait of John Wayne hanging on the walls; in that decade and a half the baseball stars had changed, but not John Wayne: there he still was, legendary, imperturbable and dressed as a cowboy, with a dark red bandana knotted at his throat and an invincible smile in his eyes, like an abiding icon of the triumph of virtue. I put out my cigarette, took a sip of beer and suddenly had an icy feeling of dizziness, of unreality, as if I'd already lived through that moment or as if I were dreaming it: a solitary bar lost in the Midwest, the light pouring in through the windows and a lazy, talkative barman who, as if he were whispering a message in my ear that had no precise meaning but for me at that moment had all the meaning in the world, gave me the news of the death of a friend who I actually hardly knew and who, perhaps more than a friend, was a symbol whose scope not even I myself could entirely define, a dark or radiant symbol like maybe Hemingway had been for Rodney. And while I unthinkingly thought of Rodney and of Hemingway – of Rodney's suicide four months before in the shed of his house in Rantoul, Illinois, and of Hemingway's suicide in his house in Ketchum, Idaho, when Rodney was just a teenager – I thought also of Gabriel and Paula, or rather what happened is that they appeared to me, happy, luminous and dead, and then I felt an irrepressible desire to pray, to pray for Gabriel and for Paula and for Rodney, for Hemingway too, and at that very moment, as if a butterfly had just flown in through the open window of Bud's Bar, I suddenly remembered a prayer that appears in 'A Clean, Well-Lighted Place', that desolate story by Hemingway I had read many times since I first read it that long ago night when Rodney's father called me in

Urbana to tell me the story of his son, a prayer that I knew instantly was the only suitable prayer for Rodney because Hemingway had unknowingly written it for him many years before he died, a bleak prayer that Rodney had undoubtedly read as many times I had and that, I imagined for a second, maybe Rodney and Hemingway recited before taking their lives and that Paula and Gabriel wouldn't even have had time to pray: 'Our nada who art in nada, nada be thy name thy kingdom nada thy will be nada in nada as it is in nada.' Mentally I recited this prayer while I watched the bartender approach from the back of the bar, fat and grave, or maybe indifferent, drying his hands on a rag, as if he'd stepped away for a moment out of the pure necessity to do something or as if he too had been praying. For a moment I thought of leaving; then I thought I couldn't leave; stupidly I asked:

'Did you know him?'

'Rodney?' the bartender asked stupidly, leaning against the bar again.

I nodded.

'Of course,' he smiled. 'How could I not know him? This is a small place: we all know each other here.' He finished off his beer and, suddenly talkative again, went on: 'How am I not going to know him? We were both from here, we lived nearby, we grew up together, went to school together. We were the same age, a year older than his brother Bob. Now they're both dead . . . Well. You know something? Rodney was an exceptional guy, we were all sure he'd do something great, that he'd go far. Then came the war, the one in Vietnam, I mean. Did you know Rodney was in Vietnam?' I nodded again. 'I wanted to enlist too. But they wouldn't let me: a heart murmur, they said, or something like that. I suppose I was lucky, because later it turned out that it was all a lie, the politicians tricked us all, just like now: all those boys dying like flies over there in Iraq. You tell me what business we've got in that fucking country. And what business we had in Vietnam. Once I heard someone say, it might have even been Rodney, I can't remember, I heard him say that when you go to war the least you can do is win it, because if you lose you lose everything, including your dignity. I don't know what you think, but it seems to me he was right. Rodney lost Bob over there, he was blown up by a mine. And, well, in a way I suppose he died over there too. When he came back he wasn't the same any more. It's easy to say now, but maybe deep down we all knew it'd end like this. Or maybe not, I don't know. Where did you know him from?'

'We worked together in Urbana,' I said. 'It was a while ago, at the university.'

'Oh yeah,' said the bartender. 'I didn't know he made any friends there, but that was a good time for him. He seemed content. Then he left and for a long time he hardly ever came back here. When he did he came back married and with a son. He was teaching at the school, I'd never seen him better, he seemed like a new person, he seemed . . . I don't know, he almost seemed like what we always

225

thought he was going to be. Until that report came out and everything got fucked up.'

At that moment two middle-aged couples came into the bar, cheerful and in their Sunday best. The bartender stopped talking, waved a greeting, turned towards the swinging door and called the girl, but, since she didn't come out, the man had no choice but to go and attend to his customers. While he was doing so the girl reappeared and took over the order, not without exchanging a couple more jibes with the boss in passing. Then the bartender returned heavily to where I was.

'Want another?' he asked, pointing to my empty beer bottle. 'It's on the house.'

I shook my head.

'You were telling me about Rodney and some news report.'

The bartender made a disgusted face, as if his nose had just detected a gust of foul-smelling air.

'It was a television documentary, a report on the Vietnam War,' he explained half-heartedly. 'Apparently it told of horrible things. I say apparently because I haven't seen it, nor do I need to, but anyway those things came out later everywhere. In the papers, on TV, everywhere. If you'd been living here you'd know about it, lots of people talked about it.'

'And what did Rodney have to do with the report?'

'They say he appeared in it.'

'They say?'

'People say. I told you I didn't see the report. What they say is that the man who appeared telling these horrible things was Rodney. Apparently you couldn't recognize him, the television people had done something so he couldn't be recognized, he spoke with his back to the camera or something like that, but people started putting two and two together and soon arrived at the conclusion that it was him. I don't know, like I said. What I do know is that before they showed that report on TV and everything got complicated Rodney had already spent several weeks without leaving the house, and then after that nobody knew anything until, well, until he got himself out of the way. Anyway, don't make me talk about this, it's a terrible fucking story and I don't really know it. Who you should see is the wife. Rodney's wife, I mean. Since you've come all this way . . .'

'His wife still lives in Rantoul?'

'Sure. Right around the corner, in Rodney's house.'

'I was just there and no one was home. Like I told you.'

'They must have gone out somewhere. But I bet they'll be home for lunch. I'm not sure Jenny will be very keen to talk about these things after all she's had to put up with, but you could at least say hello.'

I thanked the bartender and went to pay for my beer, but he wouldn't let me.

'Tell me something,' he said as we shook hands and he held onto mine a second longer than was normal. 'Are you thinking of spending much time in Rantoul?'

227

'No,' I answered. 'Why do you ask?'

'No reason.' He let go of my hand and smoothed his thinning hair under his cap. 'But you know how these small towns are: if you do stay, take my advice and don't believe everything you hear about Rodney. People talk a lot of nonsense.'

An explosion of light blinded me when I got outside: it was noon. More confused than depressed, I started walking automatically towards Belle Avenue. My mind was a blank, and the only thing I remember having thought, mistakenly, is that this really was the end of the road, and also, not mistakenly or less mistakenly, that it was true that Rodney had found his way out of the tunnel, only that it was a different way out from the one I'd imagined. When I reached the front of Rodney's house I was soaked in sweat and had already decided the best thing to do would be to return immediately to Urbana, among other reasons because my presence here could only importune Rodney's family. I got in the Chrysler, started it, and was just about to turn around on Belle to take the road back to Urbana when I told myself I couldn't just leave like that, with all those un-answered questions strung out before me like a barbed wire fence and without even having seen Rodney's wife and son. I hadn't even finished thinking that when I saw them. They'd just turned the corner and were holding hands, walking along the sidewalk that ran between the road and the front gardens of the houses, in the green shade of the maples, and as they were coming towards me, bereft and

228

unhurried down the empty street, I suddenly saw Gabriel and Paula walking down other empty streets, and then Gabriel letting go of his mother's hand to break into his oscillating run, smiling and eager to throw his arms around my neck. I felt my eyes were about to fill with tears. Holding them back, I turned off the engine, took a deep breath, got out again and waited for them, leaning against the car, smoking; the cigarette trembled a little in my hand. It wasn't long before they were standing in front of me. Regarding me with a mixture of worry and suspicion, the woman asked me if I was a journalist, but didn't let me answer.

'If you're a journalist you can just turn around and go back where you came from,' she ordered me, pallid and tense. 'I have nothing to say to you and . . .'

'I'm not a journalist,' I interrupted.

She stood looking at me. I explained that I was a friend of Rodney's, I told her my name. The woman blinked and asked me to repeat it, I repeated it. Then, without taking her eyes off me, she let go of the child's hand, took him by the shoulder, pressed him to her hip and, after looking away for a second, as if something had distracted her, I felt her whole body ease. Before she spoke I realized that she knew who I was, that Rodney had talked about me. She said:

'You're too late.'

'I know,' I said, and I wanted to add something, but I didn't know what to add.

'My name's Jenny,' she said after a moment, and, without looking down towards her son, added: 'This is Dan.'

229

I held out my hand to the boy, and after an instant's hesitation he held out his and I shook it: a soft bunch of little bones wrapped in pink flesh; when he let go he looked at me too: skinny and very serious, only his big brown eyes reminded me of his father's big brown eyes. He had fair hair and was wearing corduroy trousers and a blue T-shirt.

'How old are you?' I asked him.

'Six,' he answered.

'Just turned,' said Jenny.

Nodding my approval, I commented:

'You're a man now.'

Dan didn't smile, didn't say anything, and there was a silence during which a freight train thundered past behind me, bound for Chicago, while a slight breeze alleviated the midday heat, stirring the American flag on the pole in the yard and chilling the sweat on my skin. Once the train had passed, Dan asked:

'Were you a friend of my father's?'

'Yes,' I said.

'A good friend?'

'Pretty good,' I said, and added: 'Why do you ask?'

Dan shrugged his shoulders in an adult way, almost defiantly.

'No reason,' he said.

We were silent again, a silence more awkward than long, during which I thought the barbed wire fence was going to remain intact. I stubbed out my cigarette on the sidewalk.

'Well,' I said. 'I have to go. It was nice to have met you.'

I turned around to open the car, but then I heard Jenny's voice behind me:

'Have you had lunch yet?'

When I turned around she repeated the question. I answered truthfully.

'I was just going to make something for Dan and me,' said Jenny. 'Why don't you join us?'

We went in the house, then to the kitchen and Jenny started making lunch. I tried to help, but she wouldn't let me and, while I watched Dan watching me, leaning on the door-jamb, I sat down in a chair beside a table covered with a blue and red checked tablecloth, in front of a window that overlooked a back garden where clumps of chrysanthemums and hydrangeas were growing; I supposed that the shed where Rodney hanged himself would be in that garden. Without stopping what she was doing Jenny asked me if I'd like something to drink. I said no and asked her if I could smoke.

'I'd rather you didn't, if you don't mind,' she said. 'Because of the child.'

'I don't mind.'

'I used to smoke a lot,' she explained. 'But I quit when I got pregnant. Since then I just smoke the odd cigarette every once in a while.'

Dan wandered away somewhere inside the house, as if he'd made sure everything was going well between his mother and me, and Jenny started telling me how she'd overcome her dependence on tobacco. She barely had anything in common with the woman my imagination had constructed from the curiously discrepant descriptions contained in Rodney's letters. Small and very slim, she had the kind of discreet beauty whose destiny or whose vocation is to pass unnoticed; in fact, her features were no more than correct: slightly prominent cheekbones, tiny nose, thin lips, lustreless grey eyes; two simple earrings glittered in her earlobes and set off the dark brown of her straight hair pulled back in a messy bun. She was wearing a pair of faded jeans and a blue wool sweater that barely disguised the prominence of her breasts. Otherwise, and despite her physical fragility, she radiated a sort of energetic serenity, and while I listened to her talk I almost unwillingly tried to imagine her with Rodney, but I couldn't and, almost unwillingly as well, I wondered how that woman who seemed so cool and insignificant had managed to break through my friend's emotional solipsism.

Dan appeared again at the kitchen door; interrupting his mother, he asked me if I'd like to see his toys.

'Sure,' Jenny answered ahead of me. 'Show them to him while I finish making lunch.'

I stood up and accompanied him to the same living room with its book-lined walls, window onto the porch, leather sofa and armchairs where, fifteen years before, Dan's grandfather had told me, over an endless spring afternoon, Rodney's unfinished story. The room had barely changed, but now the floor, covered in claret-coloured rugs, was also covered in a chaotic mess of toys that inevitably reminded me of the mess that reigned in the living room of my house when Gabriel was the same age as Dan. He, without more ado, began to show me his toys, one by one, demonstrating the characteristics and functions of each with the concentrated seriousness that children are capable of at any moment and men only when their lives are at stake and, after a while, when Jenny announced that lunch was ready, we two were already linked by one of those subterranean currents of complicity that as adults it often takes us months or years to establish.

We ate a salad, spaghetti with tomato sauce and raspberry pie. Dan completely hogged the conversation, so we hardly talked about anything other than his school, his toys, his hobbies and his friends, and we didn't refer to Rodney even once. Jenny devoted all her attention to her son, although on a couple of occasions I thought I caught her watching me. As for me, at times I couldn't avoid the insidious suspicion that I was in a dream: still shaken by the news of Rodney's death, it was hard to get rid of the strange surprise of finding myself having lunch in his house, with his widow and his son, but at the same time I felt lulled by an almost domestic tranquillity, as if this weren't the first time I'd shared a table with them. The end of the meal, however, was not calm, because Dan roundly refused to take his nap, and the only thing his mother got him to agree to after a lot of negotiating was that he'd lie down on the sofa in the living room, waiting for us to have our coffee there. While Jenny made the coffee, I went into the living room and sat beside Dan, who, after furtively tapping the keys of the Game Boy his mother had just forbidden him to play with and staring at the ceiling for a while, fell asleep in an odd position, with his arm twisted a little behind his back. I sat watching him without daring to move his arm for fear of waking him, plunged as he was in those unfathomable depths where children sleep, and I remembered Gabriel sleeping beside me, breathing in a silent, regular, infinitely peaceful rhythm, transfigured by sleep and enjoying the perfect assurance of having his father watching over him, and for a moment I felt the desire to hug Dan as I'd so often hugged Gabriel, knowing that I wasn't hugging him to protect him, but so he could protect me.

'There you go,' Jenny said quietly, hurrying into the living room with the coffee tray. 'Always the same story. There's no way he wants to have his nap, and then I have a terrible job to wake him up.'

She set the tray down on the coffee table between the two armchairs and, after gently moving Dan's twisted arm so it was resting naturally on his chest, she went to the far end of the room and opened the curtains of the porch window to let the golden afternoon sunlight shine into the room. Then she poured the coffee, sat down across from me, stirring hers, drank it down almost in one gulp, let the silence linger for a while and, maybe because I couldn't find a way to start the conversation, asked:

'Are you thinking of staying here long?'

'Just until Tuesday.'

'In Rantoul?'

'In Urbana.'

Jenny nodded; then she said:

'I'm sorry you've come such a long way for nothing.'

'I would have done it anyway,' I lied.

I took a sip of coffee and then I talked about my trip around the United States, making it clear that Urbana was just one more leg of the journey; knowing that Jenny probably already knew, I explained that I'd lived there for two years, which was when I became friends with Rodney, and that I'd wanted to return.

'I thought I could see Rodney again,' I continued. 'Although I wasn't sure. I haven't been in touch with him for a long time and a few months ago I wrote him a letter, but I suppose by then . . .'

'Yes,' Jenny helped me out. 'The letter arrived not long after his death. It must be around somewhere.'

She finished her coffee and set her cup down on the table. I did the same. For something to say I said:

'I'm very sorry about what happened.'

'I know,' said Jenny. 'Rodney talked about you a lot.'

'Really?' I asked, pretending to be surprised, but only a little.

'Sure,' said Jenny, and for the first time I saw her smile: a smile at once sweet and mischievous, almost astute, which dug a tiny net of wrinkles around the corners of her mouth. 'I know the whole story, Rodney told me lots of times. He told very funny stories. He always said until he became friends with you he'd never met anyone so strange who seemed so normal.'

'That's funny,' I said, blushing as I tried to imagine what Rodney might have told her about me. 'I always thought he was the strange one.'

'Rodney wasn't strange,' Jenny corrected me. 'He was just unlucky. It was bad luck that wouldn't let him live in peace. Wouldn't even let him die in peace.'

Searching for a way to inquire into the circumstances surrounding Rodney's death, I got distracted for a moment, and when I started listening again irony had completely tainted her voice, and I had lost the thread of what she was saying.

'But, you know what I think?' I heard her say; covering up my distraction, with an interrogative gesture I urged her to go on. 'What I think is that actually it was mainly to see you.'

It took me a second to comprehend that she was talking about Rodney's trip to Spain. Now my surprise was genuine: I didn't think that I'd made the same trip Rodney had made the other way around just to see him, but I did think that in Spain I'd pursued him from hotel to hotel and that I'd finally had to travel to Madrid just to talk to him for a while. Jenny must have read the surprise on my face, because she qualified it:

'Well, perhaps not only to see you, but also to see you.' Fiddling with her hair a little while she glanced at Dan out of the corner of her eye, she leaned back in the armchair and let her hands rest on her thighs: they were long, bony, without any rings. 'I don't know,' she corrected herself. 'I might be wrong. What I do know is that he came home from the trip very happy. He told me he'd been with you in Madrid, that he'd met your wife and son, that you were a successful writer now.'

Jenny seemed to hesitate for a second, as if she wanted to keep talking about Rodney and me but the conversation had taken a wrong turn and she should put it right. We remained quiet for a moment, then Jenny began to tell me about her life in Rantoul. She told me that after Rodney's death her first thought was to sell the house and go back to Burlington. However, she soon realized that fleeing Rantoul and returning to Burlington in search of her family's protection would be an admission of defeat. After all, she said, she and Dan had their lives set there; they had their house, their friends, they didn't have any financial worries: as well as Rodney's life insurance and her widow's pension, she made a decent salary from her administrative position with a farming cooperative. So she'd decided to stay in Rantoul. She didn't regret it.

'Dan and I get along pretty well on our own,' she said. 'Besides, in Burlington I'd never be able to afford a house like the one we have here. Anyway.' She looked me in the eye, almost as if she was embarrassed to ask: 'Shall we go outside and smoke a cigarette?'

We sat on the porch steps. On Belle Avenue the air smelled intensely of spring; the afternoon light had still not begun to rust and the breeze blew more strongly, moving the leaves on the maples and making the American flag wave in the yard. Before I could light my cigarette Jenny offered me a light with Rodney's Zippo. I stared at it. She followed the direction of my gaze. She said:

'It was Rodney's.'

'I know,' I said.

She lit my cigarette and then her own, closed the Zippo, weighed it in her bony hand for a moment and then handed it to me.

'Keep it,' she said. 'I don't need it any more.'

I hesitated a moment without meeting her eyes.

'No. Thank you,' I answered.

Jenny put the Zippo away and we smoked for a while without talking, looking at the houses across the street, the cars that passed in front of us every once in a while, and as we did so I looked for the window where I'd seen a woman spying on me hours earlier; now there was no one there. We sat in silence, like old friends who don't need to talk to be together. I thought that it had been more than a year since I'd spent so long in someone's company, and for a second I thought Rantoul was a good place to live. I'd barely thought it when, as if picking up an interrupted conversation, Jenny said:

'Don't you want to know what happened?'

This time I didn't look at her either. For a moment, while I was inhaling the smoke from my cigarette, it crossed my mind that maybe it was better not to know anything. But I

238

said yes, and it was then that, with disconcerting natural-
ness, as if she were telling a remote and distant tale, nothing
to do with her, which couldn't affect her in any way, she
told me the story of Rodney's last months. It began the
previous spring, in this same season more or less a year ago.
One night, while they were having dinner, a stranger
phoned the house asking for Rodney; when Jenny asked
who was calling he said he was a journalist who worked for
an Ohio television station. They thought it strange but
Rodney didn't see any reason not to talk to the man. The
conversation, which Jenny didn't hear, lasted for several
minutes, and when he came back to the table Rodney was
changed, his gaze lost. Jenny asked him what had happened,
but Rodney didn't answer (according to Jenny he probably
didn't even hear the question), he kept eating and after a
few minutes, when he still had food on his plate, he stood up
and told Jenny he was going out for a walk. He didn't come
back until after midnight. Jenny was awake waiting for him,
demanded that he tell her about the conversation he'd had
with the reporter and Rodney ended up acquiescing.
Actually he did much more than that. Of course, Jenny
knew that Rodney had spent two years in Vietnam and that
the experience had marked him indelibly, but until then her
husband had never told her anything more than that and she
had never asked him to; that night, however, Rodney
poured his heart out: he talked about Vietnam for hours;
more precisely: he talked, got furious, shouted, laughed,
cried, and finally dawn surprised them both on the bed,

239

dressed, awake and exhausted, looking at each other as if they didn't recognize each other.

'From the beginning I had the feeling he was confessing to me,' Jenny told me. 'Also that I didn't know him, and that never before then had I truly loved him.'

Before explaining what he'd talked about with the reporter from Ohio, Rodney told her that towards the end of his time in Vietnam he'd been assigned to an elite platoon known as Tiger Force, with which he went into combat many times. The unit committed innumerable barbarities, which Rodney didn't describe or didn't want to describe, and when it was finally dissolved all its members swore to keep silent about them. Nevertheless, at the beginning of the seventies, when the Pentagon created a commission whose job it was to investigate the war crimes of Tiger Force, Rodney decided to break the pact of silence and cooperate with them. He was the only member of the platoon to do so, but it didn't do him any good: he testified several times before the commission, and the only thing he got out of it was the open hostility of his commanding officers and comrades-in-arms (who considered him an in-former) and the veiled hostility of the rest of the army (who likewise considered him an informer), because when the report finally arrived at the White House someone decided that the best thing they could do would be to file it. 'It was all play-acting,' Rodney told Jenny. 'Deep down no one was interested in the truth.' After his appearance before the commission Rodney received several death threats; then he stopped receiving them and for years he trusted that all had been forgotten. Sometimes he heard news of his comrades from the platoon: some of them were begging on the streets, others languished in jail, others spent long periods in psychiatric hospitals; only a few had managed to stay afloat and were leading normal lives, at least apparently normal. Rodney didn't want to know anything more about them, and in fact he did whatever was in his power so that they wouldn't be able to find him. But one day, when Rodney thought the story was buried, one of them found him. It was the best friend he'd had in the unit, maybe his only real friend; mentally unhinged, broken by remorse that sprouted up cyclically and gave him no respite, this friend tried to convince him that the only way they could get a little peace was to go to the authorities and get them to dig out the case, confess the facts and pay for them. Rodney tried to calm him down, tried to reason with him (he told him that too much time had passed and by that stage the authorities wouldn't even be prepared to go through the motions and wouldn't pay them the slightest attention), but it was all futile; unable to bear the imploring and obsessive pressure from his comrade, Rodney opted for the radical solution that he'd employed on other occasions: he disappeared from Rantoul.

'What was his friend's name?' I interrupted at this point in Jenny's tale.

'Tommy Birban,' she answered. 'Why do you ask?'

'No reason,' I said and urged her to go on: 'What was it that the journalist from Ohio wanted?'

'For Rodney to tell him everything he knew about Tiger Force,' Jenny answered.

241

Rodney explained to Jenny that the journalist was preparing a feature about the matter. It seems that Tommy Birban had got in contact with him and told him the story; then he had gained access to the filed Pentagon report and there he'd found out that the only testimony was Rodney's, and that, in broad strokes, it confirmed what Tommy Birban had told him. That's why the reporter asked Rodney to tell before the cameras what he'd told the commission years before; then he'd get in touch with all the members of the unit he could manage to find to ask them the same. When the reporter finished explaining his project Rodney told him too much time had gone by since the war and he didn't want to talk about it any more, the reporter insisted time and again, trying to blackmail him morally, but Rodney was inflexible. 'No way,' he said that night to Jenny, shouting and shaken and as if it wasn't really Jenny he was talking to. 'It's taken me too much trouble to learn to live with this to fuck it all up now.' Jenny tried to calm him down: it was all over, he'd made it quite clear to the journalist that he didn't want to appear in the report, he wouldn't bother them again. 'You're wrong,' Rodney said. 'He'll be back. This has only just begun.'

He was right. A few days later the reporter phoned again to try to convince him and he again refused to cooperate; he tried a couple more times, with new arguments (among them that, except for Tommy Birban, all the other members of the platoon he'd been able to locate had refused to talk, and that his testimony was essential, because it constituted

242

the fundamental source of the Pentagon report), but Rodney stood his ground. One morning, not long after the
latest phone call, the journalist turned up unexpectedly at
his house accompanied by another man and a woman. Jenny
made them wait on the porch and went to find Rodney, who
was having breakfast with Dan and who, when he got to the
porch, asked the two men and the woman to leave without
even saying hello. 'We will, just as soon as you let me tell
you one thing,' said the journalist. 'What?' asked Rodney.
'Tommy Birban is dead,' said the reporter. 'We have reason
to think he's been murdered.' There was a silence, during
which the journalist seemed to be waiting for the news to
take effect on Rodney, and then he explained that, after he'd
got in touch with other members of the unit to ask them to
collaborate with the report, Birban had begun to receive
anonymous threats trying to convince him not to speak
before the cameras; he was very scared, full of doubts, but
finally decided not to let himself be intimidated by the
blackmail and to carry on with the project, and a week later,
not two days before they were to record his testimony, as he
left his house he was the victim of a hit-and-run. 'The police
are investigating,' said the reporter. 'It's unlikely they'll
find those responsible, but you and I know who they are.
We also both know that, if you still refuse to talk, your
friend will have died for nothing.' Rodney remained silent,
as still as a statue. 'That's all I wanted to tell you,' the
reporter concluded, holding out a card that Rodney did not
take; Jenny did, instinctively, knowing she'd tear it up as

243

soon as the man left. 'Now the decision is yours. Call me if you need me.' The journalist and his two colleagues turned around and Jenny watched with the beginning of happiness as they walked towards the car parked in front of their house, but before her happiness was complete she heard at her side a voice that resembled Rodney's without entirely being his, and she knew that those inoffensive words were going to change their life: 'Wait a moment.'

Rodney and the three visitors spent all morning and much of the afternoon shut up in the living room. At first Jenny had to overcome the urge to listen through the closed door, but when, after half an hour of secret discussions, she saw the two people who'd come with the reporter go outside and return with recording equipment, she didn't even attempt to persuade Rodney not to commit the error he was about to commit. She spent the rest of the day out of the house, with Dan, and returned in the evening when the journalists had gone. Rodney was sitting in the living room, in darkness and silence, and although, after giving Dan his supper and putting him quickly to bed, Jenny tried to find out what had happened during her deliberate absence, she couldn't get a single word out of him, and she had the impression that he was mad or drugged or drunk, and that he no longer understood her language. That was the first sign of alarm. The second arrived shortly after. That night Rodney did not sleep, nor the ones that followed: lying awake in bed, Jenny heard him wandering around downstairs, heard him talking to himself or maybe on the phone;

on one occasion she thought she heard laughter, muffled laughter, like the kind you stifle at a funeral. That's how an unstoppable process of deterioration began: Rodney asked for a leave of absence from the school and stopped teaching, he didn't go outside, spent the days sleeping or lying in bed and ended up having nothing to do with Dan or with her. It was as if someone had torn out a tiny connection that turned out to be indispensable to his continued functioning and his whole organism had suffered a collapse, reducing him to a ghost of himself. Jenny tried to talk to him, tried to force him to accept the help of a psychiatrist; it was useless: he seemed to listen to her (maybe he really did listen), he smiled at her, touched her, asked her not to worry, over and over again he told her he was fine, but she felt that Rodney was living as far away from everything around him as a planet spinning in its own self-absorbed orbit. She let time pass, hoping things would change. Things didn't change. The broadcast of the television report did nothing but make everything worse. At first it didn't have much impact, because it was a local station that had produced it, but very soon the national newspapers were repeating its revelations and a major network bought the rights and broadcast the piece at prime time. Although the journalist sent them a copy, Rodney didn't want to see it; although in the accompanying note the reporter assured him that he'd fulfilled his promise of guarding Rodney's anonymity, reality contradicted him: it really wasn't difficult to identify Rodney in the report, and the result of this indiscretion or

breach of confidence was that Jenny's life became stifled by
hounding journalists and questions and gossip about her
husband's seclusion. As for her relationship with Rodney, it
quickly deteriorated until it became unsustainable. One day
she took a drastic decision: she told Rodney that it would be
better if they separated; she would go back to Burlington
with Dan and he could stay by himself in Rantoul. The
ultimatum was a last feint that Jenny hoped would get
Rodney to react, confronting him unceremoniously with the
evidence that, unless he restrained his free fall, he was going
to end up ruining his life and losing his family. But the trick
didn't work: Rodney meekly accepted her proposal, and the
only thing he asked Jenny was when she intended to leave.
At that moment Jenny understood that all was lost, and it
was also then that she had her first conversation with
Rodney in a long time. It was not an enlightening conversation. Actually, Rodney hardly spoke: he limited himself to answering, in an exasperatingly laconic manner, the
questions she put to him and Jenny couldn't get rid of the
feeling that she was talking to a child with no future or an
elderly man with no past, because Rodney looked at her
exactly as if he were trying to look through the sky. At
some moment Jenny asked him if he was afraid. With a wisp
of relief, as if her fingertip had just brushed the hidden heart
of his anguish, Rodney said yes. 'Of what?' Jenny asked
him. 'I don't know,' said Rodney. 'Of people. Of you guys.
Sometimes I'm afraid of myself.' 'Of us?' Jenny asked.
'Who's us?' 'You and Dan,' answered Rodney. 'We aren't

246

going to hurt you,' Jenny smiled. 'I know that,' said Rodney. 'But that's what I'm most afraid of.' Jenny remembered that when she heard those words she felt afraid of Rodney for the first time, and also that it was then she understood that she should leave Rantoul with her son as soon as possible. But she didn't; she decided to stay: she loved Rodney and felt that, whatever happened, she should help him. She couldn't help him. The last weeks were a nightmare. In the daytime Jenny tried to talk to him, but it was almost always futile, because, despite understanding his words, she was unable to invest the phrases he pronounced with any intelligible meaning, as they were closer to the hermetic and rigorously coherent ravings of a lunatic than to any articulate discourse. As for the nights, Rodney continued to pass them wakefully, but now he spent much of them writing: Jenny fell asleep rocked by the unceasing tapping of the computer keyboard, but when, some days after Rodney's death, she got up the courage to open his files she found them all blank, as if at the last moment her husband had decided to spare her the venomous outpourings from the hell in which he was being consumed. Jenny maintained that in the days leading up to his death Rodney had completely lost his mind; also that what happened was the best thing that could have happened. And what happened was that one morning, not long after Christmas, Jenny got up earlier than usual and, when she walked past the room where Rodney had been sleeping for the last while, she saw it empty and the bed still made.

Worried, she looked for Rodney in the dining room, the kitchen, all over the house, and finally found him hanging from a rope in the shed.

'That was all,' Jenny concluded, abandoning for a few seconds the distant manner she'd managed until then to impart to her tale. 'The rest you can imagine. Death improves the dead, so it turns out everyone loved Rodney very much. Even the journalists came to see me . . . Just crap.'

For a moment I thought Jenny was going to start to cry, but she didn't cry: she stubbed out her second cigarette on the porch step, and just as she'd done with her first, kept it in her hand; after a long silence she turned towards me and looked me in the eye.

'Didn't I tell you?' she said, almost smiling. 'The problem isn't getting Dan to sleep. The problem is waking him up.'

Dan did indeed wake up in a foul mood, but it gradually eased as he had a bowl of cereal and his mother and I kept him company with a coffee. When we finished Jenny suggested we go for a walk before it got dark.

'Dan and I are going to take you someplace,' she said.

'What place?'

Jenny crouched down beside him and, making a screen with her hand, whispered in his ear.

'OK?' she asked, standing up again.

Dan just shrugged his shoulders.

When we left the house we turned left, crossed the

railway tracks and walked along Ohio, a well-paved street, with hardly any houses or businesses, which headed towards the outskirts of the city. Five hundred metres on, across from a dense birch wood, stood a building with white walls, a sort of enormous granary surrounded by grass on the front of which was painted in large red letters: VETERANS OF FOREIGN WARS POST 6750; beside it there was another smaller sign, similar to the one outside Bud's Bar, except that it was decorated with an American flag; the sign read: SUPPORT OUR TROOPS. The building looked empty, but it must not have been, because there were several cars parked in front of the door; as we passed Jenny commented:

'The war veterans' club. They're all over the place. They hold parties, reunions, things like that. I've only been inside once, but I know that before we met Rodney used to go there quite a lot, or that's what he told me. Do you want to go in?'

I said there was no need and we walked away from the club along a dirt path that ran beside the highway, chatting, Dan in the middle and Jenny and I on either side, Jenny holding his left hand and I his right. After a while we left the highway, taking a path that went gently up to the left, between fields of young corn, and when we got to the top of a small hill we left the path, going into an irregular quadrilateral strewn with a handful of scattered graves, where there stood a couple of ash trees feeding on the earth of the dead and a rusty iron flagpole without a flag. Dan let

249

go of our hands and ran across the cemetery lawn until he stopped in front of an unpolished tombstone.

'Here he is,' said Dan when we reached his side, pointing to the grave with one finger.

I looked at the tombstone, on the front face of which was carved a boy sitting under a tree reading and an inscription: RODNEY FALK. APR. 6 1948 – JAN. 4 2004; beside the inscription there was a fresh bouquet of flowers. 'A clean, well-lighted place,' I thought. The three of us stood in front of the grave in silence.

'Well, actually he's not here,' said Dan finally. After pondering for a moment he asked: 'Where are you when you're dead?'

The question wasn't directed at anyone in particular, but I waited for Jenny to answer it; she didn't answer. After a few seconds had gone by I felt obliged to say:

'Nowhere.'

'Nowhere?' asked Dan, exaggerating the interrogative tone.

'Nowhere,' I repeated.

Dan remained pensive.

'Then you're the same as a ghost?' he asked.

'Exactly,' I answered, and then I lied without knowing it: 'Except that ghosts don't exist, and the dead do.'

Dan looked away from the tombstone finally and, sneaking a look at me, made as if to smile, as if he was as sure of not having understood as of not wanting to show he hadn't understood. Then he moved away from us and walked to one edge of the cemetery, beyond which you could see in the distance a cluster of houses with paint peeling off the walls, maybe abandoned, and he began to pick up pebbles from the ground and throw them gently onto the neighbouring fields: a succession of uncultivated plots with a few weeds here and there. Jenny and I stayed beside one another, without saying anything, looking alternately at Dan and at Rodney's grave. It was getting dark and starting to feel a little cold; the sky was a dark blue, almost black, but an irregular strip of orange light still illuminated the horizon, and only the early chirping of crickets and a dim and distant rumble of traffic perturbed the impeccable silence of the hill.

'Well,' said Jenny after a while, during which I didn't think anything, didn't feel anything, not even an urge to pray. 'It's getting late. Shall we go back?'

It was almost dark by the time we got home. I had a dinner date in Urbana, with Borgheson and a group of professors, and if I wanted to get back to the Chancellor by the agreed time I'd have to leave immediately, so I told Dan and Jenny that I had to go. They both stared at me, a bit stunned, as if, rather than a surprise, my words were the prelude to a desertion; after an indecisive silence, Jenny asked:

'Is the dinner important?'

It wasn't. It wasn't at all. I told her.

'Then why don't you cancel?' asked Jenny. 'You can stay here: there're lots of bedrooms.'

She didn't have to repeat the offer: I phoned Borgheson and told him I felt tired and feverish and that, in order to be on form for the lecture the following day, it would be best if I skipped dinner and stayed in the hotel to rest. Borgheson accepted the lie without complaint, although it took a lot of doing to convince him not to come to my aid at the Chancellor. The problem solved, I invited Dan and Jenny to dinner at a restaurant called Kennedy's, a few kilometres out of town on the way to Urbana, and after dinner, while Dan played on his Game Boy with a classmate whose family was also eating there, Jenny told me how she'd met Rodney, talked about her job, her family, the life she led in Rantoul. When we left the restaurant it was almost ten. On the way back, Dan fell asleep, and when we got to the house I picked him up in my arms, carried him up to his room and, while Jenny put him to bed, I waited for her in the living room, looking at the CDs lined up in an aluminum pyramid beside the sound system. Most of them were rock and roll, and there were several by Bob Dylan. Among them *Bringing It All Back Home*, an album that contained a song I knew well: 'It's Alright, Ma (I'm Only Bleeding)'. With the disk in my hands I began to hear in my head that inconsolable song that always used to bring back to Rodney the intact joy of his youth, and suddenly, as I waited for Jenny, remembering the lyrics as precisely as I did the music, I was certain that deep down that song spoke of nothing but Rodney, of Rodney's cancelled-out life, because it spoke of disillusioned words that bark like bullets and stuffed graveyards and false gods and lonely people who cry and fear and live in a vault knowing everything's a lie and who understand they know too soon there is no use in trying, because it spoke of all that and especially because it said that he not busy being born is busy dying. 'Rodney's only busy dying now,' I thought. And I thought: 'I'm not, yet.'

'Do you feel like listening to some music?' said Jenny as she came into the living room.

I said yes, and she turned on the machine and went to the kitchen. I avoided the temptation of Dylan and put on *Astral Weeks* by Van Morrison, and when Jenny came back, carrying a bottle of wine and two glasses, we sat down across from one another and let the record play, chatting with an effusiveness fostered by the alcohol and by Van Morrison's raw voice. I don't remember what we talked about at first, but when we'd already been sitting there for a while, I don't know exactly why (maybe owing to something I said, probably owing to something Jenny said), I suddenly remembered a letter Rodney had sent his father from hospital in Vietnam, after the incident at My Khe, a letter in which he talked of the beauty of war, of the devastating speed of war, and then I thought that since I'd been in Rantoul I had the impression that everything had accelerated, that everything had started to run faster than usual, faster and faster, faster, faster, and at some moment there had been a blaze, a maelstrom and a loss, I thought I'd unknowingly travelled faster than the speed of light and what I was now seeing was the future. And that was also when, mingled with Van Morrison's music and Jenny's voice, I felt for the first time something both unusual and familiar, something I'd maybe sensed wordlessly as soon as I'd seen Dan and Jenny coming towards me that afternoon on Belle Avenue, and what I felt was that here, in this house that wasn't my house, before this woman who wasn't mine, with this sleeping child who wasn't my son but who was sleeping upstairs as if I were his father, that here I was invulnerable; I also wondered, with a twinkling commencement of joy, whether I wasn't obliged to give some meaning to Rodney's suicide, whether the house I was in wasn't a reflection of my house and Dan and Jenny a reflection of the family I'd lost, I wondered if that was what one saw upon emerging from the filth underground out into the open, if the past was not a place permanently altered by the future and nothing of what had already happened was irreversible and what was there at the end of the tunnel echoed what had been there before entering it, I wondered if this was not the true end of it all, the end of the road, the end of the tunnel, the breach in the stone door. This is it, I said to myself, possessed by a strange euphoria. It's over. Finito. Kaput.

As soon as I finished thinking that thought I interrupted Jenny.

'There's something I haven't told you,' I said.

She looked at me, a little surprised by my abruptness, and suddenly I didn't know how I was going to tell her what I had to tell her. I figured it out a second later. I took the photograph of Gabriel, Paula and Rodney on Les Peixeteries Velles bridge out of my wallet and handed it to her. Jenny took it and for some moments examined it attentively. Then she asked:

'Is this your wife and son?'

'Yes,' I answered and, as if another person were speaking for me, I continued as a cold thread ran up my spine like a snake: 'They died a year ago, in a car accident. It's the only photo of them I kept.'

Jenny looked up from the photo, and at that moment I noticed the Van Morrison CD had stopped playing; reality seemed to have slowed down, gone back to its normal speed.

'What have you come here for?' asked Jenny.

'I don't know,' I said, although I did know. 'I was in a pit and I wanted to see Rodney. I thought Rodney had been in a pit too and he'd got out of it. I think I believed he could help me. Or rather: I think I believed he was the only person who could help me . . . Well, I realize this all sounds a bit ridiculous, and I don't know if it makes much sense to you, but I think it's what I thought.'

Jenny scarcely took a moment to answer.

'It makes sense,' she said.

Now it was me who looked at her.

'Really?'

'Sure,' she insisted, smiling gently, again digging a tiny net of wrinkles around the corners of her mouth. For a second I knew or suspected that, because she'd lived with Rodney, her words did not stem from compassion, but that it was true she understood, that only she could understand; for a second I felt the soft radiance of her attractiveness, I suddenly believed I understood the attraction she'd exerted over Rodney. Almost as if she considered the matter settled, or as if she thought it barely merited any more time devoted to it, she went on: 'Guilt. It's not so hard to understand that. I could feel guilty for Rodney's death too, you know? Finding guilty parties is very easy; the difficult thing is accepting that there aren't any.'

I wasn't sure what she meant by those words, but for some reason I remembered others that Rodney had written to his father: 'Things that make sense are not true,' Rodney had written. 'They're only sawn-off truths, wishful thinking: truth is always absurd.' Jenny finished her glass of wine.

'I have a copy of the documentary,' she said, as if she hadn't changed the subject and was about to give me her real answer to the doubt I'd just formulated. 'Do you want to watch it?'

Because I wasn't expecting it, the question disconcerted me. First I thought I didn't want to watch the programme; then I thought I did want to watch it; then I thought I wanted to watch it but I shouldn't watch it; then I thought I wanted to watch it and should watch it. I asked:

'Have you watched it?'

'Of course not,' said Jenny. 'What for?'

Just as if my question had been an affirmative reply Jenny went upstairs, after a while she returned with the videotape and asked me to come with her to a room between the kitchen and the living room, at the foot of the stairs; in the room was a television, a sofa, two chairs, a coffee table. I sat on the sofa while Jenny turned on the television, put the video in and handed me the remote control.

'I'll wait for you upstairs,' she said.

I leaned back on the sofa and pressed play on the remote control; the programme began immediately. It was called *Buried Secrets, Brutal Truths* and lasted about forty minutes. It combined archive images, in black and white, from documentaries about the war, and current images, in colour, of villages and fields in the regions of Quang Ngai and Quang Nam, along with some statements made by peasants from the area. Two threads stitched the two blocks of images together: one was a dispassionate voice-over; the other, the testimony of a Vietnam veteran. The voice-over told from the outside the story of the atrocities committed thirty-five years earlier by a bloodthirsty platoon of the 101st Airborne Division of the United States Army that operated in Quang Ngai and Quang Nam, converting the regions into a vast killing field. The platoon, known as Tiger Force, was a unit composed of forty-five volunteers which acted in coordination with other units, but which functioned with a great degree of autonomy and barely any supervision, its members distinguishable by their striped camouflage uniforms, in imitation of tiger stripes; the catalogue of horrors the report documented knew no bounds: Tiger Force soldiers murdered, mutilated, tortured and raped hundreds of people between January and July 1969, and acquired a reputation among the local population for wearing around their necks, like necklaces of war that brutally commemorated their victims, collections of human ears strung together on shoelaces. Towards the end of the broadcast the voice-over mentioned the Pentagon report that the White House had shelved in 1974 with the excuse that it didn't want to reopen the wounds of the recently concluded conflict. As for the veteran, he was shown sitting in an armchair, unmoving, backlit from a window, so that a dark shadow obscured his face; his voice, on the other hand – gruff, icy, withdrawn – had not been distorted: it was clearly Rodney's voice. The voice told anecdotes; it also made comments. 'It's difficult to understand it all now,' the voice said, for example. 'But there came a time for us when it was the most natural thing in the world. At first it was a bit of an effort, but you soon got used to it and it was just like any other job.' 'We felt like gods,' the voice said. 'And in a certain way we were. We had the power of life and death over whoever we wanted and we exercised that power.' 'For years I couldn't forget each and every one of the people I saw die,' said the voice. 'They appeared to me constantly, just as if they were alive and didn't want to die, just like ghosts. Then I managed to forget them, or that's what I thought, although deep down I knew they hadn't gone away. Now they're back. They don't ask me to settle the score, and I don't. There's no score to settle. It's just that they don't want to die, they want to live in me. I don't complain, because I know it's fair.' The voice closed the report with these words: 'You can believe we were monsters, but we weren't. We were like everybody else. We were like you.'

When the report ended I remained sitting on the sofa for a while, unable to move, my eyes glued to the blizzard on the television screen. Then I took the tape out of the video, turned off the television and went out on the porch. The city was in silence and the sky full of stars; it was a little cold. I lit a cigarette and started smoking it as I contemplated the silent night of Rantoul. I didn't feel horror, I didn't feel nauseous, not even sadness, for the first time in a long time I didn't feel anguish either; what I felt was something strangely pleasant that I'd never felt before, something like an infinite exhaustion or an infinite and blank calm, or like a substitute for the exhaustion or the calm that left only the inclination to keep looking at the night and to weep. 'Our nada who art in nada,' I prayed. 'Nada be thy name thy kingdom nada thy will be nada in nada as it is in nada.' When I finished smoking my cigarette I went back inside the house and upstairs. Jenny had fallen asleep with a book on her lap and the light on; Dan was curled up beside her. The room next to hers also had the light on and the bed made, and I guessed Jenny had made it up for me. I turned off the light in Jenny and Dan's room, turned off mine and got into bed.

It took me a long time to get to sleep that night, and the next day I woke up very early. When Dan and Jenny got up I already had breakfast almost ready. While we ate, a little hurriedly because it was Monday and Dan had to go to school and Jenny to work, I avoided Jenny's eyes a couple of times, and when we finished I offered them a lift in the car. Dan's school was, Jenny said, as we parked in front of it, the same one where Rodney had worked: a three-storey brick building with a large iron gate guarding access to the schoolyard, surrounded by a metal fence. In front of the entrance a group of parents and children were already congregated. We joined the group and, when the gate finally opened, Dan gave his mother a kiss; then he turned to me and, scrutinizing me with Rodney's big brown eyes, asked me if I was going to come back. I said yes. He asked me when. I said soon. He asked me if I was lying to him. I said no. He nodded. Then, because I thought he was going to give me a kiss, I began to crouch down, but he stopped me by holding out his hand; I shook it. Then we watched him disappear into the schoolyard with his preschooler knapsack, among the ruckus of his classmates.

While we walked back to the car Jenny suggested we go for a last cup of coffee: she still had a while before she had to start work, she said. We went to Casey's General Store and sat beside a window that overlooked the gas pumps and, beyond them, the intersection at the edge of the city; a country and western tune came quietly out of the speakers. I recognized the waitress who served us: she was the same

260

one who'd given me haphazard directions to Rodney's house on Sunday. Jenny exchanged a few words with her and then we ordered two coffees.

'When Rodney came back from Spain he told me you wanted to write a book about him,' said Jenny as soon as the waitress had gone. 'Is that true?'

I'd been prepared for Jenny to ask me about the documentary, but not for what she actually asked. I looked at her: her grey eyes had acquired a violet-toned iridescence and revealed a curiosity for more than just my answer, or that's what I thought. My answer was:

'Yes.'

'Have you written it?'

I said no.

'Why?'

'I don't know,' I said, and remembered the conversation I'd had about the same matter with Rodney in Madrid. 'I tried several times, but I couldn't. Or I didn't know how. I think I felt his story wasn't over, or that I didn't entirely understand it.'

'And now?'

'Now what?'

'Now is it over?' she asked again. 'Now do you understand it?'

Like a sudden illumination, at that moment I thought I understood Jenny's behaviour since my arrival in Rantoul. I thought I understood why she had told me about Rodney's last days, why she'd wanted to show me his grave, why she'd wanted me to stay the night in her house, why she'd wanted me to watch the Tiger Force documentary: just as if words had the power to give meaning or an illusion of meaning to what has none, Jenny wanted me to tell Rodney's story. I thought of Rodney, I thought of Rodney's father, I thought of Tommy Birban, but most of all I thought of Gabriel and Paula, and for the first time I sensed that all those stories were actually the same story, and that only I could tell it.

'I don't know if it's over,' I answered. 'I don't know if I understand it either, or if I understand it completely.' I thought of Rodney again and said: 'Of course, you probably don't need to understand a story completely to be able to tell it.'

The waitress brought our coffee. When she'd left, Jenny asked as she stirred hers:

'What is it you don't understand? Why he did it?'

I didn't answer straight away: I tasted the coffee and lit a cigarette while I remembered the report with a shiver.

'No,' I said. 'Actually that's the only thing I do understand.' As if thinking aloud I added: 'Maybe what I don't understand is why I didn't.'

Jenny's cup remained suspended in the air, halfway between the table and her lips, while she looked at me doubtfully, as if my observation was obviously absurd or as if she'd just formed the suspicion that I was mad. Then she diverted her gaze towards the window (the sun shone right in her face, inflaming the gold earring still in view) and seemed to reflect a moment, and then turned back to look at

262

me with a half smile as the cup concluded its interrupted voyage, wet her lips and put it down on the table.

'Well, I tried to explain it to you yesterday: you haven't killed anyone.' *She lied to me*, I thought in a second, in a fraction of a second. *She has seen the report.* As soon as she started talking again I discarded that idea. 'Not even accidentally,' she said, and then added: 'Besides, after all you're a writer, aren't you?'

'And what does that have to do with it?'

'Everything.'

'Everything?'

'Sure, don't you understand?'

I didn't say anything and we just looked at each other for a moment, until Jenny took a deep breath, let it out while diverting her gaze again towards the window and remained absorbed watching a man filling up his gas tank, and when she turned back towards me I was inundated with a kind of joy, as if I'd truly understood Jenny and understanding her would let me understand everything I hadn't yet understood. I finished drinking my coffee; Jenny did the same.

'It's getting late,' she said. 'Shall we go?'

We paid and left. Jenny came with me as far as the car, and when we got there I asked if she wanted a lift to work.

'There's no need,' she said. 'It's quite near.' She took a notebook out of her handbag, scribbled something on a page, tore it out and handed it to me. 'My email address. If you decide to write the book, keep me posted. And another thing: don't take any notice of Dan.'

'What do you mean?'

'What he said to you at the school gate,' she explained.

'Ah,' I said.

She made a face of annoyance or apology.

'I suppose he's looking for a father,' she ventured.

'Don't worry.' I ventured: 'I suppose I'm looking for a son.'

Jenny nodded, barely smiling; I thought she was going to say something, but she didn't say anything. She put her hand in her trouser pocket, in a gesture I thought shy or embarrassed, as if she couldn't quite decide how we should say goodbye, and then she held it out to me; when I took it, I noticed something cold and metallic: it was Rodney's Zippo. Jenny didn't give me time to react.

'Goodbye,' she said.

And she turned around and began to walk away. After a moment of indecision I put the Zippo in my pocket, got in the car, started it and, waiting to pull out onto the avenue that led out of Rantoul, I looked to the left and saw her in the distance, walking along the sidewalk in the shade, alone and resolved and fragile and nevertheless inspired by something like an inflexible, resolute pride, getting smaller as she went into the city, and I don't know why I thought of a bird, a hummingbird or a heron or more likely a swallow, and then I thought of the poster of John Wayne which hung on a wall of Bud's Bar and that Rodney would have seen so many times and Jenny too, no doubt, absurdly I thought of these two things while I kept watching her and waiting for her to sense my gaze at some moment and turn around and look back at me, as if that last gesture could also be an unmistakable sign of assent. But Jenny didn't turn around, didn't look at me, so I pulled out onto the avenue and drove out of Rantoul.

When I arrived in Urbana that morning I had already devised quite a precise plan of what I'd do over the next months, or rather the next years; as is logical, that plan envisaged the risk that reality would end up distorting it, but not to the point of making it unrecognizable. That, for better or worse – I'll never know whether it was more for the better or for the worse – is what happened though.

I returned to Spain after impatiently fulfilling my remaining commitments in Urbana and Los Angeles, and the first thing I did when I landed in Barcelona was look for a new flat, because as soon as I walked into the apartment in Sagrada Familia I realized it was an irredeemable pigsty. I found one immediately – a small apartment with lots of light on calle Floridablanca, not far from plaza de España – and as soon as I was settled in there I began to write this book. Since then I've hardly done anything else. Since then – and it's been about six months now – I feel that the life I'm living is not true, but rather false, a clandestine, hidden, apocryphal life but truer than if it were true. The change of flat made it easy to cover my tracks, so until recently no one knew where I lived. I didn't see anyone, I didn't talk to anyone, I didn't read the papers, I didn't watch television, I didn't listen to the radio. I was more alive than ever, but it was as if I were dead and writing was the only way of evoking life, the last thread that kept me joined to it. Writing and, until recently, Jenny. Because when I got back from Urbana, Jenny and I began to write to each other almost daily. At first our emails were exclusively concerned with the book I was writing about Rodney: I asked her questions, requested details and clarifications, and she answered me with diligence and application; then, little by little and almost imperceptibly, the messages began to be about other things – about Dan, about Rantoul, about her life and Dan's in Rantoul, about me and my invisible life in Barcelona, once in a while about Paula and Gabriel – and after a few weeks I'd discovered that this method of communication allowed for or encouraged more intimacy than any other. That was how I began a long, slow, complicated, sinuous and delicate process of seduction. Perhaps that's not quite the right word: perhaps the exact word is persuasion. Or maybe demonstration. I don't know which word Jenny would choose. It doesn't matter; what matters aren't the words, but the facts. And the fact is that, while I was as deeply involved in that process as in the book I was writing, I never stopped imagining my life when both were finished and I would live with Dan and Jenny in Rantoul. I imagined a placid and provincial life like the one I'd once feared and then had and later destroyed, a life that was also apocryphal and true, in the middle of nowhere. I imagined myself getting up very early, having breakfast with Dan and Jenny and then taking them to school and work and then shutting myself up to work until it was time to go and pick them up, first Dan and then Jenny, I'd go and pick them up and we'd go home and get dinner ready and have dinner and then after dinner we'd play or read or watch television or talk until sleep would overtake us one by one, and none of the three of us would ever want to admit, even to ourselves, that this daily routine was in reality a kind of spell, a magic trick with which we wanted to make the past reversible and bring the dead back to life. Other times I imagined myself lying in a hammock, in the back garden, beside the shed in which, once upon a time so long ago that it no longer seemed real, Rodney hanged himself, on a Saturday or Sunday afternoon at the end of spring or the beginning of the burning hot Rantoul summer, with Dan and his friends shouting and playing around me while I haphazardly read Hemingway and Thoreau and Emerson, sometimes even Mercè Rodoreda, while I listened to Bob Dylan and shared sips of whisky and tokes of marijuana with Jenny, who came and went from the house to the garden: from there Gabriel's and Paula's deaths would be left very far away, Vietnam would be left very far away, success and fame would be left as far away as the miniscule clouds that every now and then blocked out the sun, and then I would see myself as the hippie Rodney must have been more than thirty years ago and that he never wanted to stop being. That's how I saw myself, that's how I imagined myself, happy and a little high, somehow converted into Rodney or into the instrument of Rodney, watching Dan as if I were really watching Gabriel, watching Jenny as if I were really watching Paula. And while I was imagining my happy future life in Rantoul in those months in Barcelona and continuing the long, slow, sinuous seduction or persuasion of Jenny by the intimacy of email, not one single day went by when I did not sit down at this desk and devote myself fully to the long-postponed task entrusted to me of writing this story that maybe Rodney had always been training me to write, this story I don't understand nor will I ever understand and that nevertheless, as I imagined as I was writing it, I was obliged to tell because it can only be understood if it's told by someone who, like me, will never entirely understand it, and especially because it's also my story and also Gabriel's and Paula's. So for a long time I wrote and seduced and persuaded and demonstrated and imagined, until one day, when I felt the process of seduction was mature and that, although I didn't yet know exactly how this book was going to end, I undoubtedly almost had the ending in my sights, I decided to state my plans openly to Jenny. I did so fearlessly with no beating about the bush, just as if I were reminding her of a pledge we'd both made some time ago like someone accepting a happy fate, because by that stage, after months of writing to her almost daily and insinuating ever less cryptically my intentions, I was sure my words couldn't come as a surprise to her, and also that she'd receive them with delight.

It didn't happen like that. Incredibly – at least incredibly to me – both certainties proved false. Jenny took a while to answer my message, and when she finally did it was to thank me for my proposal and immediately turn it down affectionately but categorically. 'It wouldn't work,' Jenny wrote to me. 'Anticipating something is not enough to make it happen, neither is wanting it. This isn't algebra or geometry: when you're talking about people, two plus two never makes four. I mean none of us can replace anybody: Dan can't replace Gabriel, I can't replace Paula; you, no matter how much you want to, can't replace Rodney.' . . . 'Finish the book,' Jenny concluded. 'You owe it to Rodney. You owe it to Gabriel and to Paula. You owe it to Dan and to me. Most of all you owe it to yourself. Finish it and then, if you feel like it, come and spend a few days with us. We'll be waiting for you.' Jenny's reply left me dumbfounded, unable to react, as if someone had just punched me and I didn't know who or how or why they'd punched me. I reread it, I reread it again; I understood all the words, but found it impossible to take them in. I was so convinced that my future was in Rantoul, with Dan and with her, that I hadn't even imagined an alternative future if that one proved illusory or failed. Furthermore, Jenny's refusal was so unequivocal and her arguments so watertight that I didn't have the strength to try to refute them and insist on my proposal.

I didn't answer Jenny's message: there wasn't going to be any magic trick, there wasn't going to be any spell, I wasn't going to recover what I'd lost. I suddenly saw myself returning to my old underground life; I suddenly thought I understood it was absurd to keep writing this book. And I was about to abandon it definitively when I discovered exactly how it ended and why I had to finish it. It happened a little while after I found a cigarette packet full of joints sticking out of the slot of my mailbox as I was on my way out to have lunch one afternoon. I couldn't help but smile. The next morning I phoned Marcos, and two days later we arranged to meet for a beer in El Yate.

It was Marcos who chose the bar. When I arrived, quite a while before the time we'd arranged, my friend was already there, sitting on a stool, his back to the door and elbows on the bar. Without a word I sat down beside him and ordered a beer; Marcos didn't say anything either, or look up from his glass. It was a Thursday in the middle of October, and the last light of the afternoon was about to fade from the windows overlooking the corner of Muntaner and Arimon. While I was waiting for my beer I asked:

'How did you track me down?'

Marcos sighed before answering.

'By accident,' he said. 'I saw you on the street the other day and followed you. I knew you'd moved, but you could at least have let me know. I'm not rich enough to be throwing marijuana away.'

'You haven't thrown it away,' I said. 'I'm sure whoever rented the apartment after me was very grateful to you.'

'Very funny.' He turned to look at me. Then he said: 'How are you?'

With some apprehension I too turned around. At first

glance he didn't remind me of the aged forty-year-old of our last encounter, in the MACBA or the Palau Robert, the same disastrous night I tried to seduce Patricia; he just looked tired, maybe bored: in fact, the faded jeans, the baggy blue sweater and the lighter blue untucked shirt gave him an air of vaguely youthful sloppiness, not entirely contradicted by his thinning, grey hair or his thick and slightly old-fashioned tortoiseshell glasses; two days' stubble shadowed his cheeks. As I was studying him I felt myself studied by him, and before answering his question I wondered if I was reminding him of a ghost or a zombie.

'Fine,' I lied. 'And you?'

'Me too.'

I nodded approvingly. The bartender brought my beer, I took a sip, lit a cigarette and then I gave a light to Marcos, who stared at Rodney's Zippo; I looked at it too: for a moment it seemed a remote and strange object, a tiny meteorite or a fossil or a survivor of an ice age; for a second it seemed like the dog engraved on it wasn't smiling at me, but mocking me. I put the lighter down on the bar, on top of the cigarette packet; I asked:

'How's Patricia?'

Marcos sighed again.

'We split up a year or so ago,' he said. 'I thought you knew.'

'I didn't know.'

'Well, it doesn't matter,' he said as if it really didn't matter, running his hand over his stubble; I noticed a blotch of paint darkening his ring finger. 'I suppose we'd been together too long and, well . . . She's been living in Madrid for a few months now, so I haven't seen her.'

I didn't say anything. We kept drinking and smoking in silence, and at some point I inevitably remembered the last time I'd been in El Yate, sixteen years before, with Marcos and with Marcelo Cuartero, when he suggested I go to Urbana and the whole thing started. I looked along the bar. I remembered a luxurious uptown place, inaccessible given our destitute finances, frequented by executives and shiny with mirrors and polished wood, but the place where I now found myself seemed (or at least seemed to me) more like a dark village tavern: certain details of the decoration pathetically strained to mimic the interior of a yacht – dull seascapes, lamps in the shape of anchors, a pendulum clock in the shape of a tennis racket – but there were also horrible pink curtains tied back against window frames painted a horrible green, trays of rancid-looking tapas lined up on the unpolished bar, slot machines blinking their urgent promise of riches, the waiters' uniforms dusted with dandruff and the clientele of solitary ladies drinking Marie Brizard and solitary men drinking gin, who every once in a while exchanged comments seasoned by alcohol and cynicism, all of which drew El Yate closer to Bud's Bar than to my memory of El Yate. Suddenly I felt at ease there, with my cigarette and beer in hand, as if I should never have left that Barcelona bar with its village bar atmosphere; suddenly I asked Marcos why he'd suggested we meet precisely there.

'Why did you suggest we meet here?' I asked.

'I haven't been here for ages,' he said. And he added: 'It hasn't changed a bit.'

Perplexed, I asked him if he meant the bar.

'I mean the bar, the calle Pujol, the neighbourhood, all of it,' he answered. 'I bet even our apartment is exactly the same, for fuck's sake.'

I smiled.

'You're not going to start getting nostalgic?'

'Nostalgic?' The interrogative tone contained not surprise but annoyance, an annoyance that verged on irritation. 'Why nostalgic? That wasn't the best time we ever had in our lives. It might seem like it sometimes, but it wasn't.'

'No?'

'No.' He pursed his lips in a disparaging gesture. 'The best is what's happening to us now.'

There was a silence, after which I heard that Marcos was laughing; it was contagious and I started laughing too, and for a while a feeble, strange and uncontrollable laughter kept us from talking. Then Marcos suggested we have another beer and, while they were pouring it, for something to say I asked him how his work was going. Marcos took a sip of beer; it left a trace of foam around his mouth.

'About a year ago, just after Patricia and I split up, I stopped painting,' he explained. 'I did nothing but suffer. I hadn't sold a bloody painting for months and I couldn't even save face by blaming the market, that handy gentleman, because I felt that what I was painting was rubbish. So

I stopped painting. You don't know how good it felt. Suddenly I realized that it was all an absurd misunderstanding: someone or something had convinced me I was an artist when I really wasn't one, and that's why I suffered so much and everything was so shit. Twenty years pulling in one direction when in reality I wanted to go in another, twenty years down the drain . . . A damned misunderstanding. But, instead of getting depressed, as soon as I understood that I felt better, it was as if I'd taken a huge weight off my shoulders. So I decided to change my life.' He took a drag on his cigarette and started to laugh, but he choked on the smoke and a cough interrupted his laughter. 'Change my life,' he continued after a gulp of beer to clear his throat. 'That's a laugh. You've got to be a jerk to think you can change a life, as if after forty years we still didn't know that it's not us that changes life, but life that changes us. Anyway . . . the thing is I rented a house in the country, in a village in Cerdanya, and said to hell with everything. The first month was great: I walked, looked after the vegetable plot, chatted with the neighbours, I didn't do anything; I even met a girl, a nurse who worked in Puigcerdà. It seemed like paradise, and I started making plans to stay there. Until the shit hit the fan. First there were problems with the neighbours, then the girl got bored with me, then I started getting bored. Suddenly the days felt endless, I wondered what the hell I was doing there.' He was quiet for a moment and then he asked: 'You know what I did then?' I could imagine, I almost knew, but I let Marcos answer his own question. 'I

274

started painting. Who'd have fucking believed it, eh? I started painting out of boredom, to kill time, because I had nothing better to do.'

I thought of my interrupted book and of the two joyful kamikazes Marcos and I had imagined ourselves to be sixteen years earlier and of the masterpieces we were going to create to take revenge on the world. I said:

'It seems as good a reason as any.'

'You're wrong,' Marcos disagreed. 'It's the best reason. Or at least the best that's ever occurred to me. The proof is that I've never had as much fun painting as I have since then. I don't know whether what I've painted is good or bad. It might be bad. Or it might be the best stuff I've ever painted. I don't know, and the truth is it doesn't matter. The only thing I know is, well . . .' He hesitated a moment, looked at me and I thought he was going to burst out laughing again. 'The only thing I know is that if I hadn't painted it I'd still be living in that fucking village.'

Although the hands of the pendulum clock in the shape of a tennis racket were frozen at five o'clock, it must have been after nine, because the solitary drinkers of gin and Marie Brizard had disappeared from El Yate and the waiters had been serving dinner at the tables by the windows for a while; beyond that it was completely dark, and the lights of the cars and street lamps and traffic lights made the street look like a shimmering aquarium. When Marcos tired of his monologue about the paintings he'd done or imagined or sketched in Cerdanya, he asked:

275

'And you?'

'What about me?'

'Are you writing?'

I said no. Then I said yes. Then I asked him if he wanted to have another beer. He said yes. While we drank it I told him I'd spent the last few months writing a book, that I'd given up on it two weeks ago and I didn't know if it was worth finishing, or if I even wanted to finish it. Marcos asked me what the book was about.

'Lots of things,' I said.

'For example?' he insisted.

That was when, at first reluctantly, almost just to repay Marcos's confidences, then enthusiastically and finally transported by my own words, I began to talk to him of the apartment we shared on the calle Pujol, of our encounter with Marcelo Cuartero in El Yate, of my trip to Urbana and my work in Urbana and my friendship with Rodney, of Rodney's father, of Rodney's years in Vietnam, of my return to Barcelona and then to Gerona, of Paula and Gabriel and my encounter with Rodney in the Hotel San Antonio de La Florida in Madrid, of the two tragedies there are in life and of the joy of success and its euphoria and humiliation and catastrophe, of Gabriel's and Paula's deaths, of my purgatory in the apartment in Sagrada Familia, of tunnels and undergrounds and stone doors, of my trip to the United States and my return to Rantoul, of Dan and Jenny, of the crimes of Tiger Force and of Tommy Birban's death and of Rodney's suicide, of my return to

276

Barcelona, of my frustrated return to Rantoul, of the illusions of algebra and geometry. I talked to him of all these things and others, and as I did so I knew that Jenny was right, that Marcos was right; I should finish the book. I should finish it because I owed it to Gabriel and Paula and Rodney, also to Dan and Jenny, but most of all because I owed it to myself, I would finish it because I was a writer and I couldn't be anything else, because writing was the only thing that could let me look at reality without being destroyed by it or having it collapse on top of me like a burning house, the only thing that could give it meaning or an illusion of meaning, the only thing that, as had happened during those months of seclusion and work and vain hope and seduction or persuasion or demonstration, had allowed me to glimpse for real and without knowing it the end of the road, the end of the tunnel, the breach in the stone door, the only thing that had got me out from under the ground into the open and had allowed me to travel faster than the speed of light and recover part of what I'd lost among the crash of the collapse, that's why I'd finish the book, and because finishing it was also the only way that, albeit enclosed in these pages, Gabriel and Paula would somehow stay alive, and I would stop being who I'd been up till then, who I was with Rodney — my fellow, my brother — to become someone else, to be somehow and partially and forever Rodney. And at some point, while I was still telling Marcos about my book, already knowing that I was going to finish it, I was struck by the suspicion that perhaps I hadn't given

277

up on it two weeks earlier because I hadn't wanted to finish it or wasn't sure if it was worth finishing, but because I didn't want it to finish: because, when I was already glimpsing its ending – when I almost knew what I wanted this story to say, because I'd almost already said it; when I'd almost got where I wanted to get to, precisely because I'd never known where I was going – the vertigo of not knowing what would be on the other side got to me, what abyss or mirror was waiting for me beyond these pages, when I again had all roads before me. And that was when I didn't only know the exact ending of my book, but also when I found the solution I was looking for. Euphoric, with the last beer I explained it to Marcos. I explained that I was going to publish the book under a different name, a pseudonym. I explained that before I published it I'd completely rewrite it. I'll change all the names, the places, the dates, I explained. I'll lie about everything, I explained, but only to better tell the truth. I explained: it will be an apocryphal novel, like my clandestine and invisible life, a false novel but truer than if it were true. When I finished explaining it all, Marcos remained quiet for a few seconds, smoking with an absent expression; then he drank down the rest of his beer.

'And how does it end?' he asked.

I looked around the almost empty bar and, feeling almost happy, answered:

'It ends like this.'

AUTHOR'S NOTE

Like all books, this book is in debt to many other books. Among them I should mention two volumes that collect experiences of ex-combatants from Vietnam: *Nam* by Mark Baker and *War and Aftermath in Vietnam* by T. Louise Brown. The following texts have also been very useful: *A Rumor of War* by Philip Caputo; *Vietnam: A War Lost and Won* by Nigel Cawthorne; *Dispatches*, by Michael Herr; 'Trip to Hanoy' in *Styles of Radical Will* by Susan Sontag. Furthermore, I am grateful for the disinterested help I have received from Quico Auquer, Andrés Barba, Jessica Berman, Frederic Bonet, David Castillo Buils, Àngel Duarte, Tomàs Frauca, David T. Gies, Cristina Llençana, Rosa Negre, Núria Prats, Guillem Terribas, John C. Wilcox and, especially, Jordi Gracia, Felip Ortega and David Trueba, to whom this book owes even more than they think.